War and Peace in Dodge

DAVID KURTZ

New Brevet Publications
Minneapolis, MN

War and Peace in Dodge
by David Kurtz

ISBN-13: 978-0692101735

New Brevet Publications

Cover design by Teaberry Creative
teaberrycreative.com

This book is dedicated to

my wife and best friend

Beth Kurtz

CONTENTS

WAR AND PEACE IN DODGE

(revised)

PROLOGUE: THE TREATY OF VERSAILLES

It's kind of funny when I think back on it. I mean, not side-splitting funny, since it was a tragedy and all. However, when a piece of paper is signed and sealed with all solemnity, with a view to the future, with the grand idea of peace in mind, it's amazing how sour that can turn.

That's my grandparents' will all over. Treat and Versey. Actually, Versey was a nickname, my grandmother's Christian name being Verity, but Great-Grandmother Clementine (whom I never met, God rest her soul) apparently had something of a lisp or other disorder that made her unable to pronounce Verity cleanly. Only she and Treat called her Versey—to her face—but we all did too when she wasn't around. My mother, who married into Versey's watchful eye, at times proclaimed the fear that one of us kids would call our grandmother "Versey" to her face and then we'd see some fireworks. Frankly, I was tempted on more than one occasion, but she passed her life placidly enough without that trial, except for once only.

Anyway, my grandparents' will. They hammered out the details in somewhat secretive negotiations, expressed everything in legal language, if it pleases the court, and affixed their names portentously. Grandfather Treat wanted to sign it in blood, but Grandmother Versey forbade this. Eventually the deed got done—deed is funny, too, but only because land was involved, Grandfather's purchase when he was still young, a place on which he thought he would eventually build a grand retirement home. Some "living space", he termed it. That's the translation from German anyway. Treat's dad had come from some part of Germany around 1860, as a teenager, but we weren't sure from exactly where or exactly when. Great-grandfather Wolfgang taught his seven children the German tongue, but made them all vow to three holy causes:

1.) Learn English.
2.) Marry rich.
3.) Buy stock in Coca-Cola.

Treat learned enough English to follow baseball, Grandmother Verity was dirt poor and all he ever really wanted from Coca-Cola was the refreshing zing of the cocaine brought about by downing sixteen bottles a day. (Talk about a crazy drinking problem; at 6.5 ounces per bottle, that was 104 ounces a day, drunk straight from the profits of his Five and Dime where he sold what little he didn't drink. When they removed the cocaine from the recipe, he went up to twenty-three bottles a day.)

Lebensraum. That's what Treat called his plot of ground in the north of the county, on the east side, nearly eight hundred acres of it. Pristine was an understatement. Tall red oaks interspersed with pine trees dominated the inner half, near the river, save for a clearing adjacent the waters, a place to stretch and survey. The forestland included a heavy underbrush traversed exclusively by small deer, red squirrels and others (until a lot of Smith cousins started crawling around, exploring but finding nothing interesting except ticks). The land rose gently away from the river until the woods petered out and a grassland prevailed, filled interminably with the twittering of birds I could never tell apart. Grandfather saved for it from the two stores he inherited from his father, selling the clothing store but keeping the Five and Dime. Promising to build a beautiful home there, worthy of his name, Smith (which of course it wasn't, since Wolfgang's last name had been changed when he emigrated—we think from Schnachtenvolkerfurstung, but we're not positive), he dreamed big, talked bigger and built absolutely nothing. When it became clear that he was either too old or too lazy—depending on who was explaining the situation, he or Versey—together with his wife they decided to will the land to the next generation. Turns out he also willed them the problems that went along with it.

Treat and Versey had six children, and the desire of their hearts was that all six would love each other and never fight over the inheritance. Despite some of my grandparents' legendary lapses in judgment, moral or otherwise, one has to credit them with beautiful desires. However, beautiful desires do not bring peace.

People in my family tell me that I'm just like my grandmother. She always wanted to be pithy and quotable, but somehow always stopped short. When I'm not paying attention, it creeps up like in the previous paragraph. I'll try and keep a handle on it. But back to the will.

Treat was almost seventy when he decided he couldn't run his store anymore. The Five and Dime had stayed afloat, but I guess he didn't feel confident in the money that would come his way when Aunt Winnie and Uncle Frank took over the store to allow him to move and build, so he and Versey stayed right where they were at, sat in their parlor with a huge map of their land and tinkered with different ways to splice the land between their children.

In their nobleness, they decided to divide the land evenly between the six offspring. That way, they reasoned, no one would have anything to complain about. How could there be a complaint? *His land is the same size as yours, her land is just as big as his*, and so forth.

Land, even if it's a lot of land, doesn't divide up so logically, however. There are rocks and rivers, nooks and valleys, flat land and hilly land, all jumbled together, making some imaginary boundaries sublime, or ludicrous. Above all that, there is the magnificent human drama unfolding daily, the intelligent plate tectonics, seeing the deal, the gift given fairly, even out of love, which immediately seeks self-aggrandizement. In other words, there are plenty of cheap bastards out there and who knew but there was one in my family. Well, more than one.

I've often wondered, how does a gift turn into a privilege? An offering into a demand? I suspect Treat and Versey knew a little bit about human nature—having worked retail for all those years—and so they kept their will from their children's knowledge. Anytime any one of the six broached the subject of Treat's land, the two of them would shake their heads and say something along the lines of: "Tut tut, don't you worry your pretty little head about it. We've got it all worked out." When they died, their solicitor, Mr. Chamberlynn, produced the will, laid it before the heirs, beamed and said, "I believe this is pieced for all time." Or something like that; I was still pretty little then.

Aunt Winnie was the oldest of Treat and Versey's children. She was older than Uncle Frank by almost five years, I think. Aunt Winnie—she was born Winifred but only used that when she signed Christmas cards—was a heavyset woman with thinning gray hair pulled back in a tight bun. My cousin Laura thought she looked like a balding man. That perception certainly wasn't helped by the fact that Aunt Winnie smoked cigars, and not those little things the second cousins swiped from the Five and Dime, but big, thick, smokestack types. Lasting two hours and able to fill a hot air balloon with smoke, Dad said they were her trademark.

I don't know why, but Aunt Winnie never married. Considering her blatant characteristics, not many people wondered. However, I always had to spend the summers mowing her lawn and painting her many fences (she had a fence for every occasion, I swear, from her summer garden fence to the miniature one that went around her Yuletide manger scene), and she'd always make me sit down with her afterwards, in her kitchen that took up half of the first floor of her house. Letting me drink lemonade and making me eat cookies (while she sipped brandy and smoked), she'd tell me lots of stories about Treat and Versey. She was very loyal to her parents, and to her siblings as well. The ones they married, well, perhaps a little less so. They were all right—like my mom—as long as they upheld what Aunt Winnie called "the pillars of the family"; namely, anything to which Treat or Versey had adhered. My personal theory—which I've never shared before, except once with my cousin Davey—was that Aunt Winnie was just too darn loyal to Treat and Versey to marry. She considered herself something of a guardian to the rest of us. Being the firstborn, she styled herself the "Prime Sister". Naturally, her nieces and nephews spoke of her behind her ample back as the "Prime Spinster", but that's something to regret, I guess. I wish more of my cousins had spent more time listening to her stories. I guess they didn't want to because they could get long, and there was plenty of daylight left to play down by the river. It also could be that she had some unpleasant things to say about some of their parents (and some of them, too). Looking back, she was right about most of them.

The most punishing thing for my generation, I suppose, was that Aunt Winnie knew her Shakespeare, and she'd quote liberally from the Bard as she doled out lessons, both historical and moral. Of all my cousins, I was the only one who in college became an English major. I like to think Aunt Winnie was at least partially responsible.

Uncle Frank was the second oldest, and the oldest male. His hair thinned and grayed prematurely—much like his sister's—but as he got older he looked grander and grander. The same could be said of his wife, Aunt Ellen, who was more silver on top than gray, not trim by any definition but the nicest of my aunts (though always under slight suspicion from Aunt Winnie for some reason). All in all, a dignified couple.

At his heart, Uncle Frank was a fisherman. In our town there was only the river, but that was good enough for him. He had a boat—the *Arizona Kid* he named it—that was his pride and joy. Easily the largest boat in town (though that wasn't saying much), he of course kept it at the local marina (such as it was), and he'd spend as many days out on it as possible, sitting back in his custom-made chair (Dad told me years later that it was really an old barber's chair Uncle Frank had fished out of the dump), casting and reeling over and over (sometimes even catching something; sometimes even a fish). Only Aunt Ellen and Aunt Winnie knew how bad his degenerative hip got, and how much of his fishing was done because he could sit down while doing it. He had a cane, too, and that should have been a clue to the rest of us, but Uncle Frank smiled so broadly that when he said he only used it for the "dramatic flair" it leant to his walk, we all believed him. Whenever the family started taking pictures, however, it almost always disappeared.

Most of the children—I mean the grandchildren of Treat and Versey—loved Uncle Frank very much. In the winters, when he couldn't take us fishing, we'd go over to his house and sit in a semi-circle around him, beneath his chair where he huddled up in an afghan, appearing grandfatherly, and he'd tell us stories by the light of the fire and we could interrupt and ask any question we wanted. Even cousin Gracie, who had asthma, rarely missed one of his fireside chats with us, right up in front, staring at the flames, until her wheezing became too noticeable and she was sent to the back.

His neighbors too were particularly fond of Uncle Frank. In fact, of all of Treat and Versey's children—and all six stayed in town, or on nearby farms—the townsfolk probably liked Frank the best. That's probably why they kept re-electing him as mayor (which was not really a full-time job in a town like ours). Anyway, they, the townsfolk (as well as Aunt Winnie and Uncle Joe), were always borrowing things from him. Aunt Winnie, with her nearly impeccable manners, always asked, but Uncle Joe and the neighbors never did. Mostly they borrowed his hose, because he had a beautiful one. I don't suppose many people have ever considered a hose to be beautiful. Hoses are pragmatic and utilitarian. Uncle Frank's was too, but it was more than that. Shimmering like a snake in the sand, coiling almost on its own and stretching out for over one hundred feet, his hose was the marvel of the whole county.

It was never around when Uncle Frank needed it.

One time when Aunt Winnie was over, and smoking, she dropped cigar ashes all around, and one hot one landed on Aunt Ellen's new curtains she had just had delivered from Sears, Roebuck & Company. A little fire started. Everyone rushed out screaming, but Uncle Frank said not to worry, he'd put it out in a jiffy with his hose . . . which turned out to be four blocks away. He ended up having to rip the burning remnants of the window dressings and beat them until they were extinguished. Aunt Ellen lost one set of curtains that day, and Uncle Frank part of one eyebrow, but otherwise we all survived (except for my cousins and me who had to repaint the singed walls).

Next in line of Treat and Versey's children were the twins, Uncle Joe and Uncle Benny. They were fraternal twins, and they spent a lot of time and energy trying to prove it. That is, to dispel the rural legend that they were identical. I was never too sure. Standing side by side they hardly seemed to be brothers at all, superficially, but that was because they worked hard at appearing different. Maybe they were both six feet tall with broad shoulders and the same small potbelly, but Uncle Joe, for instance, grew a shaggy mustache, while Uncle Benny shaved his head. Still, when I watched for it, I found little things that were eerily similar that wiped out the physical distinctions, as if hair appeared on Uncle Benny or Uncle Joe got a close shave (and so the two became mirror images). It was things like how they walked, stiffly, swinging straight arms and legs too far up to be comfortable, or the little-boy thrill they both got when watching a parade, even the shoddy high school homecoming ones, as long as there were fireworks at the end; lots and lots of fireworks.

I don't know why they did it—tried to make the world forget they were so oppressively similar—but they weren't the only ones. My Aunt Hilde really exacerbated their differences. She married Uncle Benny, and though I don't think she really liked anybody in our family, she truly despised Uncle Joe. When I was big enough to see this, but still pretty young, this perplexed me to no end, because I could swear that Aunt Hilde had a mustache like Uncle Joe did. Hers was smaller, a little darker even, matching her straight black hair, and squarish, as if she had sniffed a black magic marker once and had gotten too close, leaving a permanent stain on her upper lip. I always thought, *Why, they could be twins themselves!* That's pretty silly, but I guess I figured all people with mustaches were alike, or should at least like each other.

Aunt Hilde was the bane of my existence. Actually, she was for the whole family, maybe even for Uncle Benny, who had always been something of a troublemaker, but nothing compared to after he got entangled with Hilde. The whole family all but hated her, though maybe that was just me. They were all at least wary of her. Whenever Aunt Hilde was near, Aunt Winnie would mumble (almost under her breath), "'Double, double, toil and trouble.'"

I could never get away from Aunt Hilde. She married my dad's brother, but she was also my mom's sister. They weren't all that close, as my mom was more than ten years younger than

Hilde (and a lot prettier, too, I thought). Nevertheless, my folks felt compelled to strengthen the bonds that gagged us by making Uncle Benny and Aunt Hilde my godparents. Though my parents hated it almost as much as I did, the "Triple Alliance" (as Aunt Winnie called it once) meant many picnics and photographs together. Most of Treat and Versey's grandchildren were somewhat spellbound by Aunt Hilde, but I spent too much time with Aunt Winnie to fall myself (I also spent too much time with Aunt Hilde!).

Oh, she was nice enough, I suppose, but she spooked me. Maybe her stare was too intense, what with her somewhat bulging eyes framing her bulbous nose; I don't know. All I knew then was that I was afraid of her, from the torrid speeches she could give to the dictatorial manner in which she ran her kitchen and her own side business. Though she and Uncle Benny were technically farmers, Aunt Hilde also ran a retail outlet in town and sold nothing but insurance losses and factory close-outs.

The Liquidation Store stood, or I should say slumped, in the block behind our main street, Washington Avenue, on a little off-shoot not officially named but that the old-timers called "Arnold Way" for some reason. Other buildings seemed to give it some space and so alleyways surrounded it, the darkest parts of our small town. Three stories above-ground, brown and dingy, I loathed going in there, but hated the basement entrance along the side more, where I once saw a rat. Sometimes Aunt Hilde would call our house and I'd soon be sent on my way to provide some free work there (we cousins snidely called it "slave labor"). I used to have to shovel out the wood-burning stove in the back, a huge monstrosity that belched black fumes and smelled like death. I couldn't believe anybody ever went there willingly! Who could possibly shop there? Folks did though, drawn in (ensnared, I suspected).

For twelve years, she had a giant red, white and black banner that read "Liquidation Sale!" plastered in the front window.

Advertisement execs swore to her that she needed new signs and slogans every few months, but she stayed with her own method. Years later, after the creditors had seized the business and opened the books, we were all surprised—nay, as Aunt Winnie said, horrified!—to find out exactly how much business she had done, right under our noses.

Uncle Benny was always something of a mystery to me. He attracted a crowd wherever he went, I think because he dressed so sharply. I mean, Uncle Frank was natty, but his suits were rags compared to Uncle Benny's outfits. Everything matched. I mean, everything! He had eighteen different tie-clips in order to match his socks. That was rare in a farmer.

His farm consisted of a few dairy cows, but never more than six, which was all he could stand to milk in one morning, and fruit trees and vines. He had a crazy dream of building an ice cream empire. It would span from California to New Mexico, and on to Florida and up into Maine and all through the Midwest, circling the map, he said, like the fruit-flavored swirls he'd put in his ice cream. I have to give him credit, though, because he actually built his own ice cream maker out of an old rain barrel. He installed a crank through a knot in one of the planks, and nailed a container on the side where he could put his mashed fruit. He planned to dish the syrupy pulp—or pulpy syrup, depending on which of the kids had helped him mash it—liberally as he turned the crank, grinding the salt and ice and rich milk from his cows.

A neo-Platonic ice cream label existed in his mind. He would call his hard-packed desserts "Benny's from Heaven", and the names of the flavors would be equally dreamy, like "Tango-rine" and "Straw-burr-y Swirl" and "Grape-ple Nut Fudge". Yep, grape, apple, walnuts (or whatever kind he had around) and Aunt Hilde's own hellish version of fudge. (Psst, Aunt Hilde, there's sugar in most kinds of fudge! It just wasn't a big hit with the kids. Honestly, we never knew what horrors Aunt Hilde would brew up in her kitchen, but we kids suspected that many of them were lethal in large doses.)

Actually, Uncle Benny almost made some money once off his homemade ice cream. His farmhouse was right across the road from the Lutheran church. In back of that they had a softball diamond, where every Friday night during summer the farmers played pumpkin ball against the townies (only we kids called them that, even though some of us were townies). Pumpkin ball was almost the exact same as softball, except for the size of the ball, which was about 4 inches bigger in circumference. The pumpkin ball pitcher arched the ball at least fifty feet in the air so that it came almost straight down over the plate (at least, that's what it seemed like when I was younger). Then, as the ball came down, the pumpkin ball batter walloped it into the woods beyond the fence. The kids were always sent to look for balls after a game. About three dozen pumpkin balls were kept in the church basement, many having been hit into the woods hundreds of times over their careers, and nearly all had to be found after each game. Looking for one during the game took too much time, and if a kid were out there, he was liable to get struck by the next dinger. I think if a batter hit a grounder he was automatically out, because the crowd came to see homers, and the guys playing were just too old, fat and pooped from the day's labor to try and beat out a two-hopper to third. When I was young, I thought the Major Leaguers had nothing on those guys.

Anyway, one game night, Uncle Benny had a burst of inspiration. It was a sweltering, muggy night, right? Everyone was sweating profusely and panting, right? What cools a body down better than a refreshing dish of ice cream? In Uncle Benny's mind: nothing. Thereupon, he went through the stands and the two benches (Uncle Benny didn't play, because he thought cleats would hamper his balance), talked up his current flavor ("Apri-cadapri-cot") and took pre-orders for the seventh inning beer guzzle (where as long as one was stretching, one may as well stretch for something to drink). By the middle of the sixth, Uncle Benny had almost a hundred orders to fill. He scampered back to his barn, where he kept his equipment and started churning. It was a long-remembered inning in local pumpkin ball lore as not a single home run was hit. Each side sent three up and three quickly back down again. Later on, Uncle Benny took credit for this, saying they were all thinking about the apricot ice cream, but it really wasn't much consolation for him. He couldn't get a batch together until the ninth inning (by which time the normal scoring had recommenced), and then he could only run over two dishes at a time. By the time he had crossed the near football-field distance, the ice cream had either melted or was covered with horse flies. When he handed his first customers their treat, he had the audacity to ask for correct change (and for the dishes back as soon as they were done, because they were Aunt Hilde's good china).

Uncle Joe was a farmer, too. Unlike his twin, he was a chicken farmer. As I've mentioned, he had a mustache. It was big and burly, as he was as well. While he and his twin were virtually the same size, Uncle Joe was stronger; I mean more muscular. He always said that he had gotten that way from his farm work, but it made no sense to us kids. Really, we thought, what was he doing, bench-pressing a dozen chickens in his barn at night?

Aunt Winnie told me that Uncle Joe was a real cute kid once, playful and cuddly. She made him a Teddy Bear when he was three, and she said that he held on to that bear night and day. They were inseparable. I asked Aunt Winnie over sandwiches and lemonade what had ever happened to the bear. She said he had stopped playing with it when he had become conscious of it as an "extraneous attachment". I asked her what she meant and she said, "'What man dare, I dare; Approach thou like the rugged Russian bear.'"

"Aunt Winnie, stop talking riddles!"

She threw me a wicked look. "Riddles, boy? It's Shakespeare. Hasn't your father ever read you Macbeth?"

I wasn't sure my father even knew who Shakespeare was, but I wasn't about to tell Aunt Winnie that.

"Oh, oh, Macbess, of course."

"Macbeth! 'Ow, Tom will make them weep and wail.'"

(I didn't know Tom. Aunt Winnie often spoke like this; one had to either get used to it or spend time around her simply confused.)

I never found out from her what happened to Uncle Joe's bear, but my cousin Jimmy once said that he had seen it in the back of Uncle Joe's closet. He laughed when he told me, when we were out camping in the woods in back of the pumpkin ball field. I wasn't sure why he laughed then, and I'm less sure now.

Anyway, Uncle Joe's chicken farm was the largest one in our county. We all thought it was the largest one anywhere. Aunt Hilde said that his place was filthy and smelly, and Uncle Benny would nod and smile. I don't remember it being smelly, but I suppose it could have been. Things that I think are bad smelling now weren't always so bad when I was younger. However, it could have smelled bad and I could not have known for another reason: I always got away from his farm as fast as I could. Okay, Uncle Joe, personally, he seemed nice whenever I could understand him, but of all my creepy relatives, he was perhaps the king. Aunt Hilde was the bane of my existence, but if I had spent more time with Uncle Joe, history sure could be different.

What creeped me out most about Uncle Joe's was his gigantic chicken pen. There were rows and rows of individual buildings, each housing from twenty to a hundred chickens, and they were all dilapidated, desperately in need of a fresh coat of paint, oil for the door hinges and straw that was younger than Uncle Joe's old dog Goat. Around this entire chicken megalopolis was not one, but two, electrified barbed wire fences. He had a whole shed built to house the generator he used to power his fences. He said it was to keep the foxes out, but, looking at the chickens, it seemed designed to send them a message, one which they could understand as it kept them in.

"Chickens," he said to me once in a rare interview, "are the backbone of society. They can provide eggs, their feathers can fill the guest beds, their manure can help grow crops, their meat and skin is delicious when fried. If they ever figure out how valuable they are, the whole system might fail."

When I asked him what system, he gestured around himself, to the chicken coops, smiling as if he were in the lap of luxury or something. He lorded it over his chickens, and almost every single one of them seemed to sense it. Walking about listlessly, pecking at the dirty feed left in the barren coop-yard, they looked not just white, but deathly pale, with a pallor of hopelessness, assured of their doom. To top off the macabre scene, smack dab in the middle of the pen was a stump that we kids thought had once been a Giant Redwood (though it would have been the only one within a thousand miles). My cousin Davey suggested once that we count its rings, to see how old it was, and maybe see if it had survived any fires or other disasters, but he was too chicken to step inside the pen-yard and find out. That's because the stump got used whenever the family came over for a chicken dinner. None of us kids were ever brave enough to look up close. All we could see was the axe buried an inch or two into the stump. Cousin Laura said that Uncle Joe always picked out the chickens that he thought were trying to be leaders in the coop, and would relish chopping off their heads (the "coop d'grace" he called it). Actual reports were hard to come by, because Uncle Joe didn't seem to care for witnesses to his executions.

When I said earlier that Uncle Joe had told me about his chicken beliefs, that's true up until a certain point only, after which I have to fill in based on post analysis (and my best guess). The reason for this was that, once, he took a trip down to the Deep South. When he came back, he spoke differently, using this thick, nearly unintelligible accent. He called it his Georgian ("Joh-jahn") accent, although I think he went to Alabama. It was about the time that he came back that he made a public announcement to the family. He had a plan. This was the start of his famous "Five-Year Plan", as Aunt Winnie styled it. Dad said that nearly every year Uncle Joe had a new five-year plan. They were pretty much always the same. He'd take his eighty acres not devoted to chickens and raise grain for five years, selling it all. Then he'd take the money he made from that and expand the chicken operation until he had enough chickens to provide eggs and fried chicken to everyone in the county.

It almost worked, too. Dad said his brother had it all backwards. He said that Uncle Joe was a lousy farmer, but he couldn't fail to grow good grain because he was sitting on the best topsoil within a five-state area. He should have bulldozed the chicken coops and grown grain as far as the eye could see.

"No, no," Uncle Joe would say. "This is a chicken's paradise!"

At least, that's what I thought he said. He could never get that accent down properly.

My dad was the next in line of Treat and Versey's children, the fourth son and fifth child overall. My dad's name was Harry. People asked him if Harry was a nickname, and what was it short for? But it was his Christian name. I once asked Aunt Winnie about that—it wasn't the sort of thing I could ask my dad directly—but she didn't think anything strange about it.

"'What's in a name?'" she said. "'That which we call a rose By any other name would smell as sweet.'"

I'd look at her as if we were each on a different conversation and she'd grimace and add, "Besides, 'Harry' came from the same people who decided upon 'Winifred'."

She laughed then, but she also took out the brandy.

Anyway, my dad was a great guy, but he sure could be mean. Mom explained once that he wasn't so much mean as he was stubborn and bureaucratic. It wasn't so much that there was a certain way things should be done, as there were certain things that should get done regardless of how or whom they hurt.

To impress my favorite aunt, I once dropped the term "Machiavellian" into her lap when describing dad. She raised one eyebrow, but Uncle Frank was around and he heard, too. Boy, did he laugh then.

"Your father," he said with a look both condescending and dapper, "will never be Machiavellian. He may want to be the eldest son, but he'll always be second in my book. I mean, fourth. He's short and bad-tempered is what he is. Ahh, but we all love him dearly, of course."

I don't think Dad ever heard this, but I think he knew his older brother Frank saw him as young, untested and overly emotional. See, when Grandfather Treat retired from his Five and Dime, he told Aunt Winnie and Uncle Frank to run it together. Aunt Winnie told her brother, "I'll take the Five. You be the Dime." Uncle Frank didn't know what she meant until he noticed she only worked half the time he did. Thereupon Uncle Frank hired his brother Harry, my dad, to help at the store. It was about the time Uncle Frank was first elected mayor anyway, and he didn't want help doing that job, so he made concessions with his store. He made Dad his Assistant Manager, which mostly meant he locked up at night and got there in time for any early deliveries. Dad said it was like being Vice-President: Close enough to look in on the Oval Office from time to time, but not close enough to use the private bathroom.

Maybe Uncle Frank was right that Dad didn't have any experience to run the store himself, but I always thought he'd do okay. Of course, I was young then, and really just wanted free peppermint sticks like Treat always handed out (Grandfather had a "one for you, two for me" mentality). Dad also kept the books at the Five and Dime, so that made him especially a genius in my eyes. One time, Dad said he went over the accounts from the first few years of the store under "new management" and compared it to earlier years. According to his calculations, they went through almost exactly the same amount of dry goods as Treat had, only they were 33% more profitable. That wasn't until after Treat and Versey had died though. One of my chores when I was seven was to haul over a case of Coca-Cola and a jar of peppermint sticks from the back of the Five and Dime three whole blocks to my grandparents' home every other day. Grandfather would always tell me to go back and get myself a peppermint stick, and fish out two bits from the register, for my trouble. I saved up for the whole last summer Treat and Versey were alive and bought myself a baseball mitt and hat, from the store Treat had sold years ago after he had inherited it.

He was short, though, my dad, I mean. Uncle Frank was right about that. He had the same thin hair that all the Smith's shared, except Uncle Joe maybe, with temples that grayed early like all the Smith's did, except most of Aunt Patti's, making me think of my father as old, think of all of them as old. Dad was six inches shorter than the average Smith height to boot. Mom towered two inches above him; eventually I did as well, but not until my late teens. I don't know if the height and the hair caused the lines in his forehead, but they couldn't have helped.

Anyway, Dad met Mom in the eighth grade, when her family moved here briefly. This was quite apart from his older brother Benny meeting Mom's older sister Hilde (I really have no idea how that one came about). By the time high school rolled around, they were sweethearts. It's kind of weird to talk about, but they're still remembered at our high school for being homecoming king and queen two years running, the only time that ever happened at Fillmore Senior High. When the dreamy talk got embarrassing, I'd usually say something aggravating like, "That's because they both flunked their senior years," but it's not true and I guess it was more like the whole senior class ahead of them were pretty much nondescript, and since they made such a cute couple, the whole high school voted them in as juniors.

I just didn't know how Mom could be related to Aunt Hilde. Okay, okay, I knew they were sisters. But they were so different! Mom was quiet and unassuming, but could get me to do things with one quick glance out of the side of her eyes. She really loved our family, too, and was happy to be part of it. Versey always treated her like another daughter. And Mom came the closest of any in-law to being accepted by Aunt Winnie, which was nice.

The last of Treat and Versey's six children, and their second daughter, born when they were past forty, was Aunt Patti. Tall for a Smith, she had dark hair just fringed on the sides with silver, a dainty nose and dark eyes that seemed to shine out of a face normally flushed from constant motion. She loved to drive. Aunt Winnie quipped that she drove people mad, but I think that was just because of the speed which she usually attained. Aunt Patti could drive cars, trucks, boats, airplanes, tanks; you name it, she could operate it. That's why people all said she loved driving, but I'm not so sure. To me she always seemed to love arriving at a place a lot more than driving there; that's why I think she went so fast. Uncle Frank always said that she was going to kill herself someday with her recklessness, but Aunt Patti was somehow inspiring as she raced along, sweeping you and everything with her. One could be for Aunt Patti, or against her. There wasn't really a middle ground with her. She had spunk like Aunt Winnie and guts like my dad, and her tongue was a combination of the two: The profanity was Dad's, the poetry was Aunt Winnie's. It was the strangest combination. Needless to say, Aunt Patti was a favorite of the next generation, as long as we weren't ever afraid to jump in the passenger side and ride along with her (we kids used to call her "Old Blood and Guts", because when you rode with her, all the blood drained out of your face, and your guts felt like seeing the light of day). She was also a firm believer in the Almighty, which, after scrambling out of her passenger side door, seeking balance, solid ground—anything not moving—all of us kids wholeheartedly endorsed. We had to, otherwise the whole speeding trip would have been a sermon, the kind laced with profanity but wasn't really noticed until later, having been so wrapped up in the glory and all.

Aunt Patti told me once that if she could have been a traveling evangelist who was allowed to swear, her life would have been complete. As it was, she married Stan Bradley, who owned the only car dealership in town. It had been a failing business before Uncle Stan allowed Aunt Patti to drive cars around town painted with "Stan the Man's Cars are Going Fast!" People around town first had to get out of the way, then they had to watch for her to come back, often two or three times, before they were able to read the whole slogan. For some reason, people stopped going to Dodge City in the next county to buy cars and came to Uncle Stan's establishment. Aunt Hilde was indignant that it had worked, but Aunt Patti said, "Bulldozers! The working man's spirit is fired by burning rubber! They follow me to Stan's like a jackrabbit in heat!"

At times like those, Aunt Winnie would usually intervene to keep the conversation polite.

Uncle Stan died when I was nine (and it was only just before the troubles began that Aunt Patti came out of her doldrums, looking for love again). He suffered a stroke or a heart attack, or some such thing, and died peacefully in his sleep. I hated his funeral, because he was a nice guy, and the only uncle who had never made me do a chore just because I looked like I had nothing better to do.

Treat and Versey's six children were the driving force of the whole family for many decades, even before Grandfather and Grandmother passed away, which happened at one of the church potlucks. Fortunately, they were the only ones who ate that potato salad, which I guess had sat out in Clara Hinkle's car too long (she thought the potluck was on for the week before). No charges were filed, and the doctor told Clara that it probably wasn't just the potato salad, because both had been sick for a long time, but Aunt Winnie made sure that Clara understood that two beloved relatives dying at the church potluck who both happened to have a last meal consisting of week-old potato salad was too much of a coincidence not to reside on one's conscience for years. Aunt Winnie never failed to call Clara on the anniversary of her parents' passing, just to say hello, ask her for her recipe for potato salad and invite her over to sample it the following week. Clara never failed to have a prior engagement.

I loved my family, mostly. When one's whole family lived nearby, all of us staying in and around the same town, it was certainly possible to achieve overexposure. However, apart from Aunt Hilde, I never thought when I was younger that we would have any serious problems, much less a family feud. That was exactly what happened, and it turned out to be, in Aunt Winnie's words, "A sad story of complicated idiocy."

I don't think she intended to paint her own actions in a poor light, or of anyone's on her—I mean *our*—side. What I think she meant by that was that the whole thing seemed preventable! Or rather, she insisted, it would have been had we all obeyed the last will and testament. She always said things would come to a breaking point if we didn't stick to it. I don't know now. Maybe it had to happen, maybe it was bound to happen.

Oh, it didn't happen right away after Treat and Versey died and their will divided up the land with pen strokes, once and for all. Mostly, we all thought they had been pretty wise. As the years trickled down, and Treat and Versey's children's own retirements loomed large (or at least as inevitable, whereas, when younger, they appeared at worst as improbable), thoughts about the land—so near to us, and yet so isolated—percolated up into family gathering conversations more and more. Aunt Winnie said again and again that someday things would break if we didn't stick to the will. Up front, everybody agreed. No, it didn't happen right after Treat and Versey died, but when it did, it began with a bang.

CHAPTER 1: BLITZKRIEG

I t started at a family picnic down by the Obeg River. That's what we called it as kids, anyway. We had a hard time pronouncing its real name, so we picked up on Uncle Frank's way of calling it the "Old, big" river, and then quickly put it into the vernacular from "Ol' big" to "O' beg" to "Obeg". Pretty neat, huh? Etymology was always a forte of mine.

Anyway, picnics were really common for us. During the Depression, the picnics were the best overall way to gather enough food to feed everyone, plus have a good time and keep the mind off of money worries. Aunt Patti always brought a bunch of pieces of rope from Uncle Stan's car lot (he always had rope because he also used his lot to sell Christmas trees in the winter, and if he could seal the deal by throwing in some rope which cost him about two pennies each, he'd do it; of course, he'd make us all mad by constantly saying he was "putting in his two cents' worth") and we'd split it apart and jump rope, or wind it together and play tug-o-war. When food got more plentiful in better times, the picnics continued. They were good ways for one of the families to pass off unwanted leftovers to another. We weren't the only family to do that in Dodge. That was our town,

Dodge, not to be confused with Dodge City which was about fifty miles away and much bigger, or Dodge Center which was eighty miles away and much smaller. In a geographical oddity in the United States, the west side of town was settled first and built up, then the east side. We lived on the west, and almost all of the town proper was on the west bank of the river. ("West is best" we said in our little rivalry with the east-siders, "and East is least." We didn't take it seriously, but I always suspected that they did. It was just like those losers to get an inferiority complex from that, resent it for years and finally lash out. Aunt Hilde and Uncle Benny lived on the east side, and so did Uncle Joe.)

Whereas Dodge City and Dodge Center were both founded by brothers of the Dodge Family (once popular off-Broadway actors), they never neared our own fair town. Apparently, we were called Dodge because all the westward-bound settlers missed this locale; they "dodged" it on the way out to California and only found and founded it on the way back (hence the west side developed first). Then the railroad dodged us, then the telegraph, then the state highway system. Oh, eventually we got these things—well, not the railroad—but it took some time. When we finally got the radio tower for KOBG, the contractor looked down on us and said disdainfully, "Welcome to the twentieth century." Dad said that was in 1935.

We didn't care much about the outside world, though. We had everything we needed, or we thought we did. Outside broadcasts were nice, and most of us followed the baseball scores religiously, but we had little hustle and less bustle, and when we had visitors, it usually caused a stir. Not for long, though, because normally it was just somebody who was lost.

Most of our picnics were held in a small park on the east bank of the river. We'd take a boat across or walk across the bridge, everybody carrying something. On the bank there was always such a nice view of Dodge, with the tallest points being the church spires and the radio tower. Our church, St. Paul's, had the tallest spire, topped with this white, shining cross that caught the sun and reflected it everywhere I went in town. I climbed up the belfry once and sat next to the bell, looking out from near total darkness into the bright world around me. It was like a metaphor for something, but I was young at the time and didn't know what. At the picnics, after boating or swimming (if there was no current), I'd always take a peek up and nearly get blinded by that cross, unless the sun was low enough. That would usually be about the time that the conversation started in earnest.

Treat and Versey's children—Treat and Versey being dead of course, so their children were the "parents" or the "adults" or, more usually to us kids, "the other generation"—would usually spread three or four blankets together in one big square where they could gather and relax, leaving one end for kids who were screaming or soaking wet (or both). They'd always talk business first. I suppose it was a derivative of the "business before pleasure" saying, what for us kids was the "chores before baseball" rule, but they did it unfailingly. Of course, they followed it up with a discussion about church, the pastor's sermon or, more frequently, who put what in the offering plate. Anyway, by business I mean the Five and Dime. There was no mention, at least no serious digression into, Uncle Stan's cars or Aunt Hilde's Liquidation Store. The farms could certainly be discussed during the day, but for some reason they weren't considered business, but were an entire subset in and of themselves. They came immediately after the church talk. The food and the kids came after the farms, and could come in either order, depending on which was upsetting Aunt Winnie the most right then.

If there was time left in the day, and the voices and the brains held out, the other generation allowed a sort of open forum discussion. The kids could participate—technically—but were not encouraged to do so. Mostly we kids were too tired and crabby to bring anything interesting to the fore, but sometimes we listened with zest.

It was during one such open forum when the conflict erupted. Aunt Hilde started it. I swear on something holy she started it. Oh, she said often how Aunt Winnie provoked her, but I was there, I was listening to everything that was going on. It was all Aunt Hilde's fault.

I was almost twelve at the time (well, a couple months shy). I was not yet old enough to sit all the way on the other blankets, but I was old enough to be closer than any of my other cousins. Sure, I was still soaking wet from swimming in the river (and my cousin Laura and I had NOT tried to drown my cousin Davey that day; he just gulped down a whole bunch of river water, that crybaby; yes, we swam in the river, but not in a big current; I wouldn't do it at all, nowadays), but I had for some time been getting a sense that, at these picnics, history was being written. Actually, what I knew at almost twelve was, it was being written without my participation!

These things tend to happen, as Grandmother Verity liked to point out, though she did so less succinctly than I've managed this time through. Let's see, what did she say? Oh yes, "The willingness of the one means not the directive of many others." Well, she was old when she said it, anyway. I am inclined to give her the benefit of the doubt and say that the wisdom of her experience was talking. Maybe it was the medication. Anyway, I digress, and I apologize.

Aunt Hilde, carefully repackaging her picnic basket and taking with her the Polish sausage that we had brought, said, and without looking anyone in the eyes, "You know, with that land up in the north of the county, I think Benny and I should manage it for the family."

Aunt Winnie dropped her stogie right in her lap. It fell from a mouth wider than a pumpkin ball.

"Yes, I've been thinking about it for quite some time," Aunt Hilde declared, straightening her little jacket and calmly smoothing the already slick jet part in her hair, "and it makes ever so much more sense than what Winnie wants to do, keeping it undeveloped and all. Don't you think so, Joe?" A cruel little smile played under her queer mustache while her eyes nearly twinkled as she looked upon her formerly despised brother-in-law.

Aunt Winnie gaped, Uncle Frank raised an eyebrow in stunned silence and my knees knocked together violently. The blows came fast and furious; we were all ill-prepared. The shots Aunt Hilde gave came from all sides and it seemed a monstrous machination, a divide and conquer attack. For see, in hindsight how clear, but the subtlety of her touch was evil genius. Starting her attack when everyone was so sleepy, on such a beautiful, peaceful day, too, she achieved her desired surprise. Quick, rapid-fire blows knocked the wind out of poor Aunt Winnie (a rare occurrence, it was reckoned by us kids). Then the real twist: Aunt Hilde turning to Uncle Joe for succor and support, the one she had always looked down on the most.

Aunt Winnie told me later that she had sensed malevolence from Aunt Hilde (she even showed me some past letters Aunt Hilde had written to Treat and Versey's lawyer, about the solidity of their will and deed, and how she would follow it always), but since she was part of the family, we all had to work for the best. I asked her what gave Aunt Hilde away—apart from the fact that I had always been convinced she was the anti-Christ, or a rough facsimile thereof—and she told me that it was Aunt Hilde's unnatural interest in chainsaws, cement-mixers and electrified fences.

"Uncle Joe has an electrified fence around his chicken coops," I reminded her.

"Yes. Maybe that's what brought them together."

At the family picnic, however, Aunt Winnie was flabbergasted for a few minutes. Uncle Benny filled the silence, as if on cue, by stating that, apart from Uncle Frank's portion, Treat's land would make a good international headquarters for the new family business: Benny's from Heaven Ice Cream, Incorporated.

Aunt Winnie finally gasped and sputtered, guttural noises meant to search out and find her voice if nothing else. Luckily, Shakespeare saved her.

"'This is the excellent foppery of the world!'" she declaimed, striving to rise.

"That's Macbeth," I said with a wink to Cousin Davey.

Uncle Joe said, "Sooo, sis-tah Winifred, y'all like this h'yeer plan o' Hilde's?"

Aunt Winnie stared at him, jaw agape. "'Fools by heavenly compulsion! Knaves! Thieves!'"

"Whoa, whoa, Winnie," Uncle Frank said, leaning on his cane as he too struggled to stand. "Let's stay calm, here. We don't even know the facts yet. Let's please withhold judgment."

"Thank you, Frank. You see, I'm merely trying to tell you that there's a more equitable, much more profitable solution to our problems."

"Problems?" Aunt Winnie was going positively berserk, but was on her feet. "We weren't having any problems! It seems like you were just looking for a solution, Hilde! And," she cried, rounding a fierce gaze directly at me, "that was King Lear, not Macbeth!"

I crawled away sheepishly (but not far away enough to lose the conversation, although it was pretty loud at that point). I knew Aunt Winnie was on my side, or at least that I was on hers, but it still hurt when an ally stung you. I fought back a tear and remembered the true enemy: my double-aunt godmother!

"I think it's a perfect plan, I really do," Aunt Hilde said.

"Ah say, Ah must agree h'yeer with mah sis-tah-in-law," drawled Uncle Joe.

Treachery is an amazing thing in a family. The unthinkable goes to the commonplace in a split second. Whereas Uncle Joe and Aunt Hilde had always sparred, they suddenly purred like two contented kittens, nuzzled together for mutual warmth. What had moments before seemed ludicrous—"Pish-posh! Hilde and Joe agreeing about anything? That'll be the day!"—now made complete sense. Yes, they were both insane. Even later on in the fight when Aunt Hilde had destroyed their alliance, it was hard to go back to the original viewpoint. The new one stayed, because it seemed to fit so well.

And they really were insane. They had riled up my aunt Winnie something fierce; that was something people just didn't do. If Uncle Frank felt the same way, he could probably carry my dad and Aunt Patti with him. There's no question that if they were united, Aunt Hilde's plans would be dashed. The children of Treat and Versey—especially if Uncle Joe could be brought back into the fold—would scold Uncle Benny, maybe even to the point of shaming him into the "d" word (something unknown in my family at that time—though the statistics may have been helped along by the fact that Aunt Winnie remained unmarried), and rid us of Aunt Hilde (though she'd still be my aunt on the other side of the family). But what would happen to Treat's land that touched on her own property? Surely we couldn't go back to the idyllic days of, well, of that morning, before the peace had been shattered, because now no one was satisfied with Treat and Versey's original intentions.

"For such reprehensible, unprovoked idiocy, I shall see that land undivided!" Aunt Winnie vowed, although I think she may have meant "unspoiled" because undivided I thought was what Aunt Hilde was talking about. Aunt Winnie was under tremendous pressure, though.

It was at this point though that I watched Uncle Frank pace. As he paced, he veered further and further away from the picnic blankets. Dad told me he looked troubled, and reported after a quick conversation with his eldest brother that things were moving too fast for him. Aunt Winnie's words seemed harsh and drastic, although certainly Aunt Hilde and Uncle Benny's tactics were seriously troubling, too. Saying he needed more information and hoping that cooler heads would prevail, he nevertheless shrank back from the fray.

Uncle Benny said, "Okay, so what have we all decided? Putting the land together again seems the most sensible thing to do. And so does developing the site for our headquarters."

"Ah must agree," said Uncle Joe.

"Yes, that is what Treat and Verity, God rest their souls, would have wanted, had they been able to do this themselves," Aunt Hilde added.

My uncle Frank was almost at the river, headed straight for his fishing boat, isolating himself. Dad and Aunt Patti really didn't have a voice without Uncle Frank there. It's funny thinking about that, because they were so spunky themselves, but for some reason they were under Uncle Frank's authority. He was the oldest male in the family, and they were the two youngest, by a fair number of years; it was a different generation with different values, I guess, some of which I don't fully understand, but many of which I am secretly envious, missing something in my own character and life.

Anyway, Aunt Winnie found herself alone, devoid of support, while the full ravages of the family rift (we were not yet calling it a feud, but it wouldn't be long) were sketched out in her presence. Her dress wrinkled, her graying hair coming out of its bun, the cigar she had been chomping on a sad mess, my aunt sat on a lone island. She looked like a lost waif (albeit an old one), but then I saw her eyes narrow slightly and turn cold, like steel. One hand made a fist at her side before unclenching.

I think Aunt Hilde knew Uncle Frank would try hard to avoid a fight, and that she also thought that Aunt Winnie would crumble when she saw she stood alone. Many people through the

him, but he stood over me and was something of a comfort. Except I didn't know what he was telling me.

"What?"

"Done," Kirk said again. "The picnic's done. You look tired. Come on, we can rest on the boat."

"What boat?" I asked wearily, desperately propping my elbows behind me.

I followed Kirk's finger as he pointed out at the water. It was Uncle Frank's boat, and he was piloting it toward the bank. As he approached, he waved at us, motioning us to come toward him. He was going to give us a lift.

We were in awe of the boat, all of us kids, not just Kirk and me. When we were little, it seemed the most powerful, biggest, most stupendous thing afloat. When we heard talk about battleships, we pictured Uncle Frank's boat with guns on it. Ah, the *Arizona Kid*. Really, life couldn't have gotten much better for any of us if the boat had been armed. The experience of that may even have been too much. As it was, however, the closest thing to guns were the fishing rods in their permanent anchors, or the sound of the motor. When I was older, and looked back at old photos of the boat, l had to admit that it looked in need of a paint job and some minor repairs and was somewhat less than grandiose. But it sure was a fine boat back in the day, with a loud, powerful motor, one bought from Ole Evinrude himself in the early years of boat motors. It even had a little cabin space below, where Uncle Frank kept brandy in what he called the "gallery". (The sides he called "left" and "starward", so you can forgive Uncle Frank his lack of nautical depth.) Up front, ahead even of the windshield, were two small seats, which all the kids vied for. Uncle Frank only let one kid ever sit there at a time, however, and this time, after we had run into the water just a few feet to the boat and climbed aboard, he picked Kirk, which seemed a supreme rip-off to me.

Uncle Frank paid my grimace nary a heed as he chugged back out into the middle of the river again. He started talking almost at once, however, and I quickly lost interest in the faces Kirk was making at me from the coveted holy seat. I don't know if Uncle Frank sent Kirk up there intentionally, or if he didn't consciously realize his need for someone to listen, but if he had, the choice was a no-brainer. I mean, really, Kirk picked nose, toes, ears, belly button and butt. Most people did at least one, and one is forgivable, but all five, even in a ten-year old, is too much. I don't know if my second cousin really was stupid, but that's how all of Treat and Versey's children treated him. Their grandchildren did, too, for the most part.

"I just don't know what Benny and Hilde have gotten themselves into," Uncle Frank began his ruminations. "Their plans don't pass mustard, or any other kind of gas, those windbags."

He didn't speak for a good long time after that, though, and I almost thought I had miscalculated. I almost thought I was supposed to answer him. But then I looked sidelong at his firmly-set jaw and hard eyes—the muscles around one eye socket literally gripping his monocle—gazing out at the water ahead.

The Obeg walked along its course, slate gray and calm. At times it could gush forth, green or brown or sometimes even a heavy shade of blue. At its stillest, one could see down three or four feet, but mainly it was as mysterious as it was wet, singular in its placement in our town and our lives as it cut through the county. On board the *Arizona*, I could see the easy boundaries of the west side of Dodge, the storefronts with windows peering back at me, a few scattered three-story brick edifices popping over them like prairie dogs on alert. There was St. Paul's again, there was Our Lady of the Something or Other (I always got that name wrong). Green was all around though, some within the town, but wide swaths on either end, parks, grassland and woods. It looked calm, but naïve, like a fellow crossing the street who doesn't see the bus barreling down the road.

Craning my head around I looked upon the suddenly darkened east side of the river. There were fewer buildings, and only the one church spire, but there were more than I had recalled; the east side was growing. Beyond more of the green that remained I could see the start of the farms, similar lands of which I knew bordered all the town. We had no purple mountain's majesty, but we had amber waves of grain aplenty. All sorts of shades of brown dominated the land, earthy, real . . . and for the first time in my imagination, vulnerable, combustible, soon to be swept away.

When Uncle Frank sighed mightily, I spun my head and attention back to him as he started his real ramble.

"The thing about it is, Hilde and Benny are family! You have to accept that different members of the family are going to have different opinions. That's natural in a family, even a close one like ours, you know. You accept it; you let your differences become a strength to the entire family. Like Stan's business sense was, or Harry's propensity for swearing."

Okay, that wasn't a new one for me. But Dad never swore *at* me. I swear. And how was that a strength, anyway?

"No, the really difficult thing is knowing how to keep the peace. Nations have to do it all the time. Families should be able to do it. We can't just declare war on another part of the family, can we? Any kind of serious divergence like that, well, that's a major undertaking. It's best to be sure.

"Still, some things are just plain wrong. And not only wrong, but stupid! Sure, they're leaving my land alone, but it's not okay to try and steamroll the rest of my siblings. How could Joseph go and agree to a blasted idea like this? Hmm. And Winifred is just as obstinate, if not more so. She has no reservations whatsoever about sparring with the lot of them. Huh, I almost think she'd fight with me if I told her they were right!

"But they're not right, of course. I must help her. It's the only way. But I can't rend the family apart. Any public rift would be utterly destructive for the town. Seeing its mayor involved in this would destabilize the voters—I mean the community—during an election year. And what about the Five and Dime? I must try and keep this quiet. I am the eldest after all, practically, and I must not be partisan, at least officially. Do you know what I think I will do?"

Boy, did I ever want to answer him!

"I will lend her my help, since she's determined to fight this thing openly. She'll need a lawyer, most likely, to look over the will. If I loan her some of my overall holdings of the Five and Dime, I think she'll be able to afford someone good and hold out against Benny and Hilde, for a while anyway. If anything comes up in the town council, I can probably brush up on my rules of order and keep things in a subcommittee. Maybe when they get tired of trying to best her, they'll be a little more open to talking.

"There's no sense closing the door to communication if there's still hope."

This was too much for me, though. Hadn't I heard what had happened? My double-aunt godmother had practically declared an open war on Grandmother and Grandfather's estate! On their last will and testament! On our family land where we sometimes went hiking and camping, the land that Uncle Frank himself said held endless possibilities, and was also the fabric of the future of our family!

But that gave me pause. If Treat and Versey's children (and in-laws) didn't know how to keep the land together—or how to divide it evenly—how were their grandchildren supposed to do it? Would I watch my parents and aunts and uncles fight over something that I would inherit? Land and a fight and bitter feelings that didn't seem to end? What would I do when Davey or Laura didn't like their carved-up share which had no access to the Obeg River while mine did?

If it meant that much to Uncle Benny and Aunt Hilde, maybe they should take care of it. That way, they'd be busy all the time with the property—which, to be fair, was not easy for us to get to, so we saw it only rarely, it being north of Uncle Benny's and Aunt Hilde's farm and on the other side of the river. They'd be so busy I probably wouldn't see them for weeks at a time! That was the most peaceful, solitary thought I had ever had! If I could get Uncle Frank and Aunt Winnie to play things right, we could all be separated from my aunt! All it would cost was land which was nice, but not really in our main interests. We could isolate them!

"I think," I suddenly declared, "we should be isolationists."

Uncle Frank's monocle dropped from his eye. He stared down at me with flaming eyes, indignant, scandalized, gravely disappointed.

"Well, nobody wants a fight," I suggested lamely.

He coughed once to clear his throat, then spoke with finality: "The family will not feel that way for long."

Uncle Frank guided his craft to the dock of our town's marina. For not knowing anything about the sea, he had a deft touch with the wheel and an instinctive feel for when to cut power to the motor. Kirk just jumped off onto the pier and ran away. His house was only two blocks away, so we didn't give him another thought. I helped Uncle Frank moor the boat. He called it "moo-ing" the boat, which is maybe why he sometimes referred to his craft as an "old cow".

While we worked, he talked openly again of how he would help Aunt Winnie. He had saved up for an addition to the Five and Dime—he was going to add a second floor where he planned to sell luxury items, like car horns and swimming trunks. He thought the town could afford things like that, coming strong out of the Depression. But it would just have to wait. Aunt Winnie could use the money to hire a lawyer friend of his. He also thought she should enjoin her own land surveyor.

35

"I have the original map of the land stake somewhere. I remember looking over it with Father about a year before he died, then marking each of our shares out on it after his death. I'll dig that out and let her ponder her next move."

"So we just stand pat for now?"

"I don't know if anything will be necessary," Uncle Frank answered, and cast a sidelong glance at his boat. "We can always go out to the land and squat, right boy? Hah!"

I blanched. Whenever we went camping to Treat's land, "squatting" was not my favorite part.

"Uncle Frank, what happens if Aunt Hilde takes your land, too?"

"Well, that remains to be seen. Sure, it's dangerous now, but I don't think even Winnie's land has actually been taken over yet. I think this is a problem that should be taken care of democratically."

"How do we do that?"

Uncle Frank looked thoughtful as we left his boat and walked up the pier (the place where he always said you "peer" at all the boats), "Well, I'll just have to decide and then enforce my will upon the others."

The day that had started out as a nice family picnic had exploded into the worst family conflict we had ever seen, at least as far as I knew. As Uncle Frank walked me home, I thought sure I'd have to duck for cover somewhere along the line. Aunt Hilde had a bomb with my name on it, I just knew it. All you had to do was look at pictures of my baptism. Aunt Hilde, serving as my godmother, held me the whole time. For years, our pastor told stories of me being the loudest, crabbiest baptism on record. He shuddered every time he saw me. But of course, my aunt was to blame. I don't even blame Uncle Benny who would be a lot easier to take as a bachelor, because she'd still be my aunt. I don't think she'd live around here, though. Mom liked putting a little distance between herself and her sisters, when she could. She just needed a little more backbone when dealing with Aunt Hilde.

I found out as that day ended, and soon others did as well, that a relative calm pervaded our lives. While no one quite pretended that the feud had not broken out at all, our day-to-day lives were devoid of the immediate divisiveness of that picnic. We didn't see Aunt Hilde and Uncle Benny, but we didn't see Aunt Winnie, either. She mainly stayed at home, as if licking her wounds suffered that Sunday. I imagined Aunt Hilde enjoyed the anguish she caused her sister-in-law, and I pictured her preening herself and parading around her parlor, doing a little jig, plotting her next offensive, but giving no hints.

CHAPTER 2: THE BATTLE OF BRITAIN

I have pretty much been able to stay out of trouble my entire life. Actually, that's a lie and I'll probably get in trouble for telling a whopper like that. However, what I mean is, I never as a youngster got in the kind of trouble that really stuck. Not necessarily the kind of trouble that could land one in prison or anything like that, but more the kid kind that meant multiple weeks' worth of being grounded, or multiple times cleaning the garage or painting an aunt's fence, *etc.* I mean for the same offense. Most all my single offenses came with swift retribution, but only a fair amount and quickly over, quickly forgiven, unlike some of my other cousins. Well, all of them, actually. They may get in trouble less frequently, but that's only because they spent so much more time in their rooms (or the garage, or painting), so they were no longer taking an axe to the cherry tree (playing "George Washington") or thinking (erroneously) that the neighbors would like a game of "Tom Sawyer" (so let's paint their fence . . . with whatever color paint is handy).

No, in family circles I'm known as the "Nice One" of the cousins. At times, I have despised this epithet, mainly for some deep-rooted sense of masculinity that I feel is denied here. My cousins got worse punishments, but they probably had more fun in the things that got them in trouble than did I, and they ended up with better nicknames, too.

Life is a game, and it's meant to be played to win. Except no one knows how to win, because no one's ever been able to satisfactorily explain the rules. Without being able to win, the second-best option is to play the game by way of humiliating as many people as possible. If the people happen to be close relatives, so much the better. Thus the majority of my cousins, especially Davey.

Neither he nor my other cousins were particularly hard-hearted or evil—I reserved that right strictly for my double-aunt. They could be, at times, the most sensitive of souls. Like when the tables were turned on them. Davey was always a most obnoxious whiner, just like he had been at that fateful picnic, frowning beneath his slightly curly brown hair and abundant freckles. He was a big baby, but he was also sneaky, perceptive and capable of quite daring feats. In fact, he was the only one of us cousins to ever call Grandmother "Versey" to her face and get away with it. We nicknamed him "The Gambler" (how much cooler is that than the "Nice One"?).

See, Davey was that rarest of all children: a little boy who loved raw vegetables. He used to sneak into Grandmother's garden from mid-summer until fall and dig up carrots, parsnips, turnips, beets, whatever she had planted that spring. It was a big garden, a small farm in and of itself, really. Grandmother was exceptionally proud of it and always entered her best examples in the county fair. Every year she could count on at least two new blue ribbons which she would modestly keep framed and hanging in her own room, although on occasion when certain rivals—er, neighbors—were over, the frame mysteriously vanished from there and found its way to the main living room wall. Every year had gone like that, blissfully for Grandmother, until Davey was old enough to get out into the garden on his own and he devoured her biggest and best before they could dim the light of the fairgrounds. This made her very cross and she set about to scare him good. So she announced to the family at one of our picnics—Davey in obvious earshot—that she was worried about the "birds" that had gotten into her vegetables, and that she was going to put out a scarecrow the next day.

Naturally, we kids didn't believe a word of it and resolved to walk past her house the next day *en masse*. When we gathered together and headed over to Grandmother's garden, a shadow loomed over her prized growth as we approached. We were amazed, both at the simple fact that the scarecrow existed and that it was so hideous. There wasn't a bird—or even Davey—in sight. He had come with us but had gone missing (the rest of us figured he had gone off to cry, being scared off from his favorite haunt).

Then we caught a glimpse of a rustling from the tomato vines into the corn stalks, moving steadily toward the scarecrow. One of us, it might have been my cousin Luke, said that Grandmother Verity's place had certainly become spooky, and we all nodded in assent.

Suddenly, Davey rose up out of the garden, drew his arm back and pelted the scarecrow with a nearly ripe tomato, screaming (to our horror and amazement), "I know it's really only you, Versey!" and the scarecrow threw off a shawl and a wig and shook with rage.

It was Grandmother Versey! Davey had guessed it, had thrown a tomato at her and—much worse in the family etiquette—called her what he called her. We all thought or said quietly to ourselves, "Nice knowing you, Davey," but it turned out that Grandmother had gotten tomato juice squirted in her eyes and hadn't been able to pursue him. She was so embarrassed by the failure of her scheme to scare Davey that she never mentioned it again, not even making our aunts and uncles interrogate us to find out what had really happened; she never told anyone and neither did we.

Anyway, if a body had to guess which of the cousins was the "Nice One", most would point to my cousin Gracie. Only six when the feud started, she was a shy, asthmatic thing, and cute as a button, too, what with her blond pigtails and a little gap in her front teeth. Her blue eyes were always wide; she seemed to stare at everything in awe, as if the world were one big, magic kingdom unfolding before her in a never-ending splendor of childish delight. We all felt swept up in her joy and innocence, just because of those beautiful eyes. Then her doctor discovered that she had a retinal sensitivity which caused her pupils to dilate.

She might still have been in line for the daunting "Nice One" definition had it not been for another curiosity about her: pyromania. Oh, she had never done any significant damage. The biggest fire in the family annals had been Aunt Ellen's new drapes, and that had been Aunt Winnie's fault—well, her cigar's anyway. Gracie only set fires to leaves and grass, and sometimes in a controlled setting like a fire pit. Her sin as a pyromaniac was something akin to omission. She pretty much always did her match-lighting in broad daylight, where there were lots of people around to stamp out the flames.

Still, it was a peculiar habit for an asthmatic. Maybe she did it because it was the most dangerous thing for her—the smoke, really—and that danger brought with it a certain desire. Subconsciously we may all have thought that she was too young and sweet to understand the seriousness of her trespasses, both to herself and all the relatively dry property in and around the county. And so, out of a sense of duty or devotion or love (or fear), we all kept an eye out for her. Every so often you would hear one of the aunts or uncles exclaim loudly, "What in tarnation! Where did she get those? Dog-gone it all but I locked up every single one of my matches before she got here—and I frisked her, too!" They would grab her and hold her up high, above their heads, while they stomped out whatever poor, unfortunate vegetation had gotten in Gracie's way.

The kids fully expected her to do some serious damage someday, but she was just so cute we could hold no animosity in our hearts against her. Still, she wasn't the "Nice One". She was just plain old "Pyro" (still cooler than mine). To make her feel better, we sometimes emended that to "Ultra Pyro" or "Dynamite", but she didn't like charity any more than the rest of us, so she stayed just plain "Pyro".

I was unmatched in being the "Nice One".

The main reason I got stuck with that was Aunt Winnie's fault. If she had had kids, it may have been different. Though I have a hard time contemplating what those cousins would have been like (running around grimacing and quoting Shakespeare), I wouldn't have continually been sent over to Aunt Winnie's house to do chores for her if they had existed. It was always the same before the feud. She'd ring up my folks and say her back had gone out, and since her garden was in desperate straits, could she borrow her nephew to do some "desperate straightening?"

My father always gave me a stiff shove on the way out the door (which always shut rather quickly, and he probably just didn't want me to be accidentally hit with it on the way outside), and when I'd arrive fifteen minutes later, Aunt Winnie was at the door, moaning, saying, "You're just in time, boy. The garden's an awful mess, and my knee is acting up again, you know."

"I thought it was your back?"

"What? Yes, that's acting up, too."

That truly taught me something about acting.

Anyway, the only thing about that situation I wish to point out is that I was never asked if I indeed wanted to go help my poor aunt. I suppose most days I would have said yes. Possibly I would have said yes every time after the first time—based on what my parents' reactions might have been to my demurring. However, I was sent off like a bad vaudevillian by a producer with

Danny Kaye on the phone. Here's the nub: The rest of the family assumed that I had been asked and had always said yes. Hence the "Nice One".

Well, everyone knows what happens when one assumes. That's right, they get it wrong.

After the feud had started, my whole attitude changed, of course. Aunt Winnie needed my help? I'm already on the way! She's one of the biggest talkers in the family! I was bound to pick up any number of juicy tidbits!

Hoeing it and mowing it, I had helped clear out her garden earlier that spring. It was time for a major weeding. I had a special pair of overalls that I always wore for Aunt Winnie's garden. Thick and heavy, originally blue but faded from sun and wear, and now an earthy brown from the many hours spent kneeling in dirt, they were my uniform of choice. The knees had been patched over, of course, and one buckle was helped along by one of my mother's bobby pins, but they had a certain feel that no other pair of overalls would ever achieve: broken in, familiar, a soothing confidant. Okay, in other words, they fit nicely.

I always wore them over a white t-shirt, and my mother told me I ruined more white shirts gardening—more than what she never did say, nor, however, did she keep me from my appointed rounds. With the feud full on, I was out the door before she could even give me one "tsk" for the amount of bleach she would need later.

I ran down Madison Lane to Washington Avenue, our main thoroughfare, lined with the oldest and best buildings in town. Most of these were two-story affairs, stores beneath and apartments above and very little room between them. A few buildings were bigger, but not by much. Almost all still had their original façades, but lack of paint and plaster had left many of them looking dilapidated. A few had been re-done all in brick fronts, but these weren't my favorite. Before these came along, I could walk slowly down Washington, pretending it was an Old

West town, sans taverns, troughs, sheriffs and bad guys, manure in the street and tumbleweeds. Actually, it didn't look much like a Western scene at all, but it wasn't that big of a stretch of imagination for a boy, anyway, and it remained my favorite street.

I skipped along until I got to Ben Franklin Street. If I kept going down Washington, I would get to the Five and Dime. As I made the turn, I saw Mr. Larebil and his wife on the opposite side of the street. They went to our church, and I knew their sons, so I waved to them.

"Hello, Johnny!" Mr. Larebil called.

"Good morning, sir."

"Say, son, we hear there's a little ruckus in the family. That true?"

Up went my antennae. Proceed with caution. Dive! Dive! Dive! Loose lips sink . . . hmm, something anyway, I forget what.

"Oh, you know my aunts," I said. "They're probably just fighting over whose recipe for three-bean salad is best."

Recipe for three-bean salad? He wouldn't buy that, but I'd have to stick to my story.

"Hmph. Not likely. I heard some talk about that land old Treat had. I heard that Hilde has made quite a stink about it. Yep, land'll always do that to a family. Land and power, of course, but you know all about that."

Eh? I know all about, um, what was that last part?

"Oh, um, yes sir, I guess I do."

Now just refresh my memory slightly, would you? So kind.

"Yes," Mr. Larebil said, "you better settle in for a long one. I wonder if this one will be as bad as that first one."

First one? What in the world?

"Oh, now Jim," Mrs. Larebil scolded as she straightened her flowered hat. "Don't talk so! Let's never have a fight like old Treat and Willie fought. Heavens! I never saw such a thing, back and forth, back and forth, until you never knew what street was what. Why, when we'd walk downtown it felt like land no man belonged in."

No man's land? These streets? Grandfather Treat? And the other name . . . Willie? Strangely enough, I also had a Grandfather Willie, my mom's—and Aunt Hilde's—dad.

"Lord preserve us from that," Mr. Larebil said, surreptitiously making the sign of the cross, though they and we weren't Catholic.

"Amen," Mrs. Larebil said and also crossed herself deftly. Then they walked on.

I turned and walked quickly toward Aunt Winnie's house. In less than a block, I was in an all-out run. Down Commodore Perry Way to Grover Cleveland Boulevard, back out nearly to the country. Aunt Winnie's white Victorian two-story house—so out of place with the meadow and wheat fields behind it—stood like a bastion of light overlooking its own island of the Obeg River valley.

Well, it was not much of a valley in that part of town, and it quickly turned into level farmland and plains, but her house was imposing nonetheless. I've often wondered if it would have been less daunting were I not related to Aunt Winnie, or if she had lived elsewhere. Every time I saw those front windows like two angry, ever-watchful eyes, I felt like I could circle the whole world, but the sun would never set on that house, waiting for me.

I kind of liked it.

I ran up to the gate, somersaulted over it (careful where you place your hands), and gasping, hopped, skipped and tripped my way to the front porch.

"Ow!"

"Careful!" Aunt Winnie said as she opened the door.

"That last one was supposed to be a jump."

"So I gathered," she said.

She helped me up, made me brush off my knees before letting me inside, then poured me a glass of lemonade. Her lemonade was fabulous: strong, tart and pulpy. My cousins didn't much care for it, but as soon as Aunt Winnie withdrew Grandmother Versey's old glass pitcher from the ice-box, my mouth watered with my cheeks and lips set to pucker. Anticipation made life sweet, especially when it only lasted as long as it took Aunt Winnie to find a glass she wouldn't particularly mind me breaking.

"Can I have some more?" I gasped as the glass thudded back down onto the counter. My throat actually burned from downing the lemonade so fast.

"May I," Aunt Winnie said with a thin, strained voice, looking up to heaven.

"May I have more?"

"Absolutely not," she said and swiped away the glass. What, was she rationing it? "You know the house rules," she said, as if knowing my thoughts. "One glass before we battle the weeds, as many glasses when the war is won. Now march."

For a woman—strike that, a sophisticated lady, she would have herself styled—she sure used a lot of military terminology. We always "battled" weeds in her garden. Whenever we finished planting, we had "reached our objective". When we watered, we were "strafing" the vegetation. And so on.

My aunt Winnie was pretty neat sometimes.

Anyway, she led me through the kitchen and down the hall to the back door. The landing consisted of three wooden steps, the top one of which wouldn't even hold an unfolded lawn chair. Every time I looked at her house from the back, I envisioned a deck that covered half her yard. It would have worked, too, and she would have had it built, but she loved having an extensive garden too much.

"I have plenty of room to sit in the house," she'd say. And if asked what she did when she wanted to sit outside, she responded coolly, "'Let us sit upon the ground and tell sad stories of the death of kings; how some have been depos'd, some slain in war, some haunted by the ghosts they have depos'd, some poison'd by their wives. . . ." and on and on until she had either finished Richard II or the inquirer had walked away.

Aunt Winnie had a lot of free time to read.

As we "marched" over hill and dale—well, the stone walkway dividing her miniscule lawn and the garden proper—I remembered my encounter on the street with Mr. and Mrs. Larebil.

"Hey, Aunt Winnie!"

"Excuse me?"

"I mean: Aunt Winnie."

"Yes?"

"Who was the Willie that Grandfather Treat fought?" I asked, and Aunt Winnie dropped her hoe. It clattered on the stone walkway and fell dead at her feet.

"What did you say?"

I forgot. The other reason why I'm known as the "Nice One" is that, while most of the family believes I'm at least somewhat intelligent, all my cousins know that I rarely use that intelligence within the family to analyze what I was about to say, and whether I should say it or not. They think that's "nice" because I ended up asking a lot of things they desperately wanted to ask, but wouldn't suffer the embarrassment and/or punishment for it for anything. I'd been consciously working on that for some time—I felt I had made great strides in front of Uncle Frank, and also outside of the family, like with Mr. and Mrs. Larebil. Consistency, however, was hard.

"Er, well, it's like this."

"Don't tell me what it's like," Aunt Winnie suggested (I'm kind of giving her the benefit of the doubt when I say she "suggested" anything). "Tell me what you heard."

"Well, I saw Mr. and Mrs. Larebil on the way over, and they, well—"

"They wanted to gossip about us, is that it?"

"Kind of."

She raised one fierce eyebrow at me.

"I mean: Yes."

"Those vultures! Always ready with news of our destruction, words of our doom! In peacetime they make endless toasts at parties to our glory and strength! But they are the first to believe bad news about us!"

Aunt Winnie reminded me just then of Mrs. McCormick who taught us Sunday School at St. Paul's. She thundered the lessons down from Mt. Carmel at us, like she was Moses or one of the nastier prophets herself. And always my second cousin Kirk or his sister Lucy was there to interrupt her, asking her when we would get the caramel. Kids.

"Mark my words," Aunt Winnie said. "They are no kind of friends who do that, who believe the worst of you at the drop of a hat. Oh, they'll take your charity, easy as pie, but get in a real fix, and they look out for number one."

In thinking back, I spent too much time with Aunt Winnie. That was where I gained my propensity for stating clichés. Anyway, I didn't think that at the time. I noticed the worry lines on her face, the rage fixed just beneath her skin, shuddering her body as it struggled to fly loose. Only it had no victim in view, nothing untoward upon which to set its sights, only a helpful nephew.

Aunt Winnie always regained her composure quickly; her grimace softened and her fists unclenched. She fixed her bun and re-rolled one of her sleeves as a smile returned. Pragmatic to the core, she hated idle hands and many weeds about, so she got us working among her beans and peas. Maybe it was only to get her mind off her current problems that she told me of past glories—I guess that's my word, not hers—although I like to think it was because I was something of a confidant to her during the family crisis. But as we systematically pulled weeds and made little piles for each row completed, she told me what my mother never had.

"Your grandfather—and Johnny, I mean your mother's father, William—used to live in this town, the same as your grandfather Treat, long before your mother was born. Yes, both your families lived here, and Treat and Willie (that's what he liked to be called, the funny old cow) were sure friends. They shared many similar habits, including a fondness for costumes and for growing out their mustaches and making them flounce when they talked.

"Oh, you should have seen them! To think of all the wonderful moments we all spent together. Perhaps that's why it hurt so much, feeling a friend's betrayal. Oh, it's not like we shouldn't have seen it coming, forgive the double-negative. No, if we had been sagacious enough, we would have known William to be, at his core, shall we say, desperate for attention. Don't ever forget, Jonathan. Someone who needs to be in the thick of things will never change—perhaps if supremely humiliated, but perhaps not. Water finds its own level, and your mother's family (much as I like her), well."

"Aunt Winnie, it's like you're giving a speech."

"Don't complain so. You want unembellished facts, eh? Well, I happen to like painting pictures with words."

"I know, I know. Like Shakespeare."

"Well, I should say I enjoy many a fine poet, Chaucer and Milton, Yeats and Herrick, and—"

"—and Tennyson," I concluded.

"Tennyson!" Aunt Winnie spat. "Hackneyed old fop! Now, where was I? Get that little one right there, Johnny, that's a good boy. Oh, yes. Treat and William. They had the same laugh, you know. Sort of a deep-throated, long-winded affair. It started in the bowels and came creeping up, through a dry larynx, as if someone had hit them in the belly and knocked the wind out of them. Drove my poor mother to distraction when those two got together to tell stories.

"It seemed natural. William was always something of a braggart, but everyone knew it and they all forgave him it. That's because everyone thought that he knew as well."

"Knew what, Aunt Winnie?"

"Everyone thought that William knew what he was, a loud-mouthed fool. But he didn't. What a tragedy. He took himself seriously, and so wanted everyone to take him seriously, too. That's a sin, child."

That didn't ring a bell as being one of the commandments, but having been stung by Aunt Winnie's tongue already that morning, I bit mine.

"I still remember being a young lass, having dinner in the other room with my siblings because my parents had company, just William and Edna again. The whisper of the two men's laughter swirled through the house as they exchanged fish stories. We all liked William then, mind. His shop had done all the electricity for the town, installing all the new lamps and street-lights. He truly brought enlightenment to our dreary little town. The town elders appreciated his work, but still looked upon him as something of an upstart. Maybe that's why he decided to challenge your grandfather. I mean, your other grandfather. Treat."

I couldn't take this pussyfooting about anymore. What had happened? A challenge? Did she mean a duel? Had my grandfathers nearly killed one another?

"What!" I screamed, throwing a fistful of weed entrails up into the sky, merely to fall and stick to my hair. "What happened? Tell me quick!" The tension was too much—I really needed to learn to relax.

My aunt looked at me with what I first thought was amazement. After a moment, I knew it was closer to annoyance. If I didn't apologize, I was liable to get spanked—I wasn't kidding, either. My aunt Winnie didn't think my dad was too old to spank, and for her to do the spanking, too!

"Sorry, Aunt Winnie."

"Yes, rather. So, anyway, it was a sincere shock to me and the rest of the family when—even from the other room we heard this—Willie stood up and announced that, since my father had decided to run for city alderman, he would put up the challenge."

Huh? That was it?

"Oh, we were struck to the core! Never had such guile been delivered in our own town, in our own house even! My father was so incensed and he stood up so fast the chair on which he had been sitting collapsed behind him. He pointed to the door and shouted at Willie that if he knew the way so well to the polling place, he should just as well know the way out the door."

That's how I learned what passed for wit a couple generations ago.

"The battle lines were drawn quickly then. It seems that Willie had been prepared for the opening salvo for quite some time. He advanced quickly and ruthlessly. On the steps to the museum the very next morning, he gave a speech that vituperatively attacked my poor father!"

"What museum?" I asked and Aunt Winnie whirled on me. Dang it, I had done it again. She meant the little storeroom that Grandmother Versey and she had put together a long time ago of a few framed photographs of what our town founders looked like. Our family didn't even get to Dodge until twenty years later. The little storeroom was in the back of the city building which also held the courthouse, sheriff's office (when he visited), town hall, mayor's office and what passed for a library—which was actually the original first building in the town, they just added on to it— and the war memorial, which was actually two replica Civil War swords, tacked up on a wall and crossed with some red, white and lavender streamers surrounding it. I reckon that last one was either blue at one time, or maybe someone a little colorblind bought the supplies and not enough was allocated to cover any mistakes. I think I heard one of my uncles say once that there were about a thousand rolls of lavender streamers still in the basement of the city building. Anyway, the whole complex was known to everyone else as just the Town Hall.

"He gave a terrible speech at our lovely museum," Aunt Winnie insisted forcefully, to which I added my own vigorous nod. "It was a political maneuver of the most diabolical kind, aligning himself falsely with patriotic trappings, speaking in solecisms to an unregenerate and pusillanimous crowd who—"

"You're losing me, Aunt Winnie."

"What? Oh, sorry, my boy."

It was a forgivable trait, of course, Aunt Winnie getting carried away like that. It especially happened when she talked about the past, our family's history or a few other topics. Sometimes one needed to interrupt and bring her back, reel her in. Otherwise, she could go on for hours. I'm not exaggerating, either. Hours. She really missed her calling; she should have run for Congress and spent her life filibustering.

My aunt settled down when I stopped her. She finally got to the real story about my grandfathers' early duel. My grandpa Willie—whom I never knew—incited the townsfolk with his bold idea to rename all the city streets. Apparently, it was unfair to the famous Americans who did not have a street named after them. To fix that, he formulated a plan to begin in the center of town with First Street, and move outward with higher numbers. That way, Patrick Henry (or at least his descendants) would never be offended at our town, and curse us for seven generations.

"Why seven?" I interrupted.

"What? Er, I think it was perhaps a metaphor."

"Oh."

My aunt had clever ways to quiet down her nephews.

"It was a frightful attack, it was! The townsfolk screamed—they had never considered such a possibility! Offend some of the Founding Fathers? Sacrilege! It must not be, it could not happen to us!"

Aunt Winnie's arms pointed with a familiar flair—she and Uncle Frank shared a sense of occasion—and I know now why all the townsfolk called her a thespian. They called her that and an old maid, but they were just mean.

Then Aunt Winnie ran around the edge of her row of pea pods.

"The dreaded attack was pressed home dearly. We feared we would lose our town's history and traditions in an awful scourge of irrationality." She ran back again. "I mean, really! Johnny, have you ever heard of such nonsense? 'Tis a true 'Comedy of Errors', eh, lad?"

I gave her an appreciative laugh as she smiled. It was the correct response—thank goodness—because I had no idea what she meant.

"Can you imagine? People actually got it into their heads that they could be offending some of the Founding Fathers because we had a Washington Avenue and a Jefferson Street, but nothing for good old Josiah Bartlett or Button Gwinnett. Really, we are just a small town."

"Who?"

"What? What are saying, John?"

"Um. Who are—"

"Josiah Bartlett and Button Gwinnett?"

I nodded.

"They're Founding Fathers not important enough to get a street named after them. Not in our town, anyway. Now come on, we've got bean rows to clear."

"But what happened?" I asked, stepping over to the beans.

"Well, we were nearly lost, boy! It would have been like the lights going out in Paris, or the Trevi Fountain running dry in Rome. Your Grandfather Willie had all the street signs torn down. He put up all new numbered ones. Ah, but that's when your Grandfather Treat stepped in, took down Willie's signs, and put up the real ones again. Oh, he may have been taken unawares, but he showed his true mettle. When all others cowered and faltered, he flourished.

"See, what he wanted to say was: 'You brainless imbeciles, why are you listening to this buffoon who is beguiling you!' No offense to your mother's side in you, dear boy."

"None taken."

"Your Grandfather Treat wanted to beat his fellow townsfolk over the head, he was so angry with them, falling for all that balderdash, as if you should manipulate a constituency with made-up guilt! Huh!

"But he didn't say that, not at first anyway. Grandfather Treat started by reminding the folks just why the streets had been named after the Founders in the first place! If it was tragic that Oliver Wolcott didn't have a lane to bear his name, wouldn't it be more tragic to erase George Washington's name from a marker, any marker? How would they feel, telling their children that they were the ones who decided to take down the great Thomas Jefferson's name from Jefferson Street, simply because Benjamin Rush didn't get the same treatment (especially when Benjamin Rush would have been the first to laud the lord of Monticello)?"

"So," I ventured slowly, trying to formulate what I heard, "Grandfather Treat fought guilt with different guilt?"

Aunt Winnie shot me a look. I am the "Nice One" even when my cousins aren't around to hear me ask the really stupid stuff.

Then she laughed; a deep, guttural pleasure that rolled into her belly and dissipated. "I guess you're right, Johnny. But desperate times, you know. Now pay attention, you're missing many weeds."

I turned my attention back to my task, but it wasn't long before I was pressing Aunt Winnie to continue the story. I had no idea walking down my town's streets that they themselves had once been a battleground. It's amazing what one misses when history is unknown. Or when parents decide to edit the past a little bit. My mother had only told me that Grandpa Willie had never much liked our town. I thought that had meant he had never spent much time here in order to know us (and love us). I didn't know it meant he had quarreled with Grandfather Treat.

What Aunt Winnie told me, however, was even more drastic. The townsfolk listened to the mammoth debates between my two grandfathers all through that summer. She said that every other night, Willie would take down the correct signs and put up his own. Then Treat would respond the next night. Everyone felt spent, and the town was running out of nails. Election Day loomed, however, and Grandfather Treat was cautiously optimistic that that would settle things. He had, Aunt Winnie declared decisively, logic and tradition on his side.

"Usually," she confided, "logic is the enemy of tradition. But on this glorious occasion, my father was both right and patriotic."

"But Aunt Winnie," I said, dropping my dredges of weeds, "isn't it—"

I stopped. My wide-eyed stare must have rankled my aunt.

"What is it, dear boy?" she asked, forgoing even to scold me for the discarded weeds.

"Nothing, Aunt Winnie. Please continue."

Hah! I had stopped myself! It was truly a proud moment for me. I had been about to tell her that it seemed far more logical to have streets named 1st, 2nd and 3rd, all in regular order, instead of the hodge-podge collection of historical names. I mean, in most towns, the presidents and others were arranged alphabetically, at least. In our town, they were arranged by the order of their births. At least, that's how it started. It worked fine as a system until someone said, "Oops! What about good old Martin Van Buren, b. 1782?" when they've already nailed up the signs for John Tyler Avenue b. 1790.

Don't get me wrong. The idea of all my town's streets being 1st, 2nd and 3rd Streets, running perpendicular to 1st, 2nd and 3rd Avenues was disconcerting. I much preferred the name medley we employed. However, my aunt was patently biased when she stated that it was the more logical of the two.

Not that arguing the point was healthy, which was why I smiled all the way through three rows of red cabbage.

"We all thought Father was in the right and would eventually prevail," she continued, oblivious to my normally intoxicating smile. "But that slick Willie had shown no compunction for admitting he was wrong. Twice he had called secret sessions of the town council, telling them he had invited Father—those simpletons who believed him!—and then hammering him before the council when Father failed to appear as, quote unquote, 'promised'.

"Willie knew that if he could get the current council to approve just one permanent street name change, then the tide of public opinion would flood his way. Treat wouldn't be able to change the sign back because he was a law-abiding citizen. The townsfolk, sick of seeing their society split, would eagerly retire to their rest, claiming a *fait accompli*, and the election would fall to Willie. Then, all the street names would be forever changed.

"But both times, your noble grandfather—Treat, I mean, of course—sniffed out the nefarious plot and burst in on the unsuspecting coward! See, Father had been sagacious enough to keep close tabs on the council. He'd send your Uncle Frank or myself—the twins and your father were too small yet—around to their houses, offering to do small chores, or to deliver something Mother had baked.

"'Hello, Mrs. Newton,' I would say. 'This is a nice rhubarb pie Mother baked that she wanted you to have. I hope I'm not disturbing your family's dinner, am I? Father will be so cross with me if I had!'"

Aunt Winnie giggled, reliving her golden moment. I knew she was a ham.

"'Oh no, Winifred! Thank you so much for delivering this. We haven't had our dinner yet, as Mr. Newton was called away to the council on some urgent business. I imagine he'll see your father there.'

"'Oh yes, I imagine he will!' I'd answer and then scamper away, racing home and breathlessly blurting the news, like the Marathon runner bringing news of the Persians."

A strange vision of cats with numbered placards running in the Olympics flashed through my brain. I can still see it vividly, to this day. Quite odd.

"There was one more important speech to give to the assembled masses. It was to be at 11:11 in the morning—all the really important announcements in town are scheduled for palindromic times, you know. Father went to town early. He stood at the podium well before the appointed time, standing formidably, whispering his speech under his breath to practice: 'Four-score and seven streets ago our fathers brought forth in this river valley, a new town, conceived in a library, and dedicated to the proposition that all streets are named after Patriots.'

"Then, five minutes before the debate was to begin, and with Willie a no-show, a note was handed up to Father. It was from Dr. Kenyon. Willie had suffered a heart attack and had withdrawn from the election. Father was unopposed and captured a landslide majority! Oh happy day!"

Hunh. I still wasn't sure what to do with all that.

"Four months of awful slander were over. Willie moved to Holland, Michigan to convalesce—I think he said the Tulip Festivals were very comforting—and we thought we had won forever."

"I didn't know Grandfather Treat was on the council. You'd think I'd have heard about that already."

"I'll think whatever I please, thank you very much!" my aunt scolded. "Anyway, Father couldn't stand the council and resigned after two meetings. I'm not surprised you haven't heard of it. The joy was quite short-lived. Of course, when Willie's family showed up again after his death, we all remembered the pain we had gone through.

"Then, of course, Benny went and married Hilde, and your father married her younger sister. Don't worry, Johnny, your mother's the nicest one. I've always sort of thought of her as the 'adopted' daughter. Anyway, your aunt Hilde's got Willie's gumption, that's for sure, launching this attack where it stings the most—at Treat and Versey's last will and testament. She could be even worse for me than Willie was for Treat. Is that someone coming to the door?"

I looked up as she made a beeline for the house. How in the world could she have heard someone coming to the front door from six rows deep in her garden out back? But she had many hidden talents. I would have to pass on her "advanced hearing" to my cousins. (We'd often huddle together at family outings, away from the children of Treat and Versey, in order to exchange information about their habits and plans, in order to make it easier for us to get away with things. We called this the "O.S.S.", or "Opportunity for Sneaky Stuff".) However, it was then that I heard the doorbell. Was that the second ring or only the first? Did Aunt Winnie have amazing hearing or did she have some kind of radar that gave her the ability to intercept visitors? Pretty spooky either way to a nephew.

Soon I heard voices, sharp and high-pitched like upset cats. Only one person made Aunt Winnie screech—the same person as made me do it: my double-aunt godmother. What was she doing here? It seemed entirely wrong, but then again, she often did head-scratching things.

For example, every time she talked to one of us kids—ordering us about to do something—she pointed. If she wanted us to go clean the barn, she pointed. If she wanted us to go find Uncle Benny in the back Forty, she pointed. However, she didn't point in the direction of said activity. No, it was always off to the right and—bizarrely—at an angle shooting up. Every time she did this, she snapped her heels together frenetically, making this hideous clicking sound that set my teeth on edge.

Or think about how fanatical she was about dressing up my cousins. Though none of them were twins to one another, Aunt Hilde always made sure to dress them in matching clothes. First they were all dressed in brown shirts, but later she switched it to black shirts. The poor fools always looked so uncomfortable and hot. When she announced that she was getting them play clothes (so maybe they could do better at baseball . . . at least when they were on my team), we all cheered, thinking they would finally be able to smile about something. The rough corduroy turned out to be horrendous for the summer, of course, and as it had to be matching, she chose field gray for them all. They were like a little army all marching to the ball field, lining up at attention behind home plate as captains tried desperately not to pick them. To console them as they stood unflinchingly, sweating profusely, I told them that at least they'd likely be prepared for winter sports. When winter rolled around, however, their gray uniforms were all they had; Aunt Hilde had forgotten to get them new overcoats and to knit them new mittens, the poor devils. They fared poorly in the family snowball fights.

Eager to see what strangeness had brought my double-aunt godmother out (and to see her get her comeuppance . . . though I wasn't sure what that was, to be honest), I grabbed one glove with the other, tore it off, threw down its mate and scrambled to Aunt Winnie's back door. Cautiously, I peered through the screen. The voices were in the front parlor, so after a quick brush-off, with a steady hand I slowly opened the door, hoping to hide the squeaks and so escape detection.

I made my way to the kitchen, which was the perfect place to spy on them; it was merely a short hallway from the parlor, and there was a pantry with a sheet for a door in which to duck should the need arise (the sheet being Aunt Winnie's succumbing to her reigning hip-size, having once got caught in the narrow doorway and needing to unhinge the former closet-like door in order to extricate herself). I held my breath and leaned toward the parlor.

"—that isn't at all why I came, Winifred dear, and you know it."

"Oh, Hilde, you take the cake. By Jove, you've got my dander up! And this morning I think I've worked it all out."

"Worked what all out? What are you talking about?"

"It's jealousy, that's what it is, Hilde."

"Jealousy? Which one of us is supposed to be jealous?"

"Owf! By dander, you've got my Jove— Oh, confound it all. You're the jealous one! It's envy or an inferiority complex or just plain malice the way you want that land. And you're doing it because my father beat your father; he beat him and nearly killed him, too! I only wish he had had the opportunity to finish the job! One more speech would surely have done him in! But now that 'my father is gone wild into his grave', you weave your little schemes to make up for it all!"

Wow! This was good stuff! Oh, if only I could see Aunt Winnie's face as she emptied both barrels into dreadful Aunt Hilde's smirk! If I were careful, I was positive I could stand flat against the wall in the hallway without being noticed, and so catch a glimpse of the battle.

"Oh, Winnie."

"Don't you take that deprecating tone with me! I never trusted you for an instant! You've got Benny wrapped around your little finger, you have. Well, he's my brother and I love him, even if he is a fop. You may have lulled Frank to sleep and I don't know exactly what you've done to Joseph, but you've never pulled the wool over my eyes."

Growing up and going to church and having family picnics, I never realized what an adult world could really be like. When we kids had tantrums, they would tell us: "Act your age," or "Grow up," or "Why can't you be more like your cousin Johnny?" (Well, neither my mother nor I knew where that one came from, because the first two were used aplenty on me—another aspect of my accursed nickname, I suppose.) Whenever they said those things, I guess I received the subtle impression that an adult would never act that way. Everyone was nice, polite, civilized. Events were almost scripted they were so uncontroversial. It made all of us kids think long and hard and deep, and then come to the barely conscious conclusion that we better have all the tantrums possible and get them out of our system while we were still young because adults were incapable of such acts. Adulthood, when it eventually came, was an eye-opener and no doubt.

Aunt Winnie was a new hero, not only standing up to the evil that was my godmother, but doing so with such tenacity and voracity; she was pure inspiration. I felt like if this feud came to actual Hatfield and McCoy's, I would fight for her. I would fight for her on the beaches, in the fields and in the streets (oh, so apropos!).

I peeked around the corner and saw both aunts' backs. Aunt Winnie was at the window, her hands clasped fiercely behind her in a manner which more than suggested her scowl, hidden from me; Aunt Hilde was between Aunt Winnie and me, her words and tone promulgating a plea, but her hands worked in opposition.

"Winifred, I came here to diffuse such a situation! Honestly! I don't have a quarrel with you. Even before I married Benny I thought of your family as my own, you as my own sister."

"Hmph!"

"Come now, Winnie," Aunt Hilde said, and I watched as she pulled open the drawer of Aunt Winnie's end table, where she kept her bridge decks and scoring pads for the Ladies Auxiliary bridge group from church that met at Aunt Winnie's once a week to gossip . . . er, to play a friendly game of bridge. They'd be by later in the afternoon.

Aunt Hilde continued to talk in a soothing, hypnotic tempo, lulling me into relaxation, so much so that I hardly recognized at first what I was seeing. I had expected her to steal something from Aunt Winnie—instead, she was putting something into the drawer. I couldn't quite tell what it was, though.

I forced myself to slink back into the kitchen. I needed to think. The aunts were starting to battle. If they didn't settle it— and they both seemed too powerful to me for either one to succumb, much as I wanted Aunt Hilde to crumble—who knew how long it would last, or how it would end? One thing seemed clear though, Aunt Hilde wasn't on a mission of mercy. This had been a raid. Aunt Hilde was trying to take Aunt Winnie unawares. And since she was evil (well, I had been convinced of it ever since I could remember), that would mean that she would try and hurt Aunt Winnie where she was weakest. The question was, where? I slipped back into the pantry to think.

"Really, Winifred, you should know me better than that. You know I would never do anything to harm this family. All I do, I do because I know it's right. You see, I was given something by your father before he passed away."

"What? What do you mean? What were you given?"

"He left me certain, shall we say, instructions."

"Come clean, Hilde! What are you gabbing about?"

"Well, let's just say that he wanted me to carry out certain plans, so he left me his true last will and testament. The one you have is false, as it predates mine."

"What? Balderdash! I— I— Oh! Show me this monstrosity!"

"Now, now. This is why he left it with me. He knew you and your siblings were too insular, too oppositional and didn't have the kind of vision and drive that his plans called for."

"Hand it over immediately! I insist!"

"Ah ah! Insist all you want, Winifred, but the will was given to me and is for my eyes only. If I give it to you, Lord only knows what will come of it. See, Treat was a very wise man, knowing his daughter so well, knowing that she'd invent any lie to tell—even about her own father—to keep her worldview intact. What he wanted was much bigger, and he knew that his children, and especially you, would be unable to accept it, though it was his fondest hope that one day you too would share his vision the way I do now. Yes, he was very wise."

"Oh, that's fine coming from you, Hilde! I think you've worn out your welcome here for the last time!"

"Yes, I must be going," I heard my double-aunt call, her footfalls signaling her imminent departure. "I think I've closed the book on this visit," she added cryptically.

The door shut and I—like a dream in which I was both participant and viewer—both heard and sensed my aunt Winnie storming from the hallway, through the kitchen, then out the back door. After a few seconds, the back door creaked open again and slammed shut.

"Johnny? Where are you?"

That's when the dream-like part ended and I fell off the orange crate upon which I had been perched, bringing down a thunderous clatter of canned goods around my head.

Aunt Winnie whipped aside the pantry sheet. She looked down on me with something mingling between anger and dread.

"Are you all right, my boy?"

Remarkably, I was, though I wasn't able to state as much with any distinction. But my nodding was clear enough.

"Good heavens, you're lucky I've so few rations left."

I looked at the clutter of cans on the floor beside me. I did count only three cans of beets and two of water chestnuts. (Aunt Winnie put those in everything, not just pot roast and stew, but every kind of soup and once she tried to dry them out and put them in cookies, covering up her baking *faux pas* by claiming they were just "biscuits"—I shuddered every time I thought about it.)

"Once I get my canning done, I should be able to make it through the winter—I'm not as well-off as it might appear, Johnny. I need every last one of those things in the garden!

That's why we need to weed so strenuously. By the way, boy, what were you doing in the pantry?"

"Uh, looking for a biscuit?"

"Oh! I haven't made biscuits in ages! Remember how much you loved my Water Chestnut Surprises? I gave you one, then I turned my back for a moment and they all vanished! Poof! I knew I should have entered those in the county fair."

"Yes, ma'am."

"Well, you've been working hard, and I'm pretty well beat myself. We deserve a break. There's not much lemonade left in the pitcher, but I think we can squeeze out a little more from somewhere in this kitchen, even if we have to get a little creative. 'A Persian's Heaven is easily made; tis but black eyes and lemonade.'"

"Shakespeare?" I ventured.

"Good heavens! Certainly not. It's Thomas Moore. Why on earth would you say Shakespeare?"

I shrugged, even though Aunt Winnie frowned upon shrugging. We set to work in the kitchen and actually found lemons. I could tell Aunt Winnie was still smarting from Aunt Hilde's attacks, because she chopped each lemon in half with a vengeance, and then squeezed them against the juicer until they were drier than a raisin. We made two quarts and I hardly had to lift a finger. Aunt Winnie could be tireless when occasion demanded.

We sat out on the back-porch steps and sipped our lemonade. The day was passing along. I knew that if we didn't start right away, we'd never get all the weeding done, and I'd just have to come back and give up another summer vacation day. But it was an eye of the storm time, very peaceful. Most people think an adolescent boy has no appreciation for such times, but I did. I had worked hard and learned a lot—I felt very satisfied with the day. Except there was something on the edge of my mind, tugging at me, like a favorite song to which I had forgotten the opening line.

It had something to do with something. . . . That's all the further I could get. My mind was stop and start, like Uncle Joe's Studebaker. It was something, and it had to do with something. Hmm.

I shrugged my shoulders again, causing my aunt to glance sidelong at me. She seemed about to ask why I shrugged—or tell me to desist—when Aunt Winnie suddenly stood up. Then there came another knock at the front door.

"Ow! That Hilde's back for more, is she? Well, I can give as good as I get!" Aunt Winnie said, setting her lemonade down with a smack and rolling up her sleeves as she stood on her top stoop. She marched into the house, but when I strained my ears to listen, I heard something unexpected: Not Aunt Hilde, but a chorus of cackles the likes of which I had never imagined.

I ran inside and as soon as I got to the parlor, I stopped dead in my tracks. There stood Mrs. Belgem, Mrs. Norge and Mrs. Frank. They were some of my aunt's closest friends. They were, in fact, her bridge club.

"Ladies, ladies, you're so very early!" Aunt Winnie scolded, but with a tinge of playfulness.

"Well, we came as soon as we could," Mrs. Frank said. "As soon as we heard."

"Heard? Heard what?"

"What your sister-in-law Hilde did!" Mrs. Belgem exclaimed. "It bowled us over, truly it did!"

"Completely!" Mrs. Norge agreed.

"Hilde! What's she done now? As if any outrage would surprise me."

"She's bought KOBG," Mrs. Frank said.

"What! The radio station? Bought it?"

I went into the kitchen to sit down as Aunt Winnie scrambled for her own seat in the parlor. (I would be able to hear these ladies just fine from the other room.)

"That's right. Ben Arnold signed the deed over to her this morning. She came and told us about it herself."

I could actually feel my aunt's suspicions growing by great bounds from twenty feet and two left-hand turns away. As she rose and crossed the room, the floorboards groaned their displeasure, and her hands—I just knew—knotted behind her back like sentinels awaiting an ambush.

"She came and told you this?"

"Oh, yes. One by one."

"And you believed her?"

"Well, Winifred, we saw the deed."

"Yes," Aunt Winnie said, "the deed was done, eh? Well, what of it?"

"She, uh—" Mrs. Norge began, but apparently looked to her fallen comrades for help.

"She wants us to go on the air tonight at eight," Mrs. Frank finished.

"What?" Aunt Winnie exclaimed. "All of us?"

"Well," Mrs. Belgem said, "not quite all of us."

"The three of you?" This time, Aunt Winnie screeched. They must have nodded, for Aunt Winnie continued, "But why? For what purpose? What did she say?"

"She only said that she wanted a local talk show about, well, bridge, and thought that we'd be the perfect hosts."

"She's never been interested in bridge before."

"That's what we thought, but Hilde told us to go and play some bridge with you, then come immediately to the radio station so we could talk about it."

"And you didn't find that peculiar?"

"Oh, Winifred, we found it most peculiar, but the chance to be on the radio on Saturday night, well, you just don't pass that up."

"But it doesn't make sense," Aunt Winnie continued to protest. "Saturday night is the most popular radio night; it's usually Benny Goodman or Bob Hope from New York! Why would she pre-empt that for you three?"

"She said she's bringing in a lot of new talent. Personally, I think she's just really interested in bridge," Mrs. Frank said.

"Oh, that's fine coming from you, Fifi," Aunt Winnie said. "But why didn't she invite me, then? She was just over here!"

"Oh ho! So someone's a little jealous, eh?"

"Jealous? Absolutely not. I just know more about bridge than all three of you put together."

"What?"

"Oh heavens!"

"That certainly is false!"

"Well, I've beaten you all in round-robins for the last couple of decades, so I don't know with which Winifred you play."

"Maybe you'd like to back up that statement with a little card playing?" Mrs. Frank said.

"Oh, with pleasure, Fifi, with pleasure. As you always say Fifi, and so needlessly rigorously, too: 'This is something up with which I will not put!' My table is right here. You know where the cards are kept."

Yeah, I thought, the cards are kept in that drawer where I saw Aunt Hilde put something.

"Wait!" I shouted and jumped up from my chair.

I ran as fast as I could. Knocking my flailing hands against the table and running into three separate walls (kitchen, hallway left side, hallway right side), I thundered through the house. I must have appeared to the bridge club like a Nordic berserker, more shocking for this being small-town America, for they screamed and turned piteously to Aunt Winnie for support.

Mrs. Frank had her hand out, had drawn open the drawer to fetch the cards, but she abandoned it and threw up her hands, as if in surrender. I swooped in, grabbed the top-most item and kept going, reaching the stairs and climbing skyward, practically soaring until I reached the relative haven of Aunt Winnie's bedroom. Only then did I look down to see what Aunt Hilde had planted.

It was a book. *Shakespeare for Beginners.*

It was not brand new, either. It looked thoroughly thumbed through. Why would Aunt Hilde plant this, though? Aunt Winnie knew everything about Shakespeare; at least, that's what she told everyone, with great pride, too.

The light dawned on me like the click of the bedroom light as Aunt Winnie discovered me. She towered and seethed and strode toward me as if the only thing walking erect amidst rubble and ruin.

Normally, I greatly appreciated her indomitability. My father had it, but I guess we were too close for me to really appreciate it until I was older. But it was hard to admire in her as well when I had just acted like an idiot and was sitting in the middle of my maiden aunt's bedroom where I wasn't allowed to go (was I the only one to ever have had this experience?).

"What is the meaning of this, boy?"

"It was Aunt Hilde."

"What? Has she gotten to you?"

"No. When she was over. I saw her put something in your card drawer. I just remembered."

"Let me see that, Jonathan."

Jonathan! Well! I handed over the book gleefully, now that I was suddenly important enough for my full Christian name again.

"*Shakespeare for Beginners!*" Aunt Winnie cried. "That devious minx! Jonathan, you'll have to finish weeding another day. I've got some card playing to do."

She had me duck out the back way (it was, in fact, years before any of her bridge ladies could see me without making a cry). I ran home and headed straight for our living room. Mom and Dad were already there, listening to the radio.

"Well, so you're home," Mom said. "Did you have fun at Aunt Winnie's?"

"Mom! She had me weeding!"

Mom winked at me. "I know, but I also know you get some interesting stories out of the deal. I'm making you meatloaf for dinner."

My mom was the best. I always suspected she was adopted.

"And what am I having for dinner then?" Dad said.

"Oh, Harry, you know you're getting meatloaf, too."

We settled in for a lovely time at home, just the three of us. In fact, if Mom hadn't made me take a bath, it would have been one of my most enjoyable evenings ever. Of course, I was waiting with quite a bit of anxiety for eight o'clock to roll around. Would the bridge ladies really be on the radio? Did Aunt Hilde really set them up to tell the whole town a lie about Aunt Winnie not really knowing Shakespeare, but only pretending, having to rely on a help book?

Mom tuned the radio. That is, she moved the dial around from 680 up to 740 or so, then back down to the far edge, finally resting back on 680 (where we always tuned the radio). KOBG was the only radio station we could get in well, except late at night when we'd get other signals, but two on top of each other, making music one moment and speeches in German the next. That was nothing but a headache.

"KOBG, your local voice!" came the canned sound of Stewart Swisland. He was the main announcer for the station, always had been. I was actually a little surprised to hear him, though I hadn't consciously considered that beforehand. I mean, that Aunt Hilde would get rid of Stewart, as he had been there since KOBG had started and comforted everybody. Aunt Hilde was the sort to get rid of institutions, but Stewart was still there. Maybe he begged her to keep his job, or promised to work for free (saving a buck was worth almost as much to Aunt Hilde as being a pain), but he was there, introducing Aunt Hilde and seemingly giving her a fiction of legitimacy in the radio industry.

"Beginning tonight at eight o'clock, the premiere of The Bridge Hour, followed by Last Will and Testament, a new theatrical production! It's 7:57, and here is KOBG's new owner and station manager with some important announcements!"

I bristled. I could hear Aunt Hilde sidling up to the microphone as if caressing it, if the microphone could be tied up and held against its will.

"Hello everyone."

Mom and Dad perked up.

"Hilde?" Mom gasped. Dad picked up the newspaper and buried his nose in an article in the middle. He never found the front page as interesting as pages four and five.

"I know you're all looking forward to our new line-up of shows. We'll have all your old favorites still, as well as many new ones that I'm sure will become ever more important to you. This week we'll be bringing Mrs. Norge, Mrs. Frank and Mrs. Belgem in to enlighten us in the wit and wisdom of their bridge club that has graced our fair town for years. Even if you don't play bridge, I'm sure you'll learn many interesting tidbits. You'll be talking about this show with friends and family tomorrow, I assure you!

"Finally, be sure to tune in next Saturday, when I'll be proudly introducing our new announcer—"

Ah. So Stewart was being terminated. Now why did I choose that word?

"—and I promise you, you will be mesmerized!"

Really? I could almost picture Aunt Winnie, hunched in a chair, chomping on a stogie, her ear nearly affixed to the radio, her brow deeply furrowed. What was Hilde plotting? She was certainly looking to entrap her, and the entire family, but how? Was the radio station part of it, or had she finally flipped?

I didn't know. I sure hoped Aunt Winnie did, or would at least figure it out soon.

"Now," Aunt Hilde said, obviously dispensing with Stewart's services already, "it's eight o'clock, and time for The Bridge Hour. Hello, ladies."

We all heard a little titter over the airwaves.

"Ladies. Hello," Aunt Hilde said with an edge of force to her tone, like a bayonet up against one's back.

"Hello," one of them said, tentatively.

"Hello, hee hee hee," said another, probably Mrs. Belgem.

There was a lengthy freeze of dead air, the foremost sin of radio, and I could feel the whole town leaning toward their sets, fine tuning, frowning, thumping the set. What was this gag of Hilde's? Was it for real? Everyone was still trying to choke down the news that she had bought the station, shifting the whole scene of the town's foundations. Hilde's Liquidation Store was a dank building on a dingy street—perhaps not the only one in the town, and one that had once been bright—but it only darkened the light of day if one went there intentionally. Now it covered the whole countryside, unless one could ignore the signal call of clear radio, something none of us achieved for long. We were a small, dissolute community, desperate for entertainment. Sears, Roebuck & Company got major looks if not much business. We wanted it all, but were poor in cash, if not in spirit.

"Well?" Aunt Hilde finally demanded. That shocked everyone back to dire reality.

"Oh, I say, absolutely," said Mrs. Frank, and we all pictured her hiking up her considerable bosom, as an old man gathers up his sinking trousers. "We had a wonderful game today, ladies and gentleman. And, as this is our very first show, I thought the girls and I would chat a bit about the general rules of our club."

"It's bridge," said Mrs. Belgem, I think.

"Yes, of course, dear, they all know it's bridge. We've had the club for twenty years."

"Well, I thought—"

"Ladies!" Aunt Hilde spat, and we all heard them snapping to attention at their mikes. "There's three of you here. Don't you need a fourth to play bridge?"

"Oh yes!" cried Mrs. Norge. "Yes, you do indeed, Hilde. Thank you for bringing that up. Oh, that's exactly the sort of thing we thought we would let everyone know. Seeing that you invited three of us, people might think three played the game. Though of course, with you here, there are four of us."

"But!" Aunt Hilde spat again. I pictured her furrowing her brows furiously, slapping her forehead and making fists. "I am not your fourth, am I?"

"No," all three whispered.

It was so patently obvious what she was getting at, I could hardly stand to listen. In fact, I lay down in front of our set, enthralled. They wouldn't be able to gossip about the planted book of Shakespeare quotes; how would they fill up an hour for Aunt Hilde? Finally, something to entertain the whole family at once on the radio!

"So . . . who . . . is . . . your fourth?"

They all paused as if looking at each other. They spoke in unison, "Winifred, of course!"

"And isn't there anything you'd like to say about her RIGHT NOW!"

Again with the dreadful dead air.

"She makes a lovely orange whipple," Mrs. Norge volunteered.

"That reminds me," Mrs. Frank said, "I had some of Cecilia Johnson's orange whipple just last week. It was simply awful! I was so taken aback because her jams are always excellent, and her egg salad is passable."

"But she hardly ever ventures outside of that repertoire, does she dear?" Mrs. Belgem said.

"Get out!" Aunt Hilde suddenly erupted. "Get out all three of you!"

"But what about The Bridge Hour?"

"It's been cancelled permanently! Out out out!" she shouted and the whole town heard gasps, grunts and a chair tipping over, plus a heavy, "Well, I never!" as a final fling from Mrs. Frank.

"Hurrah for the good guys!" I whooped.

"What was that all about?" my father asked.

Turning sheepishly to him, I shrugged my shoulders (as best I could—I was still lying down in front of the radio), but suggested that my aunt Hilde was a lot less sure of herself now.

My father whipped off his spectacles, dabbed them with a handkerchief he always carried with him in his back pocket and cocked his ear toward the radio. Then he held out his glasses, checking the light through them, and soberly readjusted them to his nose. It was a habit I was to see many a time during the feud—I knew he was thinking (I also knew his handkerchief was so filthy it only made the streaks on his lenses worse). He was buying time to gather more information, or at least to put his speaking words in order. Save for my youthful impeccable vision, it was a ploy I would have copied.

Finally he spoke. "It sounds to me as though your aunt Hilde is still perfectly sure of herself."

My head swung slowly around, my attention focused again. He was right. Though her plot had failed to the wide-eared town-wide audience, she had fallen like a cat, claws first. With a voice like a drum beat, her words marched forth along the radio waves, drilling into every home in the town, possibly the whole county.

"This is only the beginning!" she thundered. "The entire programming schedule will be overhauled! Every aspect of broadcasting is in my control, and will be launched toward better goals! The whole township—no, the entire county—will benefit from my management!"

It was a little creepy, especially the way some of her sentences seemed to mimic my own thoughts. Or maybe it was the other way around. As my mind started to wander along this tangent, I almost missed the more complete hint of what would become the most listened-to radio broadcast ever on KOBG next Saturday. Of course, I didn't know it at the time; none of us did, because she refused to give us full details. The apprehension, she said, would make our knees buckle!

"Be prepared next Saturday night," Aunt Hilde said in an evil whisper. "For though there will be no more ladies of The Bridge Hour, a new hostess will be unveiled. She will be very soothing to hear, and I'm sure she will eliminate your opposition to the new schedule . . . by how delightful she is, of course!"

She?

My mother crossed the room and switched off the radio.

"I wonder which 'she' she means by that?" she said. Man! Not even her own sister could figure out Aunt Hilde.

"Go on up to bed now, Johnny," my mother said.

Boo. No matter how diabolically interesting things got around here (and that wasn't often), nothing could shatter the sacred commitment of sending the children to bed.

This was how life was supposed to be for generations (this might be in the Bible, I'm not sure):

Mother: It is time for you to sleep, young Johnny.

Johnny: But Mother it is only half past eight.

Mother: Do not argue with me, but be sensible. You have been up since early morning; it only makes sense that you should now retire.

Johnny: Mother dear, I am not tired. All of the most interesting things in life take place after half past eight.

Mother: That's only true if the children fall asleep.

Johnny: I knew it!

Mother: Ha ha! Yes, you have uncovered our sinister plot to have fun without you!

Okay, so I can get carried away—and be a little melodramatic—at the end of the day. I won't say "when I get tired," because even though I had to go to bed, I would never admit I needed sleep. Not even if I yawned through all my protestations, yearning to stay by the radio just five more minutes.

Of course, when I was older, I did figure out that the most interesting things did take place after the kids were finally asleep (like "Santa Claus" came and put presents under the tree, what else?).

"What are you doing just standing there?" my father said in a loud voice—not a yell, but definitely heading toward that border—while beginning to roll up his newspaper. "Didn't your mother tell you to go to bed?"

"Y-y-yes, sir!" I stammered and bolted.

Oh, Dad wasn't going to hit me or anything—I don't think—but there was something firm about a father's voice that put the fear of God into a boy like nothing else. I suppose the unscrupulous (or immature?) man could take advantage of that position, but with my dad, well, let's just say I obeyed him when I was young and I respected him when I got older. How often does that work out?

After breaking the world's record for the swiftest brushing of teeth (but oh so thorough), I lay in bed and tried to fall right to sleep. Really, I tried. However, my body started shaking. Perhaps "tremoring" would be closer to the mark, except I was unsure of being able to verb "tremor". (Wait, could I verb "verb"?)

Anyway, I closed my eyes and I guess I eventually fell asleep, until in my dreams my sheets were suffocating me. I kept clawing at them, kicking at them, trying desperately to loosen their stranglehold, but every move I made seemed to tighten their twisted grip upon me. A bolt of adrenaline woke me. Reaching for my bedside lamp, I turned it on and sat up in one swift motion.

Sweating and panting, I looked around with wide eyes. The sheets were all off my little twin bed except for a tangled mass wrapped around my foot so tightly it was cutting off the blood supply. I hacked at it, feeling that I would gladly sacrifice my foot to be free. Eventually it came undone and fell limply over the precipice that was the end of the bed into shadows.

I took huge breaths, slowly inhaling and exhaling, trying to force myself to calm down, to relax. When I lay back down, I recognized what a dilemma we were in. I had grown up in blissful ignorance, thinking the family was the family was the family. Aunt Hilde had always been there, had always been a pain in the rear with the way she talked and strutted, but I had never imagined that the eerie feeling her presence put in my spine would ever be more than a child's disaffection for having his aunt kiss him and rub her mustache roughly across his cheek.

This was real, what was happening to us! Aunt Hilde was out to destroy the family, to rule it like a despot, even though she had only married into it. And I wasn't sure that Dad and Uncle Frank and Aunt Patti could see this. Were they blind? Were they afraid? Why didn't they act to stop this lunacy? I mean, Aunt Hilde had blatantly attacked Aunt Winnie, who—her water chestnut cookies aside—was the most sensible among us, and felt most keenly the desire to transfer to the next generation intact the wisdom and faith of her parents.

Fine, so what I remember of Treat and Versey—plus some stories told by Aunt Patti—make them out to be a little beyond the edge of loopy, but I also had seen Grandfather Treat and Grandmother Versey praying before every family meal, letting the hot dish lose half its name while they pestered God about each and every member of the family. They would pray out loud—the only ones who did so routinely in our mainline Protestant family—speaking as if they were trying to see into the future, determining the mind of the Almighty in regard to the ones they loved. *Hey, God, remember little Johnny? Make sure he doesn't get malaria, or smallpox, or die in a horrible train wreck, or. . . .* It could go on and on, but we got the idea that they just wanted to embrace us until we were all grown up. They couldn't do that—either physically, or in sensing their mortality—and so they asked God to do it. There was a time when I figured that for ignorance, but I neglected to accept pure chance as the only reason why I sat at home on Sunday evenings when grown, eating chocolate sundaes and puzzling my way through the New York Times crossword found in my local paper's "Entertainment" section, page 2 (the answers on page 7). Maybe they hoped for the future; maybe they had a good reason.

I felt, lying there in cotton pajamas, that my grandparents would have roused my folks and my aunts and uncles into a unifying stance. They would have probably placated Aunt Hilde—for the sake of family peace—but not once she became unreasonable, borderline criminal. Uncle Frank was upset, but urged caution. He was the leader, even more so than Aunt Winnie. She was independent enough to stand up to Aunt Hilde on her own, but was she strong enough to thwart her by herself? If even Uncle Joe were swayed by Aunt Hilde's crazy schemes, was part and parcel with them, how could Aunt Winnie stand? Maybe Dad and Aunt Patti didn't like what was happening, but they always felt compelled to follow Uncle Frank's lead.

I was just a boy, piloting my way through the uncharted territory of a family feud. I had heard the tales from Aunt Winnie that day, but they were long ago and bore little resemblance to the current clash. I was up in the air, soaring above the battles, circling around the island fortress that Aunt Winnie had become; I would be ready to swoop down and strike whenever opportunity presented itself. It gave me great pleasure to thwart AH (so I would call my double-aunt godmother in code . . . I pretended to use code a lot), as I had that afternoon. As so many were blinded by her, mesmerized perhaps, I would do what I could to assuage their guilt, cover their sin of inaction, so that when the feud was over, they could emerge from the ashes shaken, but with souls intact, because someone had done something.

I knew it was pretty big talk coming from a little kid. I could only think that way consciously when I was safe at home, harbored in my bed. From day one I had been taught to love my family, to be loyal to them. Who else, my parents and aunts and uncles had taught me, could you count on if not your family? Who else indeed, had always been my answer. Friends went home at night to their own families. Strangers did the same thing, I guessed. But what happened to the Sheep Family when a member of the McWolves started dining incognito with them? It was a dangerous game with a terrible price—even if one recognized the costume early.

Anyway, all I knew that night was that AH had been blocked from humiliating Aunt Winnie before the whole town. I knew Aunt Winnie was strong enough to withstand that singular attack, but the loss of esteem would be dear; all her friends laughing at her (and worse, laughing with AH), and Uncle Frank hemming and hawing even more. I had to go back and help her finish weeding Monday morning—we wouldn't work on Sunday, and school was already out. While there, I would relive my part in our victory, just the two of us (and Aunt Winnie would hold up two fingers, me and her). I soon fell back into slumber with that comforting thought, one of few in those dark days.

*　　*　　*

On Monday, after Mom fixed me her special hearty waffles (a little gesture, I assumed, for having to go weed again), I in my overalls ran the usual route to Aunt Winnie's house. There were fewer stares this time around, or possibly I was more inured to them and so didn't notice. However, as I rounded the corner onto Madison Street, my radar caught a whish of a familiar shape slipping into a nearby storefront. It was Aunt Hilde (I mean, "AH"), and I imagined a foul stench wafting in the air behind her. The location that had caught my attention was our post office. I knew AH had her mail delivered to her Liquidation Store, and normal things like letters picked up, too (hey, I had to do chores for all the aunts; though Aunt Hilde never let me touch anything, or go exploring in all her back rooms, which she usually kept securely locked), so the only reason for her to go to the post office was to send out a package.

This being the feud and all, we hadn't seen her Sunday like we normally would have. None of us had even had a picnic. I heard my dad say something about Aunt Winnie and Uncle Frank meeting together on his boat, but nothing about AH, not even her radio shows. So I was immediately curious as to what she would be sending, and so found my feet straying from my intended path and down toward the post office, across the street (dodging two cars and one bicycle, a traffic level we called "busy"), and up against the exterior glass.

There didn't seem to be anyone else inside, for AH banged on the service bell sharply, several times quickly, in staccato bursts like machine-gun fire. Bill Mallard was the chief postman in town. He didn't often do routes anymore because he was getting a little hard of hearing, but from what Aunt Patti said, when he did he earned his name well, as he was a little roly-poly and tended to waddle.

I thought, *If I time it right, I can open the door, and the jingle of the bell attached to the top will be drowned out by AH's droning desire for attention.* I saw her hand rise and begin to fall, as if in slow motion. My heart raced. I closed my eyes, pushed open the door and slipped in as quickly as possible, staying hunched over, low to the ground. By some kind of intuition or miracle—my eyes still squeezed shut—I skipped in three steps around the corner of the local P.O. boxes, out of sight of the counter or anyone standing right at it as AH was.

I pried open one eye and forced myself to take a slow breath—as I realized I hadn't taken one for who knew how long. My aunt was still at the counter, oblivious to me as good old Bill finally either heard the ringing or simply passed the front counter by chance.

"Howdy Mrs. Smith! What can I do for you?"

"You can start by answering the front counter when you're called!"

"Oh. Is there somebody here?"

I froze.

"No! I mean, yes! I'm the one who called!"

Whew.

"Yes, ma'am, and here I am!" Bill Mallard announced as if he were the Christmas angel.

"It's amazing anything ever gets done in this office," my aunt mumbled, loud enough for me to hear, but I doubt Bill could. "The inefficiencies are simply appalling. I would run this place much differently. . . . Look here, Mr. Mallard! I need this package delivered, priority!"

"Oh, yes ma'am, yes ma'am. Let's see here, out to New Mexico, huh?"

"It's not New Mexico, it's New York!"

"Oh yes, so it is. New York."

New York? I didn't think she knew anyone in New York.

"Well, let's just weigh this beauty up. What 'cha got in here, Mrs. Smith? Papers? A book?"

"It's none of your filthy business, Bill Mallard. Just weigh it, please. I'll need insurance on that, too."

"Insurance, huh? Must be important, then." Old Bill Mallard was still sharp as a pointed stick!

"You're real sharp, Mr. Mallard," AH said. "Sharp as a sharpened piece of wood."

Ugh! It gave me the willies to think I came close to sharing a thought with my double-aunt.

Bill must have had the scales out and his tattered postal regulation chart, battered from its many battles with his morning coffee and doughnuts (or those bits that were spilled and/or smeared). He muttered and said, "Let's see," a half-dozen times. Insurance evidently wasn't called for much in our town. It was that morning that I learned that things put in the mail could be insured. It would be a few years yet before I knew exactly what was meant by that.

"That will be one dollar and sixty-three cents, Mrs. Smith," Bill announced proudly after he had figured the final sum.

"What? That's blackmail! I mean, that's an outrage! You better be telling me the truth, Bill Mallard. If you aren't, well . . . I have ways of finding out."

"I thought it was wrong, too, ma'am, so I double-checked it. Twice. It's one whole dollar plus sixty-three cents. Do you still want this all?"

My aunt didn't answer him. I risked peeking around the corner. She mumbled and fumbled in her purse, a deep, dark place that didn't divulge coins willingly, even if she had plenty to spare. I pulled my head back sharply as she slapped something down and, in the same instant, turned and strode out of the store.

"I'll have to get the one dollar stamps from the back if you really want it," Bill said, but it was mostly to himself. He made some kind of sniffling sound—the kind Aunt Winnie prohibited in her house as "most unceremonious and possibly unhygienic"— and shuffled away to the back room.

I acted—or maybe I meant I reacted—without thinking, letting my daring or own niche of talent take over my conscious actions. Staying low for cover, I darted from my hiding place, over to the front counter where I raised up, exposing myself to danger only long enough to grab AH's package. It seethed and frothed like molten metal in my mitts, or at least it seemed so. I gulped and stood like a statue for a few seconds, moving my eyes but not my head back and forth from the front door (expecting the enemy) to the back room (fearing the civil servant), but no one appeared. So I bolted.

I didn't expect Bill Mallard to hear the jingle of the front door as I rushed out (he hadn't heard AH when she had come in, had he?), but I dashed as fast as my legs could carry me, clutching the package tightly to my chest, peering behind me for any possible pursuit.   I ran about twelve steps before my head swiveled around, a lucky prescience, and I screeched to a halt about three inches from my aunt Hilde's rear end as she waited at the corner.

I was a dead nephew, no question about it.   I sweated and prayed simultaneously.   Cruelly, I felt the undeniable first tickling of a major sneeze about to engulf me—it was the musty smell from my aunt's dress, the same as in her Liquidation Store.   It always made me sneeze, and that always grated on AH's nerves (I knew because she made it a point to tell me).   One sneeze and she would know I was behind her even before her spotlight glare could swing round and frame me.

Suddenly, something cool and hard slipped beneath my t-shirt and slid down my chest, tickling me, but also fortuitously eliminating the urge to sneeze.   It was a coin.   I realized that AH had put her money on top of the package; I had grabbed it all, clutched it all to my chest.   I had a dollar sixty-three, all in coins it seemed, either precariously placed between the package and me, or swiftly sliding down into my underwear.   Thinking of all those coins balanced just so made my palms immediately sweaty.   Everything started to slip.   A moment or two longer and I would start screaming, "It's me!   It's me!   I did it!   Waah!" just to get it over with.

The coin that had gone beneath my clothes bypassed my unmentionables and dropped quickly down my left pant leg, landing on the top of my shoe and rolling off with a tiny plink onto the pavement, tiny enough to be unnoticeable.   It was a penny, and it continued rolling until it went between Aunt Hilde's legs, over the curb and into the street.   She noticed it then, and as a penny-pincher she went after it like a dog to scraps from Sunday dinner.   As she walked right out into the street and bent down, a car hooted its horn at her and swerved away. I thought she made some sort of gesture with her hand, but I didn't stick around to see the whole thing. I turned and ran until I got to the nearest corner of a building and ducked in there. Somehow I had survived the most dangerous mission I could have hoped to imagine (and thankfully knew nothing at the time about blood pressure, which undoubtedly had climbed sky high).

After a few minutes, when my breathing rate had returned to something approaching normal, and sure that I had not been pursued, I readjusted my grip on the package and put the one dollar and sixty-two remaining cents into my pocket (the one on the right, not the left which I knew had a small hole in it after losing a great agate in the spring). Peering out to left and right, just to make sure, I went back to my original course, to Aunt Winnie's house.

Boy, was she going to be happy! I was sure I had just stopped a major offensive by AH. She'd have to turn to some other fiendish plot, because she wouldn't defeat us! So thinking, I ran the final blocks to the edge of town where Aunt Winnie's house sat. I swooped down on her house like an eagle returning home, a warrior flush with victory, having faced fire and survived. And not only survived, but come home to roost with plunder . . . except I may have filched Aunt Hilde's tax returns or some old National Geographics she was sending to a pen pal on the East Coast. That would be total lunacy; I couldn't believe it, I wouldn't. She had no pals, and wouldn't waste the time writing to one if she did.

"Aunt Winnie! Aunt Winnie!" I called out breathlessly as I skipped up her front porch steps. She met me at the door, drying her favorite coffee mug on her apron (apparently I had arrived early enough to still be in the middle of the morning washing up; forgetting my victory momentarily, I envisioned another chore at the sink awaiting me).

"Good to see you, Johnny," Aunt Winnie said. "No need to shout, I'm not deaf like your great uncle George."

"But Aunt Winnie!"

"Tut tut!" she admonished immediately. "Wipe your feet and help me dry dishes in the kitchen."

Oh well, drying wasn't so terrible. I diligently did as she advised. In the kitchen, I set my package on the table and picked out a dish towel from the drawer just below where she kept the silverware.

"What did you bring me?" Aunt Winnie asked me as she handed me a set of sopping spoons.

"That's what I've been trying to tell you! It's a package!"

"I can see it's a package, boy."

"It's from Aunt Hilde."

"What? Let me see that."

Aunt Winnie brushed her hands against her apron quickly, grabbed a knife from her knife-block (something she would never admit in the future, assuring everyone she had had a proper letter opener and scissors on hand) and deftly severed one edge of the package, spilling forth its contents. I caught myself whispering another prayer of deliverance; I was a firm believer in the need for salvation from the Almighty, as there were just too many ways for a young boy to screw up in my family and in my town.

Aunt Winnie lifted up a stack of paperwork, bound by a piece of rough twine. She pulled a cover letter off the top and scanned it. Her face drained of color. I was secretly elated.

"Good heavens, Johnny! This is from Hilde!"

"That's what I told you, Aunt Winnie."

"Yes, that's right. But it appears to be addressed to someone named 'Groebels', some kind of lawyer back in New York. She's very vague, alludes to some past business that she agrees to. Good heavens, what are all these documents? I most definitely need to go see your uncle Frank."

In my pride and joy, picturing the soon-to-come praises from Aunt Winnie, I also envisioned an afternoon opening up, free from weeding, free to roam around, down to the river or—

"Jonathan!" her cry broke my reverie and she advanced on me while I suddenly trembled. "Tell me exactly how you acquired this prize. You said it was from your aunt Hilde."

"Yes, ma'am. It was."

"But she obviously didn't give it to you. I opened it up assuming she had given it to you to give to me, but that isn't even close to the truth, is it?"

"Um, I kind of found it."

"'Kind of'? Speak clearly, boy. Where did you happen to come across this? In Hilde's store?"

"No, ma'am."

"At her house, in her kitchen?"

I shook my head violently. I wouldn't risk being in Aunt Hilde's kitchen voluntarily for anything. Aunt Winnie's cookie concoctions were truly a test of strength, but Aunt Hilde I swear was purposefully mean in her baked goodies.

"Out with it," Aunt Winnie ordered.

"The post office."

It was about the only time in my life that I completely flustered my redoubtable aunt. She stammered for fully a minute (something else she would deny vehemently in later times).

"The post office? Are you telling me you stole this from the U.S. Mail? Good Lord!"

She looked over the package.

"Oh, wait. There's no postage on this. So at least she hadn't officially handed it over to the mailman."

I put my hand in my pocket and slowly pulled out a handful of coins, setting them carefully onto the counter, hoping fervently that they wouldn't make any noise or roll off onto the floor. A dime and one of the quarters both did that, though.

"I see," Aunt Winnie surmised. "She paid for the postage and left, but old Bill Mallard had ducked out of the room early and you somehow managed to get your hands on it, is that accurate?"

"Yes, ma'am. Pretty accurate."

She sat down heavily in a chair and grabbed me. I shook with trepidation, but she pulled me firmly to herself and hugged me like she never had before. I could feel her great heart thumping madly, her arms trembling, her clenched sobs coursing through her.

"These are truly desperate times for our family, Johnny. You really are about the only one who understands how desperately we need to band together. Otherwise, we'll all be brushed aside by that tyrant Hilde. She'll rule the roost, she will. Every legacy that my beloved parents strove to give us—give us all—will be gone. Their greatest dream was for family cohesion, but not one in which some would have to kowtow to another to the detriment of all. 'For the life to come, I sleep out the thought of it. A prize! A Prize!' Winter's Tale. By rights," she declared as she finally let me go, "I'll not sleep and let Hilde do this to us. That land in the north of the county is all of ours. Your uncle Frank knows this, Johnny, he does, but for right now, he's unable to speak as head of the house. Thinks it will ruin his re-election chances. So it's up to us, and I think what you found will convince him; it must. Never, Johnny, in the course of our family's history has so much been owed by so many of us to one as small as you."

I smiled at her and a tear welled up in my eye. Then she grabbed me again and straddled me over her lap and began laying to with her stout hand onto my rear.

"Hey!" I shouted.

"All may be fair in love and war," she said, "but stealing is always wrong. Especially for you."

I lost count around twenty-five or so, and it couldn't have gone much beyond forty whacks. When she felt like I had paid my penalty, we both rose. She donned a hat then and announced that she had to go into town to the Five and Dime.

"I want the weeding finished by the time I'm back," she said.

What a crock.

CHAPTER 3: OPERATION BARBAROSSA

I didn't think things could get much worse than they were. Hardly anyone in the family was talking to one another, our Sunday picnics had gone the way of the dodo and that's what Uncle Frank kept calling Uncle Benny and Uncle Joe, too. My father was anxious all the time. He felt excluded from the decision-making his elders were doing, together or apart, and my mother was surly because Dad was so ornery (but I think also because her own sister was being such a turncoat). I think she felt that the rest of us looked to her for some kind of guidance in understanding what Aunt Hilde was going to do next or why she seemed to crave power over us insatiably, but Mom was a sister genetically, which is only a strong bond if you work on it. Until they were both married into the same other family, they had rarely spent time together, being ten years apart in age. Now, Mom felt like we held her responsible for the feud somehow. Later on in life, I would be able to recognize the symptoms of clinical depression, but at that age I just knew that I had to tread lightly around my folks.

I guess it didn't help that I had become a criminal.

I had finished weeding for Aunt Winnie. My hands and knees were exceedingly sore, but it had given me an excuse not to sit down (and not sitting down for the whole morning had allowed something very sore indeed to heal, something besides my psyche). My actions were not something I could easily forget. I was not proud of them; at least not very much. I mean, I probably had single-handedly won an important victory over my double-aunt godmother and saved the family from ignominious ruin, but that was nothing to be overly proud about.

Okay, so I was still dealing with things a little bit. I didn't understand why I couldn't have a parade staged for me, but then I could see everyone clutching their own little packages to their breasts, eyeing me like a little thief, and an unrepentant one at that.

Returning the parcel and confessing my deed to AH was, of course, entirely out of the question. Besides, Aunt Winnie had taken authority over the package and had gone to consult with Uncle Frank. I don't know exactly what they discussed, but my cousin Susie told me that when Aunt Winnie had gotten to the Five and Dime, Uncle Frank hadn't been there, but had been out on the Obeg River on his boat, the *Arizona Kid*. Aunt Winnie's rush was such that she had gone immediately out to meet him, going in someone else's craft out into the middle of the river and climbing aboard Uncle Frank's boat.

That must have been quite a sight. I mean, I loved Aunt Winnie, but she didn't seem like the nimblest of women. She was always gung-ho, though.

Anyway, things seemed to settle down for a few days after that. I mean, despite my father's anxiety, my mother's depression and my own guilt-laden, megalomaniacal conscience. Mom was touchy, though, so I spent most of that week out of the house, either at the river with some of my cousins and second-cousins, or at my aunt's and uncle's store.

The Five and Dime, the store Treat had inherited from Great-grandfather Wolfgang and then had given to Uncle Frank and Aunt Winnie, was a sort of combination drug store and department store. It was two stories of capitalism, only one of the stories was actually the basement, with a counter along one side that had an old National cash register and plenty of room to lean on. The room behind the counter was called the "Back Room" (even though it wasn't close to the back at all) which was half office, half warehouse. Throughout the store there were many departments, including hardware, dry goods, clothing and others, but all small. There was only so much shelf or rack space for any one type of item. The furniture department was folding furniture only. The only thing that was always in abundance was candy and soft drinks (probably dating from Grandfather Treat's habits); if anyone wanted clothes, there were a few stores in town one could go to, not just the Five and Dime, but if anyone wanted candy or soda, the best stop (if not technically the only one) was our place.

People liked to hang out there, sometimes under the front awning, sometimes in the back lot. They'd amble in and out as regulars did in many stores in town, and that's how Aunt Winnie learned so much of the goings on in town and Uncle Frank sometimes took unofficial meetings as mayor.

When they had first taken it over from their father, Uncle Frank and Aunt Winnie had argued over almost everything concerning the store, what hours to set, how much to charge, when to close, *etc.* They only agreed on the color scheme: red, white and blue. However, Uncle Frank liked his colored stripes horizontal, throwing in some stars in a field of blue, while Aunt Winnie disdained this, opting for mostly crisscrossed stripes. However, as with most things having to do with the Five and Dime, as Uncle Frank paid for more of it (and earned more out of it), his ideas usually carried the day.

These days, Uncle Frank was there more than ever. Dad was there a lot, too, because he did the books for Uncle Frank and

Aunt Winnie, and Uncle Frank was riding him pretty hard. They were in a tizzy over something (obviously the purloined package!), and were testy with everyone.

Since I was handy, I was set to work stacking the empty glass Coke bottles into the casements and setting them out back for the delivery man to haul away. For some reason, he hadn't been by in a while, so there were lots of bottles about. Putting the empties all together was about the last thing that Uncle Frank liked to do; I guess it came from Grandfather Treat's Coke habit, which wasn't only the scores of fluid ounces per day, but meant leaving the bottles everywhere. They mostly ended up in the basement (I have no idea how), but a goodly number of them could be found behind the counter and in various places around the store. It's amazing anyone could find what they needed in the Five and Dime without the shattering of glass, but I suppose that's what one finds in a town where everyone knows not only one's name but his or her personal habits as well. If anyone found a bottle, he would just take what he needed from the shelf and put the bottle back.

Now for some reason, they needed all the deposit money. I think it was only a couple of quarters per case, but Uncle Frank was very insistent on needing every dime he could scrape together, so off to the chore I went.

I had hauled out about six cases when I felt I deserved a break. It may have been a little warm, but I took an unopened Coke for my own and went behind the counter to pop the top, since that's where the bolted-on bottle opener was (as a convenience to the paying customers, anyway). Uncle Frank and Aunt Winnie were outside as it was nice out and there were no customers. I watched them walk to the back of the building while they grumbled. Dad was in the Back Room pouring over the books. Beneath the register, and to the left of the permanent bottle opener, were the remnants of the package from AH. The package looked empty, except I could see one piece of paper sticking out from it.

I double-checked where everyone was, then reached for that sheet. I couldn't help myself. It looked like a cover letter, as it denoted enclosures (though where they were, I couldn't say).

Dear Mr. Groebels:

Enclosed please find the necessary changes for the secondary prospectus for Out-Wits Corporation, making it technically a separate entity from the Greater East Dodge Co-Prosperity Sphere. As soon as the changes are made, this should be offered to the market. This is ASAP!

Previous commitments to my brother-in-law have been discontinued. As they were never legally bound, but only discussed generally, you may ignore all references in the original text to the building of the chicken pens. Instead, the factory and warehouse sizes will be increased proportionately on the original land tract, and will be added to in later phases (I will send you a re-drawn map).

Let me know as soon as this is executed.

In Victory,

It was signed by Aunt Hilde, of course. The signature was bird-scratch, but I knew it was hers. I quickly put the letter back as the front door bell jangled, announcing someone had entered, a random customer. Sidestepping my way from behind the counter, I slipped into the Back Room, sipping on my Coke.

"How's things?" Dad asked me.

All I could think about was the letter. What did it mean? It sounded nefarious, like so many things AH had said. What was she offering to market, a store to rival the Five and Dime? What was that thing about Dodge? And who was the "brother-in-law"? She had several, my dad and Uncle Frank included, but I was willing to bet my share of the Coke bottle deposit money (which unfortunately turned out to be zero) that it was Uncle Joe. Why would she double-cross her erstwhile ally? Apart from the fact that she was simply evil, that is. But what did that mean? I would have to find out. More immediately, I needed something to say instead of sputtering out that I had read a letter not quite intended for my eyes.

"Uh, want a Coke, Dad?"

"No, thanks," he said and looked back down at the ledgers and documents spread out on the table before him.

"It just doesn't make any sense," he mumbled and I hushed up, hopeful that he would continue, which amazingly enough he did.

"How can Benny and Hilde do all this? They've only got the one farm and her store. Benny's ice cream sales must be negligible, at best! The farm is small and can't do any more than keep them afloat. Yet they claim them as major assets! So maybe the Liquidation Store does make a profit, but nobody ever goes there, so how do they do it? And enough to encourage the kind of growth they're talking about? Six million? It's an enigma, but I'm sure we'll crack it somehow."

Six million? Six million what? I wondered momentarily if he could have meant dollars, but I laughed that off as there probably wasn't a total of six million dollars in the whole world.

"That's neither here nor there, I suppose. Not when we're hardly getting any supplies delivered to us. I can only call the trucking company so often. Everything gets sent off, so they say, but only so much makes it to us. It's like the whole operation has been torpedoed!"

He started scribbling some calculations on scrap paper. I hoped he would go on, but it soon seemed obvious that I waited in vain; every sound that came out of him degenerated more and more into mumbling. Again sidestepping (it was my quietest way of walking), I went back into the main room of the store.

We weren't getting all of our supplies? I darted over to the candy aisle and looked aghast at the scarcity of chocolate products. Where were the Hershey bars? No non-pareils? What about jaw-breakers and bubble-gum? Cracker Jacks? Oh look, plenty of Bit o' Honeys. Blah.

As I wondered how to deal with this new crisis, I heard a rumbling out on Washington Avenue. I walked to the front door as the clattering continued, a rising cacophony. A series of three large trucks passed in solemn formation, each spaced about ten feet apart with almost military precision. Two were flat-beds hauling parts of what looked like a steam-shovel, and the third was a dump truck.

The bell jingle on the front door of the Five and Dime was lost in the roar of the engines as I went outside. There, the passersby stood agape and stared. What was going on and where were those trucks headed? All we could tell was that they continued on down the street, toward the Obeg River bridge. I counted East Dodge as barely part of town. Yes, there were some buildings, but nothing much else out that way except farms, like Uncle Joe's, empty land like Grandfather Treat's, and miscellaneous houses like . . . Aunt Hilde's.

I did a quick about-face and ran back inside to go see Dad. The conclusion was obvious, if vague: Aunt Hilde and Uncle Benny were going to set up a steam shovel somewhere!

I stopped at the counter and realized two things at once: The first was that, even as a vague conclusion, mine stunk; the second was that Dad was so engrossed in his work, he hadn't even heard the trucks go by, so he probably wouldn't believe me.

I sighed and looked about helplessly. With no handy solutions (or distractions), I went back to getting the Coke bottles together. I went up and down each aisle, carrying a casement like a candy-striper, except collecting instead of dispensing. When I had filled it, I carried the casement past Dad into the back hallway to the landing. I was just about to turn and back into the screen door to open it when I noticed Uncle Frank and Aunt Winnie. I nearly dropped the entire load of deposit bottles when I saw them standing and talking with Uncle Joe!

What was going on here? Immediately, I leapt into sleuth-mode. Stealthily lowering my set of bottles to the ground without a single rattle and sneakily edging my way to the side of the landing, I strained to hear them (and, to my delight, I looked down and saw my own partially downed bottle of Coke, which I could finish on this lucky "break"). At first it seemed that a distant siren would drown them all out, but it turned out to be just Uncle Joe wailing.

"Oh my heavens!" he declared. "Ah do declare that these h'yeer days have goht tah be the worst, Ah say, the worst days of my life!"

What an actor.

"Say, Ah say thah John-boy!" he used to say to me, twirling one finger around the tip of his mustache, "Why don'tcha, Ah say, why don'tcha help mah feed these h'yeer chickens!"

"Uh, what was that, Uncle Joe?"

I would always pretend I couldn't understand him when he affected his Southern accent (always bad, but I found out how poor it was later in life when I spent a winter in Savannah, deciding he sounded more like Foghorn Leghorn than a passerby in *Gone with the Wind*; in fact, I'd bet anything he picked it up from the Warner Brothers' cartoons and not his own travels). Part of it was true—I couldn't understand him—but also it was to have a little fun with him. Mostly it was a desperate attempt to get out of feeding his chickens. It was a fate much worse than weeding Aunt Winnie's garden. Those chickens were the saddest things I'd ever seen. If one of us kids was stuck in the pen with them, having to feed them, we all thought the chickens stared at us nonstop, their look alternating between homicidal hunger and a pleading for us to kill them swiftly.

"Oh, Ah do declare!" Uncle Joe yelled at the top of his lungs in the middle of the peaceful haven of the back lot of the Five and Dime.

"There, there," Aunt Winnie said and gave Uncle Joe two slight pats on his shoulder. "Buck up there, Joseph."

That was the limit of her outward compassion. She would give you the shirt off her back (or, more modestly, the spare shirt in her wardrobe), so long as she didn't have to hug you or anything (nieces and nephews excluded while young).

"Ah am in desperate straits!" Uncle Joe cried.

"I should say that it seems to serve you correctly," Uncle Frank said, but I could tell from Aunt Winnie's glare that she thought it a grave mistake.

Uncle Joe was indeed most mightily offended. His tears dried up immediately (we all knew they were part of the façade, like his accent, unevenly applied as they both were). He made to walk away, around the store.

"Ah will just sign it all over to her! Ah'll take the lump-sum buyout, Ah swear Ah will!"

"Franklin!" Aunt Winnie said, a one-word rebuke of her brother. "Now, Joseph, hold up. You know we can't go making a separate peace with her. That's exactly what she wants. It's how she'll win. We must stand united!"

"Ah need the land for mah birds."

"All right, Joseph," Uncle Frank said, fanning himself with a set of papers. "Just calm down. I'm sorry for what I said. I'm as opposed to what she's done as you all are."

Uncle Joe came back, muttering something I couldn't pick out, but Aunt Winnie ignored whatever it was.

"Do you really think so, Franklin? Are you really that involved?" my aunt asked, rounding on her other brother.

"Well, I've got a business to run, haven't I? I've got an electorate to placate. Do you think I can take the lead in this?

You two have both had your share of squabbles with her in the past."

"As have you!" Aunt Winnie declared. "Besides, it's part my business, too, yet I'm devoting all my time and energy to fighting her on every front I can. You will all have to declare yourselves against her sooner, rather than later."

"Mah po' chickens!" Uncle Joe wailed.

Uncle Frank ignored him. "Winifred, I'm the one paying for much of this venture already!"

"But it's to preserve—!"

"I know what we're trying to preserve," he said, raising his hands, deflecting Aunt Winnie's righteous rage. "Now please, Sister, let Joseph finish telling us what's happened."

Then Uncle Frank glanced back and spied me on the other side of the screen door, in mid-swig, too.

"Aren't you supposed to be stacking bottles, Johnny?" he asked pointedly. "Not adding to the clutter around here?"

"Yes, sir," I said after a hurried swallow.

They headed in anyway, so I quickly went about looking as busy as possible, grabbing another empty crate and gathering the low-hanging fruit (i.e. the empty Coke bottles in sight on the shelves, but also within earshot of my aunt and uncles who landed near the register). I missed some things, especially what Uncle Frank said, as for the most part his back was to me, but I overheard enough to get a clearer picture of what the last week had been like for Uncle Joe.

As the whole county knew, Uncle Joe was a widower. That is, of course we knew that Aunt Alice had died tragically inside one of the chicken pens, in what the sheriff described as a "bizarre accident, hopefully never to recur" in which she had apparently slipped, fallen and knocked herself unconscious, after which the chickens pecked at her. No, they didn't peck her to death (although this story was latently part of the reason we kids were all afraid of having to feed them), but the pricking on her skin all over must have brought her back to some sort of consciousness. She rolled around violently to get the dirty birds off her, rolled right up against the side of one of the coops, against which the axe (the instrument that provided us all with Thanksgiving and Christmas dinner) leaned, tottered and fell. Suffice to say, Uncle Joe kept that axe sharp enough to split hairs, which he usually did all the time, anyway.

When I say that the whole county knew that he was a widower, it was more in reference to the fact that he was constantly searching for a second wife. We knew it—for goodness' sake, he was SO obvious about it, always looking the single women up and down, whispering (too much aloud, of course) the details he noticed, mostly denoting all the faults he found or thought he did. He would have checked their teeth if they had let him, I swear he would have. In his "inventory" (that's what we kids took to calling it) he kept up not only on the single women in town, but also any of the married ones whose husbands he felt were each not in the best of health.

"Mornin', Miss . . . uh, Mrs. Mitchell. Mighty fine day out. Say, Ah saw Richard the other day and he looked a might bit yella. He ain't about to croak none, is he?"

"Good heavens, no!"

"Oh. Well, good, good. Well, have a nice day Miss . . . uh, Mrs. Mitchell."

It was a little macabre, of course, but in a town like ours and with a family like ours, slightly insular, not quite as powerful in the town as we once had been, but still respected for what we once were, it was accepted as merely eccentric. Uncle Joe was what he was. His kids were nice enough and his land was kept in order, if not the way that the less eccentric folks of the community would take care of it, using more manure on the fields and a little more feed for the chickens and a little less anger on both.

Anyway, Uncle Joe thought his quest for another bride to be pretty well hidden. Maybe all of our most blatant flaws are as obvious to others. Maybe deep down he really knew that we all knew. Maybe that's what he wanted because some "lucky" woman might take pity on him and agree to be the one to feed the chickens next for him.

From the way Uncle Joe carried on inside the Five and Dime, it seemed to me that he felt he had found such a woman. Apparently, he had gotten a letter of introduction from an anonymous source, who said that he or she knew of a woman looking for some rural accommodations. If he (Uncle Joe) were open to providing a little "Southern hospitality", there might be future implications.

This was, naturally enough, puzzling to Uncle Joe, but it was also tempting. So tempting that he immediately went to his old roll-top desk, cleared off a place, scrounged up some ink and wrote out his reply of acceptance. (I've seen his desk. This was no small feat finding room to write on, or ink with which to write. It's a "roll-top" desk in style only, because it's piled so high with maps he's collected from the South that there's no chance of the cover rolling back down without needing to start a major fire to clear away the brush.)

All hopped up on love, Uncle Joe dashed outside to go post his reply (even though he apparently did not know of a return address to use). As he made his way down the driveway, however, Lawrence Welcome's taxi drove up and stopped in front of his drive. Out stepped the most beautiful woman he had ever seen, though he also said her face was hidden behind a veil from her wide-brimmed hat. She held a suitcase and stood in the street while Lawrence (our town's only taxi, and that part-time whenever school was out; Lawrence was also our erstwhile gym teacher) drove off back to town.

Uncle Joe was beside himself with joy, chuckling thickly, an ugly mixture of phlegm and spit that always sent us kids running in terror. We weren't half as afraid of his outbursts of anger as we were his outbursts of joviality. The woman must have been too far away to hear or see, though, since she walked toward him instead of away.

No words were exchanged when she reached him. Uncle Joe even took hold of the suitcase for her and led the way into the house. He had had no time to make up the master bedroom (he hadn't slept there since Aunt Alice died, but instead had a cot in the kitchen), but he took her there anyway.

It was filthy, choked with dust and shadow. Even Uncle Joe was embarrassed, but I guess she finally spoke and said, "No matter," to him, and for some reason Uncle Joe seemed absolutely tantalized with this statement. I didn't catch all of the retelling, of course (being on soda bottle patrol). Based on his reactions, it was less that she was not angry at the state of her new room, but rather it was the tone of her voice. It hit some sort of nerve that thrilled him. What that could be I didn't have any clue at that time, but would soon find out.

Anyway, they spent a happy week together. Happy for Uncle Joe, anyway. No one else in the family saw him all week. He didn't go into town even once (so all the ladies who might be widows within a few years had breathed more easily for a few days).

Something happened at the end of the week, though. Something bad. Well, I'm not sure if I got this part down correctly via my eavesdropping, but he had no idea what went wrong. Nothing went wrong for him, but something must have gone wrong for her.

Early Friday morning, he awoke and immediately had a bad feeling, a premonition. He ran outside and to his horror saw a number of empty chicken pens, the doors unlatched and feathers strewn about the front lawn. Oh, the chickens were all nearby. Their one chance of escape and when they were three feet out the door they got homesick for the motherland.

Uncle Joe gathered them all up again (one of the really skinny ones was eaten by an equally skinny fox) but it took him a few hours. He got done just in time to see Lawrence Welcome's taxi again, driving away from his property.

In a panic, he ran back to the house, meaning to call out the woman's name. Too late he realized he did not even know it. When he ran inside, he found nothing but a mess. By mess Uncle Joe meant a kind of mess that neither he nor my cousins had made. Although they were very messy, they were so in a distinctive manner. Right away he knew that the woman who had walked into his life had sashayed out again, and with some very important papers.

Aunt Winnie was just beginning to question him on what papers were taken when Dad came out from the Back Room looking very grim. He told Uncle Frank that business had not been great for a while, plus the fact that many deliveries were not getting to the store. Uncle Frank told him that they would fix that problem easily, but everyone was clearly worried. That was the point when they all noticed me again.

"Aren't you finished yet?"

"Um," was all I could think of saying, so Dad waved me on out of there, telling me he would see me for dinner.

*   *   *

"Joseph's been evicted!" Dad announced as we sat down at the dinner table on Saturday night over meatloaf, carrots, baked potatoes and the hint of apple pie later on.

"What's that?" my mom asked.

"Hilde has control of his house and most of his chicken pens! And she's got some other woman working for her, too. Unless your sister can doll herself up and make herself attractive to my brother."

"I wouldn't think so." Mom was the one who said this. I worked hard to suppress my gag reflex thinking about it and so couldn't speak.

"No, nor me. But that's the thing that bothered me most," my dad continued after a short pause. "Joseph's role in all of this."

"Hmm," Mom said, not really to anyone in particular.

"I mean, I think he got his comeuppance. He's still blubbering on and on about his chickens, so it's hard to be sure. Still, he had always tried to distance himself from Benjamin before—you know his paranoia about looking like Benny—and he had always despised your sister Hilde. Then he goes and helps her to carve up Dad's land. Where's the sense in that, somebody please explain that? That was never going to last."

"What, dear?"

"Any partnership between Joseph and Benny and Hilde. It's like trying to get vinegar and oil to mix. It just doesn't take for good."

I chewed silently. I wanted to explore these thoughts some more, I really did, but it wasn't my place to tell Dad to please continue, which of course he didn't. Generally, parents never continue when they're about to get to something interesting. It must be innate; something kicks in genetically once you have children and a person loses the ability to tell the truth, the whole truth and nothing but, forgoing any consequences.

Dad fell silent, sulkily chewing some carrot while the rest dangled on the end of his fork. The sounds of Benny Goodman wafted through the air from the radio on the far side of the room (on Saturday night, we were naturally in the dining room, not the kitchen, and could hear the radio from the dining room table). As the song concluded, Aunt Hilde's voice broke through the airwaves. She tried, I believed, desperately hard to sound seductive, but she sounded more like a German Shepherd barking out orders to a bunch of sleepy sheep.

"Attention good fair folk of our village and the surrounding countryside! It is now six o'clock precisely! It was indeed a most efficient selection of popular songs that just played, as they ended exactly on schedule. Now, as promised, I have a treat for you.

From now on, every night, you will hear the sultry, irresistible, enchanting voice of our new disc jockey, a talent who has traveled the globe, most recently spinning her webs in the Far East, in Tokyo, ladies and gentleman."

"Tokyo?" my mother said and looked up sharply, the first sudden movement we had seen from her in days.

"I give you," Aunt Hilde continued, "Barbara Rose, to guide you through the rest of the night."

"Hello."

A mellow, luxurious voice full of resonance and ecstasy vibrated through the speaker and into each ear, nuzzling me. Two syllables, that's all that came out for what seemed a stretch of hours. Dead air on the local radio, but I didn't care and how could anyone? They were the most erotically satisfying two syllables any young boy could ever hope to hear. The face that must have produced those sounds, the legs! They were propelling me instantly into manhood—or at least, into the desires of manhood.

"Barbara Rose?" my mother cried, breaking the spell. I realized I was sweating. Barbara Rose started talking again, speaking to the whole town, but it seemed to have such an individualistic aim it could have been straight to my heart.

I fell off my chair and nearly threw up when my mother interrupted again.

"That's my sister!"

"What?" my father and I said together as I clambered back into my chair.

No! No, it couldn't be. That audible beacon of desire was related to my mother? To Aunt Hilde? Barbara Rose our new disc jockey who was going to be on every night with her tantalizing whispers was . . . Aunt Babs?

Aunt Babs was a myth, a long-lost Argonaut who had flown the coop years before I was born. I had never met her, never seen a picture, had only heard my mother talk of her on rare occasions, usually when I was in trouble (that is, the times she mentioned Aunt Babs were rare, not the times I was in trouble). I doubted anyone else in the family apart from us (excepting AH and maybe Uncle Benny) even knew about her.

"That's your sister?" my father cried. He pushed his plate away from him and looked over at the radio, his standard scowl of the last few weeks now extremely exaggerated.

But the scowl wavered. I saw it. It waned and petered out of existence, melted like the frost around a windowpane in winter where one sets a candle. He had heard the voice of Barbara Rose, too. For the first time in my life (and, with a violent psychological repression, the last for many years), I saw my dad as Harry, a man with all a man's normal desires, perfectly content and in love with my mother, but unable to stop the thoughts and visions that sprang to life from her words to our ears. Ewww. I shuddered and gulped, forcing myself to stare at my plate. Then I think I even gasped out loud as my mother stood up from the table and launched her chair behind her like a pinball behind a fully stretched out spring.

She walked over and shut off the radio.

"I don't want you listening to this!" (This was probably directed at me.)

Our radio had been on every Saturday night since I could remember, continuously until after I went to bed. If all the Saturday nights of my life had been stretched out and sewn together end on end, I would have had a silence-free summer, a handy-dandy omnipresent soundtrack to my every moment.

Dad's own gasp covered up my own.

"What did you do that for?" he asked, but she just gave him The Look.

The Look. I had gotten it before, my dad had gotten it before, oh yes, many times and in many places. It was one eye turned to you, with a steady, steely, nearly emotionless glare and a hint (a hint, mind you) of a frown with a touch of nostrils flared. The brow of my mother's forehead read in translation, simply: I dare you. No matter that it was an incomplete sentence, the dare was to complete that fragment. *I dare you to keep on talking. I dare you to question my decisions.* And so on. The only way out of the immediate harm of The Look was to freeze, play dead or, if one absolutely had to move, to look down.

The Look worked on everybody, too, even animals. It only didn't work on Aunt Winnie and AH. It even worked on Uncle Frank, although he got it only rarely. Aunt Ellen had her own version and threw that around her household and kept it in pretty good order.

My mother left her dinner where it was, even her chair where it was, and marched directly out of the dining room. We heard her retreat through the pass of the stairs to her bedroom. That she slammed the door was a nice touch, of course, but I felt it was a tad obvious, a cliché.

The worst part of this all-around debacle, of course, was that Dad and I were left to clean up the dishes (not our forte). The *very* worst part of this rout was that Dad was not left to clean up the dishes.

"Clean up these dishes," Dad said as he threw down his napkin and went to go assess the damage.

He was pretty brave, I thought, to go after Mom so soon. That thought vanished when he didn't follow Mom up the stairs, but instead went out the front door. It was the next day that I discovered that he had gone to see his younger sister, Aunt Patti. I found out because she came over then.

Aunt Patti was a pretty good choice. She was a lot like Aunt Winnie, just less calculating, less erudite. I don't mean any disrespect to her. In fact, I've always looked up to her; she was the first real "Woman of Action" in the county (that's a real designation we had in Dodge, though it wasn't an official appellation; everyone knew when a woman earned it, and Aunt Patti was the first, a trail-blazer).

Aunt Patti and Mom were pretty close, though nearly opposites in temperament, so maybe that helped. Aunt Patti never suffered from the doldrums if it didn't involve a loved one dying or something, and never let anyone else suffer them, either. It was a little insufferable of her.

I wouldn't see her until the morning, however. In the meantime, I had a lot of dishes to clean, which was a really rotten end to a Saturday night. However, I realized that I was alone in the dining room, and that if I tuned in the radio softly, maybe just to see what Aunt Babs was playing, that would make the work more worthwhile.

No, no music. She was still talking and it didn't make much sense. I had missed the thread of conversation, and so her words simply unraveled in my ears. The sensuousness was still there, but knowing who she was had dissipated the mystery, and the allure leaked out steadily like the air from a punctured tire. She kept promising things like, "As soon as this next song is over" and "When we are through with this set of music," but without actually playing anything. Instead, she prattled on and on about the opportunities coming to our town, how it would be transformed and last a thousand years, blah blah blah. That and how there were great deals to be had at AH's Liquidation Store for the "Down and Out".

I didn't know any "Down and Out" people in our town. I was too young to really remember the worst days of the Depression, but nobody seemed to make a big deal out of it around Dodge. Aunt Winnie told me once that our town had been something of an island in the storm, surviving on will and determination, and a little bit of self-reliance. We were never rich, but we didn't know that because we were never completely poor, either.

Finally a song came on. Marlene Dietrich. Ah, that was nice. Soon enough, however, it neared the end of the song without my chore getting completed. Or even started. The refrain repeated twice and faded out. Again there was silence over the airwaves, but only for a moment before Barbara Rose spoke again.

"We're in the middle of our evening of great hits. Once again, I am your host, Barbara Rose."

This was Uncle Joe's mystery woman. It had to be. I mean, our town didn't get many mystery women. That is, not any new ones. The women in our town that were considered by the general populace to be mysterious had been so for decades. We were told as children in various ways who they were and how to avoid them, especially on Halloween and such, but even I've dared to go ring Mrs. Simmons' bell and she'd give out money for Trick or Treating, usually dimes but sometimes quarters. Anyway, it would be too momentous for there to be two sexy, mysterious women new to the town.

So, Barbara Rose had been at Uncle Joe's for a week, and now was our radio host. And she had let all of the chickens out to distract my uncle and then had taken something important from his house and beat it out of there. A fear crept up my spine, a warning that it would be in my best interests not to meet up with Aunt Babs. I couldn't help myself, though. I definitely wanted to meet up with her. The allure hadn't completely drained away. Geez, though, why can't the evil women *look* evil and *sound* evil, like AH did? I didn't want to kiss her or anything gross like that (Aunt Babs, I mean; Aunt Hilde was a given), her being a relation and all and obviously a few years older than me, but . . . well, I wasn't quite twelve at the time and couldn't really think straight. When I was a bit older, every time my mother warned me about staying away from certain girls, I always thought of Aunt Babs at this moment. A few years after that, my mother stopped warning me about staying away from any girls, as desperate for a daughter-in-law as she became (she needn't have worried, though, as she eventually got the one that fit all the right categories; sorry, digressing again).

Eventually, I began clearing dishes from the table and setting them near the sink. I noticed with some satisfaction that I was the only one who had cleaned his plate. It meant a pretty decent pile for the compost bucket, but little gloating.

All in all, the week had not been great for gloating. Also, if I could not gloat, it would be nice to be in the know on everything. On that count too, I felt that the week had been a letdown. I did not know right then that I was soon to be the first one in my house privy to the biggest news all week.

I ran the hot water and scrubbed, whistling when there was a tune on, grimacing when there wasn't. Just as I was finishing the drying, someone rapped on the front door, not politely, not patiently, but sharply and with great insistence. It was still warm so only the screen door was shut. I thought only briefly of waiting to see if Mom would come down the steps because I knew she wouldn't. So I put down the last dish and threw my damp towel over my shoulder, wiped my hands then ran to the door when I heard it was Aunt Winnie, calling out for Dad.

By the time I was out of the kitchen, Aunt Winnie had already let herself in.

"Johnny, where's your father?"

I shrugged my shoulders, then quickly emended this by telling her, "I don't know. He went out and didn't say where he was headed."

"Where's your mother?"

"She's upstairs."

Aunt Winnie rolled her eyes, but then sighed. "Another one of her moods, eh? I guess I can understand that."

That was an unexpected piece of sympathy from her, but maybe it shouldn't have been. The next thing she did I definitely should have seen coming.

"What are you doing with this filth on?" she roared and marched over (with surprising swiftness) and snapped off the radio. "Don't you know who that is?"

"Yes, ma'am," I said.

"You do? Well, never mind that now. Listen, Johnny. I'll see you and your parents in church tomorrow."

She turned to go.

"Wait! Aunt Winnie, what did you need to see Dad about? I mean, in case he gets back soon."

She paused at the front door, turned back to me and stared at me hard. It wasn't her version of The Look, so I couldn't tell if I was in trouble for prying or what.

"Come here," she said quietly.

As I reached her side, I started to ask another question, but she hushed me, put an arm around my shoulder and turned us to face the outside, standing simply at the screen door. Puzzled, I thought perhaps Aunt Winnie had drifted further into eccentricity, but soon I heard what she must have meant. It was the sound of footfalls, out along the pavement. Our house was on the outskirts of town. Beyond us began the many farmlands of the county. There were dozens of people walking, shuffling their feet dejectedly, streaming in from the countryside.

"This is a terrible day, Johnny," Aunt Winnie said quietly. "I have just learned that your aunt Hilde has bought the bank and immediately foreclosed on over forty farmsteads, evicting all these tenants with barely a minute's notice."

"Where are they going?"

"They're going to stay at my house," she said and walked outside, leaving me to lean against the screen door, making out the ghostly outlines of the refugees and shuddering to the bottom of my soul.

I looked back toward the kitchen and glanced at the stairs. The dishes were basically done. Mom was shut in for the night. My hands shook with fear. It struck me right then how amazing it was that Aunt Winnie was so decisive. She learned of a need and leapt into the fray to provide aid. A part of me knew her mind frittered restlessly, already looking for an opportunity to move beyond aid to attack. Providing help for people one didn't even know was beyond me. As much as I had wanted to be a grown-up in the family conflict, at this moment it was painfully obvious what a child I was still.

"Aunt Winnie?" I called out to her down the drive. I gulped at the sound my own voice had made.

She stopped but didn't turn.

"Can I help?"

At this she turned slowly, her feet scraping the gravel like a lone dog barking in the night, anticipating a reply. She nodded and held out one arm. I bolted through the door and in two bounds was in the embrace of her arm.

"You'll do nicely," she said as we began the trek to her house.

As we fell in line with the sad people dragging their feet and what few possessions they had saved, Aunt Winnie called in a loud voice, holding up her two fingers in a V shape: "I've only got two spare beds! But we'll find room for you all. Somehow. Now come! 'This story shall the good man teach his son . . . From this day to the ending of the world, But we in it shall be remember'd; We few, we happy few, we band of brothers.'"

A ragged cheer went up the line of walkers. Momentarily, I was confident of the ultimate result of our feud. Nothing inspired like Aunt Winnie quoting Macbeth! Then I heard a familiar voice, a wailing really, and I felt Aunt Winnie stiffen before she removed her arm from my shoulders.

"Sis-tah Winifred! Oh, Sis-tah!" Uncle Joe moaned as he pushed aside the displaced farmers, even knocking one of them down.

"What is it now, Joseph?" Aunt Winnie didn't even break stride.

"You must, Ah say, you must leave these h'yeer folks and come to mah aid!"

"I already told you, Joseph, we're doing all we can already."

She stopped at this juncture, to square on her sibling (I hid behind her). They bickered for a minute, silently, meaning it was the age-old family practice of the stare-down. Older siblings mastered it for lifelong purposes, and Uncle Joe was bested.

"So, you refuse me, Sis-tah?"

"You were born without nerve, Joseph, I swear it! I am helping you, but I've got only so much to give. You'll just have to hold out with what Frank and I gave you today. There are urgent matters on this side of the river, too, you know!"

We rejoined the ranks of the farmers heading for Aunt Winnie's house, leaving Uncle Joe in the street. I could feel his stare boring into the back of my neck (though he was probably aiming for Aunt Winnie's).

"If Ah fall, she'll have all she needs to beat the likes of you!"

Aunt Winnie didn't respond to this, and that petrified me. She marched glumly on and I understood that all her smiles and tough talk were a brave show, for she had her doubts. My confidence ebbed, had only been propped up by brave words. There was no truth to sustain it.

I tried to calm myself as we reached Aunt Winnie's house that things could not get any worse, but the depressing sight of the broken families around me suggested otherwise. Get some sleep, Aunt Winnie advised all of them, for things would look different in the morning.

Who knew but she would be right, and in more ways than one.

CHAPTER 4: PEARL HARBOR

S unday was a holy day. Always had been, always would be. Anything that attempted to derail that solid-as-a-rock fact was evil, pure and simple. Sometimes, life is pretty black and white (of course, I "grayed" that phrase with the word "pretty"; and also the word "sometimes"). I will argue to my last breath that there are some things that are worth living for, and even some things worth dying for, namely: God, family and country. That's easy for me to say when I haven't been tested, or not much. Anyway, that idea was pretty ingrained in us, in everyone in our town, that it was the way the world worked best. We kids had that worldview put in front of our faces every week at Sunday School.

We had the best church, growing up. I've met many dispirited people, dulled by age and obligations, that feel the myth of God has been duly dispelled by the era, by technology and amorality (if not immorality). Most attended church almost as often as I did, growing up (we never missed a Sunday, except once, but we were traveling). However, they all hated their churches. I'm not sure why. I guess they compared their pastors or priests with television (when they were older) and found the memory of the clerical collars wanting. Our pastor, however, made radio, the movies, everything except real life itself, seem pretty bland. In fact, if we hadn't been having our great feud, we would have had our normal Sunday picnics, and Pastor Evers' antics may even have been topic number one.

Don't get me wrong, though, about the other things in life that we used for entertainment. We loved our radio and everything. When I was older we had a TV too, of course. Mom saw every movie that came to the Preston Playhouse, one new release every two weeks or so. However, what made them all pale in comparison was the fact that our pastor was board certified insane.

Well, he should have been.

He was a thin, pale fellow with large glasses and a balding head. He liked to wear stripes with polka dots in garish clashing colors (for a time we hoped he was simply colorblind). If one heard him on the radio, one would be hard-pressed to get that image. He was Methodist, but believed he was Baptist (we had a small Baptist congregation in town with a black minister, and when I heard him later in life after Pastor Evers had left I loved him and felt at home; I think he and Pastor Evers were friends and so maybe one copied the other's style . . . in speech, not fashion). Pastor Evers expected loud cheers and "Amens" to follow his sermons, but we were not that kind of people so he was routinely disappointed. Also, he was loud (but thought his voice soft), so that one cringed when speaking with him in private, and absolutely shuddered when sitting in the pews beneath his pulpit, where he thought he needed to shout to be heard. Plus, he often misquoted Scripture (but not obvious things, or stuff that would seriously update our moral code like, "Thou shalt kill," but more along the lines of, "Love is a patient, love is a lifeline, love does not levy or pay a fine"—first he would screw up, then try and save the matter by attempting a rhyme; sometimes it worked out all right).

If reinventing Scripture wasn't a dubious enough distinction for a small-town minister, then his bird-calling was. For some reason, he seemed to think he was a gifted aper (maybe I should say a "parrot"). I don't know why; I think it was because he believed passionately in people sharing their innate gifts, and Pastor Evers thought he was really good at bird-calls.

"As the Good Book says, 'To whom much is given is much required, so don't get weary and don't get tired.'"

So, every sermon began with one of his impressions. He said he could do any bird, but they all sounded like: "Squawk!" Even his rooster impression. Every Sunday, there was our minister, waving his arms like chicken wings, prancing about in fashion monstrosities, squawking and screaming at the top of his lungs.

Loud, gauche, illiterate (sort of) and bird-brained. That combination made Sunday mornings a rollicking good time, once one was over the initial shock. With all that going on, he still taught us a lot about the Lord; a very good pastor.

It was that Sunday morning, the 7th, the morning after we first all heard Barbara Rose's voice on the radio, sitting in the pews (near the back, to hear better), that I got an eerie feeling all over my skin that something terrible would happen.

One thing that's always bothered me about God is that He loves us and cares about us, but then can put someone like AH on the face of the planet. I believe I have a serious grievance with the Lord, and I do not take my dispute lightly. I haven't brushed off God because I just didn't like the thought of AH or because everything isn't all pretty and shiny in life. No, I've put much thought and prayer into this argument, from my boyhood on (from before the feud, even).

The closest I ever came to resolving this issue was to try on the philosophy of God loving every single person equally, without regard to race, sex, rank or rankness of body odor. That put us all on an even playing field. Then, each person would use his or her life to run higgledy-piggledy toward or away from God, by (I guess) doing good or doing evil. When one did what one didn't know was either good or evil, I think one would spin around in circles.

Look, I never said I was Socrates or Thomas Aquinas. I just had the world's lousiest aunt (both sides, remember) and the memory of her mustache to keep me frightened at night, and I've tried reconciling that against all the good things I had in life. I never said I had all the answers.

I guess I meant I was scared, but I still wanted to have hope.

Anyway, I sat there, between my folks, wedged in tight (there was, of course, plenty of room up front), licking my lips and waiting for the world to end. Craning my neck as surreptitiously as possible, I peered over to where Aunt Hilde and Uncle Benny usually sat. They weren't there, which wasn't a huge surprise (their haphazard church attendance was often remarked upon in the county), but it only heightened my sense of doom.

It also didn't help that Pastor Evers' sermon was from the book of Revelation.

"Squawk!" he shouted as he climbed into the pulpit and flapped his arms. "That was the lovely chickadee, of course. My text for today is as follows:

"'Go pour out the bulbs of God's wrath!'" he misquoted as he flipped his orange tie over his shoulder. "Um, 'And in them all the angels take a bath!'

"You see, my flock! The times they are changing! No longer do we call God 'Master'! His anger builds into great big bowls of bulbs! They don't ever! And then finally! Finally, will they be poured!"

One time, someone came from the national Methodist office and attempted to transcribe one of his sermons—so he sat up front to get a good listen, which was way too close based on our pastor's volume—and what he ended up with were pages and pages of phrases and incomplete sentences, all either ending in a dash or an exclamation point (or both). They made no sense written out, but we always took pride in being able to correctly interpret what Pastor Evers said.

It turned out that on this Sunday, the 7th, he would provide me with a ray of hope that I would sorely need in the coming hours. Heaven-sent, I would cling to it out of desperation and remember it all the days of my life. It solidified the hope I wanted.

Pastor Evers said, "But even while the days of evil grow, so too do the days of good, because God has not left us alone! The good days are just harder to see because no one tells you they are good! You have to discover that, and sometimes pursue it, fight for it!"

The rest of his sermon was something of a haze, something about bulbs again. Those words, however, struck me to the core, and I immediately thought of my family's situation. It was easy to surrender and think only of AH's early victories over us. In order to prevail, I knew I would have to focus on the good: like the interception of AH's package to New York City and Aunt Winnie opening up her spare rooms and land for the displaced people.

*   *   *

The morning had started out strangely. I awoke with sun streaming in my open windows. Struggling against the blinding light and through the fog of exhaustion, I rolled over and realized that I was on top of my covers and still in my clothes from Saturday night.

Sitting up, I began remembering the events from the day before: my parents both retreating, Aunt Winnie stopping by, the displaced farmers, helping Aunt Winnie move furniture about and get blankets and pillows and towels for folks. She walked me back home at probably two or three in the morning. She must have been on her feet for twenty hours straight, but at least she seemed appreciative of my efforts.

I changed quickly into my Sunday duds (and threw some water on my face, too) and descended downstairs where I heard more than the usual Sunday morning pre-church chatter. Were Mom and Dad both up? Who was that with them? Then from the kitchen came a dramatic crescendo of blasphemy, and I knew it was Aunt Patti.

"I will not apologize!" my aunt cried as I entered the kitchen. "Oh, Johnny. There you are. Hope I didn't wake you."

"It's time he was up, anyway," my mother said drearily. "Now you three can go. I'll just stay here." She sighed the sigh of the martyrs.

"Patti, the boy," my father said.

"Oh, fiddlesticks! I learned my swearing from you, Harry, and I bet he will, too. Anyway, the Lord doesn't mind my mouth. He and I are very close. I told Him, if He ever felt offended by my use of His Name, He could up and use my name anyway He pleased."

"And that worked?" I blurted out. Dang it, there I went again!

"Jonathan," Mom barked sharply.

I sat down to bacon and eggs sheepishly and hoped by my silence they would all forget I was there.

"Of course it worked! Like I said, the Lord and I are very close." Aunt Patti crossed over to the sink where my mother stood, staring out at the front lawn. "Now, Bess, you mustn't stay in this funk you're in. We don't blame you for the troubles that are brewing."

Holy cow! Aunt Patti said this out loud to my mother? One never openly acknowledged her funks. Was nothing sacred or taboo anymore?

Just as I suspected, my mother shot a vicious look at my dad, an automatic response that would probably never change.

"What?" my father said, a little helplessly.

"Harry's not blaming you either, are you, Harry?" Aunt Patti said, possibly mistaking why Mom was upset with Dad, but my

117

vociferous aunt also shot her own significant look at Dad. What was that about?

My fork with some egg dripping off of it seemed suspended in mid-air in front of my mouth, that long pause before an accident or collision, which one sees coming but cannot change. Dad knew why he was in trouble with Mom, though. Aunt Patti said the words and missed the meaning, but she wouldn't have said anything if she hadn't been told about it.

"Now Jiminy Cricket!" Aunt Patti bellowed, though that's a slight paraphrase. "Harry had to talk to someone, didn't he? Should he have gone to Winnie? To Frank?"

"Good heavens," my mother muttered, but a smile cracked the hard lines of her face. Mine too, as I remembered my other aunt's rolling eyes.

Aunt Patti slapped my mother on the back, then gave her a quick hug.

"That's the spirit! Now, Bessie, you go get changed and we'll pick up my kids and all walk to church together. I'll be meeting Norman there, if he's back yet."

Norman was Aunt Patti's new boyfriend. I don't know why she fretted over him so, for he looked like he could handle himself just fine. A genial dark-haired fellow with all the standard tallness, broad-shoulderedness and square-jawness (if those are terms, which they probably aren't) of a movie actor (maybe not a classic lead, but a solid supporting kind, anyway), he maybe didn't exude confidence, but he didn't lack it, either. He had retired early to our little town a few years back, saying he wanted to get away from it all, and I guess all of it was in Washington, D.C. where he had worked doing something for the government, I could never tell exactly what. He said it was important stuff, but he could never provide any convincing details. Despite his retirement, he traveled often on some business matters, but usually came back with neat presents for my cousins and sometimes even me. (Once, he gave me a set of pencils, each one stamped with a different state name and the date of admission to the Union; I was always afraid to sharpen them and use them for fear of destroying the date and then needing it for a civics test brush-up.)

Aunt Patti cheered up my mother considerably and convinced her to join us for church. On the walk there, she talked down Aunt Babs' radio stint as a cheap ploy that wouldn't work. She also tried to slip in a few subtle questions on my mother, about what Aunt Babs was really doing for AH, but Mom simply didn't know. Obviously, everyone now knew that Barbara Rose was a relation.

If it were possible, though, Aunt Patti went up in my book several points. It had been a masterful performance, really, considering it was a Sunday morning: swearing, talking down my mother and sneakily probing for information.

Anyway, we made it to St. Paul's a little early, so we took our time surveying the crowd as we passed through the propped open, large, wooden doors of the entryway and made our way into the foyer. (Well, I say "foyer" because my parents say "foyer" and so did my grandparents. I suppose if one says "foyer" often enough it sounds like a made-up word, which I guess they all are if one goes back far enough. Anyway, it's only about sixty square feet of space in front of the sanctuary proper in which to congregate, which is another odd thing to say since the congregation was supposed to go in and sit in the pews . . . and don't get me started on the word "pew".) My dad mumbled something about the light crowd—I thought it was not bad—then we went in and took our normal seats. Aunt Patti left us to try and find Norman, but returned a little later to sit with us, saying he must have been held up and wasn't back yet.

I was still buoyed by the hard kernel of truth Pastor Evers had given me when he wrapped up his sermon early (only 50 minutes). He had just said his usual ending, "Can I get a payment?" (which was the signal for the ushers to start passing the offering plates) when the explosion came. It shook the stained-glass windows and we all gasped. As I looked at the vibrating windows—the world in slow motion while the rumbling reverberated through us—the stone rolled away from the tomb and the lambs lay down with the lions.

Everyone started chattering at once and we all started evacuating our places in the pews, looking back and forth at everyone else's fearful faces, but keeping a sideways glance to the east, the direction of the explosion, toward the river. Uncle Frank's face caught and held my attention as we filed out to the rear, away from Pastor Evers' shrieking, "The bulbs are coming down! The bulbs are coming down! Hallelujah!" Uncle Frank, by quiet contrast, looked stiff with fear, as if he had a terrible premonition.

We squeezed out as a family, Dad and Mom each holding one of my hands, pushing our way between the Lards and Bumpuses (a noxious, suffocating experience) and spilling out onto the church front lawn. Everyone found a spot and stood and stared at the plume of smoke rising like a flare, the exhaust of some terrible fireworks tragedy, perhaps.

"It's the school," someone said.

"It's my house!" another screamed.

"No," a calm, resolute voice said, quieting everyone with its sureness and authority. It was Uncle Frank. "It's the marina."

We all gasped, knowing he was right. The marina had exploded? How was that possible?

Without answers, we finally figured out as a whole that we should go down and investigate. Uncle Frank led us, moving assuredly and with rapidity despite heavy reliance on his cane (no sort of act at that speed). We stayed behind him, arcing out on both sides of him like a flock of geese in flight, a venomous V pointing straight at danger. We were four blocks from the river and our town's marina. It was small and docked only seven craft (that was including the two-man dinghy that Maurice Peters, who ran the marina part-time, used as the town's "Rescue Patrol"); really, it was just a couple of piers. But it was a marina the same way that Joe Wisher's barn which held our square dances was discussed with out-of-town relatives as the "Convention Center". The nicest boat there, of course, was Uncle Frank's. The newest boat was Aunt Patti's new boyfriend Norman's boat (in fact, it was not much more than a hull), but it had been in "dry-dock" (Maurice's garage) ever since Norman had gotten it, awaiting a time when he could finish building it himself.

The smoke plume billowed higher and thicker as we neared the catastrophe. From down a side-street, we could see into the firehouse and noted (with no small sense of satisfaction) that the volunteer firemen, despite age, weight and the fact that they hadn't been needed in over eight years, were already assembling, about to set forth on our only public vehicle apart from the snow plow.

Our hearts thudded in our throats as we passed the last building to get a clear view of the damage. Our hearts then sank at the sight of the devastation of all the boats burning and sinking, the marina office nothing but a burnt-out husk, and the docks dismembered like a side of beef.

We slowed to nothing faster than a crawl—what could we do?—as the fire crew clanged their bell and blew their horn behind us. They would soon set to work. We noticed poor Maurice Peters crawling to us, his hair singed and his clothes frayed. Surrounding him—lovingly—we saw that he was unhurt physically, but that he had witnessed the horror.

"Oh, the horror!" he cried.

Uncle Frank stepped forward, his eyes wide and welling with tears. "The *Arizona*?" he asked in a quavering voice.

Perhaps he could not see what the rest of us saw plainly, the wreckage highlighted perfectly by the still rising sun, or maybe he didn't want to see. No one told him what had become of his beloved boat; in the end, no one needed to, for Uncle Frank realized his great loss.

It hit me, too. Staggering. No more boat trips with Uncle Frank. No more pleasure cruising on the Obeg, no more post-picnic fishing with men of the family, no more nostalgic trips up the river to Grandfather Treat's land, to camp or hike or just to have stories passed down to the next generation. All of that was gone in a rush, innocence vanished by a terrible turn of events. A terrible accident.

Or was it not an accident?

"Who did this, Maurice?"

I couldn't believe I had spoken aloud. Gee whiz, why couldn't I ever keep my big mouth shut! Everyone there—I mean everyone!—gasped and stared at me in disbelief.

"What did you say?" my father asked me.

I gulped. "I meant, um, it just didn't look like an accident to me."

How could anything that caused so much pain be an accident? My mind had landed again on the word "evil" and every time it did, it flitted to AH. Either I was a lot more perceptive than the rest of my family or I needed some major therapy. Most peoples' aunts are not their worst enemy. Or any sort of enemy at all.

Dad, Mom, Uncle Frank and even Aunt Patti surrounded me (not exactly the same way we had surrounded Maurice a minute earlier), and I thought I was about to get it for embarrassing everyone related to me and speaking out of turn. My unlikely savior from that mess was Maurice who coughed loudly to get everyone's attention, then said, "I did see someone very early this morning."

Everyone gasped. Momentarily, the smoke came flying toward us before returning to a more natural, upward track.

"There was this smell, like something between cookies and manure. It wafted into my house so I went out to look for whatever it was and I saw— "

"What!?!" we all cried, gasping again.

"A shadow—"

"Yes!?!" A third gasp, almost full up.

"A person—"

"Who!?!" A fourth gasp; we were about to explode.

"Well, I . . . I just couldn't see clearly," he admitted, and we all let out the air in our lungs, deflated, like a balloon that doesn't get tied up (only we didn't fly about the place helter-skelter).

"I . . . I couldn't . . . the smell . . . gagged me," Maurice added through tears as we turned away from him.

So ended Maurice Peters' moment in the spotlight. The only other tidbit of any interest about him was that the next day he went to get fitted for new glasses. The ophthalmologist swore that they weren't necessary, but apparently Maurice felt as betrayed by his eyes as we did by whatever—or whoever—was responsible for the destruction.

Uncle Frank turned to us, shocked, heroic, taking in all our frozen faces looking to him for leadership. He put a hand over his heart (a few of the hicks in our congregation took off their baseball hats, including their men, like Uncle Frank was going to lead us in the Pledge of Allegiance or something; appropriately, it turned out, for the promise he was about to utter). He cried with a voice that quivered ever so slightly, "I shall return!"

Then he turned away from the crowd and ambled down toward the smoldering ruins of the docks. Our volunteer firemen busily pumped water out of the river, onto the wreckage and back down into the river again. The good news was, Maurice's garage was only singed, so Norman's unfinished boat had been spared. Also, some of the boats could probably be salvaged—or so it seemed from our vantage point—but the worst of the damage was obviously to Uncle Frank's beloved *Arizona Kid*. That memorable vessel was ruined.

We followed behind him reverently, allowing him a little distance in which to mourn properly. Only the top pilothouse could still be seen, while bits of her floated away to the great confluence miles downstream.

Like I said, Sunday was a holy day. We didn't make a lot of jokes normally on the Lord's Day, but this one we would remember especially, and honor annually. It would be sadly famous (and, if my suspicions of treachery proved trued, infamous).

"Let's go home, son," Dad said to me, putting his arm around my shoulder and steering me away from Uncle Frank, who clearly wanted to be left alone. We walked ponderously back home, past the church with the steeple and cross looking down on us sadly. I looked up at it, dim like dross in the overcast sky, drooping or maybe even stooping down to me. Dad stopped inside and picked up Uncle Frank's suitcoat for him. I heard later that my uncle stayed all day at the marina with the fire crew, until the blaze was out and they pulled out several large, severely damaged baking pans and one nearly destroyed canister of propane.

*   *   *

"Infamy!" Uncle Frank shouted at the dinner table, banging both fists on it. We had been invited over, along with Aunt Winnie and Aunt Patti, on Monday evening. "It was a gutless, conniving, deadly attack. The only place in town that sells propane is Hilde's Liquidation Store!"

My mind tingled with all the news I received. There would be no more waffling for Uncle Frank. His hackles were up and I expected furious discussion (which they would assume was over my head, and therefore they wouldn't do much in the way of censoring themselves), but everyone buried their heads in their dinners.

It was picnic fare, basically. Spread out in large bowls and platters, the selections all tempted me right away, each making my mouth water. Well, most all of them, anyway. Uncle Frank had grilled hot dogs, and those were always delicious (piled high in the center of the table, waiting to be grabbed after grace), but Mom ladled out heaps of baked beans on my and everyone else's plate (NOT my favorite portion of the evening). Back on the plus side, luscious slices of watermelon; great big slabs, too. Nothing wussy in Aunt Ellen's watermelon chopping.

The food and trimmings made sense since it was sort of a make-up affair for the family's Sunday picnics we had missed. Aunt Winnie had strongly voiced her conviction that we should continue with as many of our traditions and routines as possible, as long as "beating the stuffing out of that windbag Hilde" came first. Everyone seemed to be in agreement, but there was no way to replace absolutely the times that had until so recently been ours. Uncle Frank had penned a note to both Uncle Joe and Uncle Benny (but separately, since they were touchy about being grouped together), inviting them to the "gathering" (the word he used in place of "picnic"). In Uncle Benny's letter he made it clear that only one person was being invited.

It must have gone something like this:

Dear Benjamin,

Seeing as you are our brother, and we have not spoken to you in some weeks, we would most sincerely like to see you join us for a gathering at our house on Monday evening.

We have generally warm feelings for you in our hearts, and even warmer feelings for your wife (as we wish her to burn in Hell). We believe that you do not really want to see our family in this present feud, but may feel somewhat inhibited by the presence of Hilde. Therefore, on your own, you should join us and we can talk as family members ought to. Winifred does not want to kick you in the behind next time she sees you, as you may have heard from talk around the town, so you can be assured of a comfortable visit.

*It would also be nice to have some of your wonderful ice cream, as we all
still have dreams about your Apri-cadapri-cot concoction.*

Yours affectionately,

Frank and Ellen

Well, I don't know if it said anything like that, especially that
one part. (I'm talking about the ice cream, of course; maybe we
do all have dreams about it, but they would be of the nightmare
variety. Oh yeah, they probably wouldn't have *written* the part
about wanting to see AH you-know-where.)

I don't think Uncle Benny had even replied to Uncle Frank,
but I guess no one was shocked when he was a no-show. Uncle
Joe was a bit more of a surprise, though. He had responded with
a reply note, however, and I managed a quick peek when we
arrived, before I had to run to the sink to be supervised by Aunt
Ellen in the first of many vigorous hand-washings that had to
take place upon every visit by another child (I would qualify until
I reached age twenty-five—Aunt Ellen was a firm believer in
both germs from someone else's children getting into her home
and killing off all those who lived there, and that boys were slow
to mature and had to be considered children longer than girls).

The note from Uncle Joe had said something about him
having to defend his "home" and "land" and that he didn't need
invitations over for a gathering, but what he could really use were
"supplies, supplies, supplies" because he was "surrounded!" It
didn't make a lot of sense to me, and when the conversation
finally continued at our "gathering", it started with Uncle Joe's
predicament.

"We must do something for Joseph," Aunt Winnie said. "He's the only one of us who's on that side of the river with Benny and Hilde."

"I know, I know, Winnie," Uncle Frank replied testily (as testily as he could get away with under the disapproving glare of his elder sister). "I just can't help thinking about how he brought this down on himself, though. I mean, he was all in favor of Hilde's plans."

Amen to that, I thought. It was true, it was relevant. Uncle Joe had been wrong and should pay a penalty. I mean, every time I did something wrong (and got caught) I had to pay a penalty. It never seemed to matter to any of the adults if I had changed my mind, or wished I hadn't done it. That change in thinking always had to be reinforced by a paddle, a switch or a garden hoe (I'd wield that one in a chore; they wouldn't beat a fella with that or anything). Hah, I'd love to see Aunt Winnie tell Uncle Joe to "pick a switch"! Wait, she would have no qualms with that.

"Of course he was wrong! No one said that any clearer or more directly than me! But, Franklin, the enemy of our enemy is our friend. And brother, of course. Now is not the time for recriminations. That time will come as soon as we've regained control of our parents' property. By God I'll spank the little brat myself!"

I wanted to cheer. Uncle Frank, however, seemed slightly less enthusiastic.

"Well, I'd like to see you try. Anyway, he already has my hose and my old pick-up truck, which he filled with canned fruit and chicken feed—and thirty-seven dollars out of the till—all from the Five and Dime. I wrote it all down on the credit board, of course, but we all know I'll never see any of that again. My poor hose."

The debate continued for some time like this. Mostly it was calls for action followed by immense amounts of indecision.

How were we supposed to fight when we didn't know what AH's next move would be?

It was a seemingly innocuous observation from Aunt Winnie that got me thinking. She made some comment about how Saturday night she had fifteen families camped out on her property or in her spare rooms, and how that had shrunk to twelve Sunday night, and was nine just before she had come over for supper.

The adults had all grunted at that information. They were trying to be pleased for Aunt Winnie, both congratulating her for her Christian devotion and that the people were vacating her premises. Mostly they failed, however, because they were tired and didn't actually care. For a moment, that frightened me. What if we were kicked out of our homes on a moment's notice? Who would care for us?

Luckily, before I could open my big mouth and ask about that, Dad answered it.

"It's a good thing I transferred the mortgage on the Five and Dime and our homes to the State Bank in Dodge City," he said between huge helpings of baked beans. Dad loved his baked beans. "Otherwise, we could've been taken over, too."

I was on the cusp of thinking nasty thoughts about Uncle Frank for doing no more than grunting agreement with my dad, whose foresight had obviously been proven wise, when another connecting thought got in its way and shoved it to the back of the line.

"Aunt Babs said on the radio that there were lots of opportunities for the 'Down and Out' at the Liquidation Store."

My cousins sitting across the table from me beamed at me, the "Nice One".

In the stunned silence of the room, the only sounds were those of forks dropping onto Aunt Ellen's plates. If I had been able to take a multiple-choice pop quiz right then, in answer to the question, "Who will be first to speak after you talk about

Aunt Babs?" with the choices being: a.) Uncle Frank; b.) Aunt Winnie; c.) Your father; or d.) Your mother; I probably would have chosen "b.)". I, of course, would have been flat wrong.

"I told you I didn't want you listening to her," my mother said through clenched teeth.

Oh yeah, she had said that. Lo and behold that had been directed at me. It was funny how parents found out about stuff. I suppose most parents have to resort to snooping or—egad!— trusting that the child will listen. My parents pretty much just waited for me to spill the beans.

In happier times, my mother liked to recite the story of me as a three-year-old asking her for a piece of chocolate. She said, "No," and so I walked into the next room and asked my father if I could have a piece of chocolate.

"Why are you asking me?"

"Because Mom said, 'No,'" I told him.

Mom always swore that the story was cute (and, no, I didn't get the chocolate).

Anyway, I was in trouble again, but my favorite aunt piped up, having caught on to why I had spoken in the first place. Did I mention that she's my favorite aunt?

"Wait a minute, Bessie! Johnny, say that again! Hilde bought the bank, foreclosed on all those farmers, then advertised on the radio station she bought that there were lots of opportunities for these people!"

Why would I need to say it again? I maybe wasn't in trouble anymore! How I loved my aunt Winnie!

"So?" my father asked.

"The Liquidation Store! That's where all the displaced families are going! It must be!"

I saw Uncle Frank and Aunt Patti exchange looks.

"So?" my father asked again.

"Harry, try to follow along!"

"I am following along! I just want to know the reason she's doing this. What does it all mean? Or maybe I should just ask my son?"

His withering look and sarcastic comment aside, I still thought my chances of not being in trouble for illicitly listening to the radio were pretty good. If Aunt Winnie knew the reason, that was.

"Well, I don't know the reason," Aunt Winnie admitted to my utter dissatisfaction. Maybe Aunt Patti or Aunt Ellen would say they had heard it on the radio, too, just to deflect some attention away from a singular listenership.

"I do know," Aunt Winnie continued as no other aunt seemed to want to join the conversation, unfortunately, "that that store will be where the answers are. We'll have to get in there. We have to do something, even if we do little."

CHAPTER 5: OPERATION TORCH

I couldn't sleep much any of the next several nights. Summer was oppressive, and it was wearing on into late July. Usually, I could sleep anywhere, at any time. It's an awfully nice trait to have; one I would learn to appreciate in college (for catching quick naps in the library or Student Union between finals after an all-night cram session). During my whole childhood, however, there was only one thing that ever kept me awake once I laid down my head: if I knew I was missing out on something.

As with other traits, people in my family blame it on my grandmother. They'd say I was just like her, being kept awake by stuff. Once, Dad had to drive across state (it had something to do with some taxes on the Five and Dime, but I was only six at the time, so I'm not positive about the details), and Grandmother Versey was very nervous about him driving out of town. She used to say how only in one's own town could you count on being safe in an automobile. That was because everyone knew who were the bad drivers and when they would be out in their "death-traps" (as she termed a car owned by one of the poorer drivers).

How was Dad supposed to know who were the bad drivers in Dodge City or beyond?

Anyway, she paced, unable to sleep until he finally made it home. She paced from her front porch to our front porch, a matter of five blocks. She'd make a round every forty minutes or so. Dad made it home about two in the morning, but parked on the street so we wouldn't be woken by him opening the garage or even by the opening and shutting of the car door so near to us. He came inside and went right to bed. Ten minutes later Grandmother Versey showed up, peeked in the garage and returned home, still fretting.

She did this until about four a.m. when she could stand it no longer. She pounded on our front door, wailing aloud for my mother, yelling at the top of her lungs that my mother needed to call all the hospitals in the state. She was more than slightly chagrinned when my father threw open the door and calmly (well, no) asked her what she was doing there in her nightgown and what in blazes was she yelling about?

Excitement or fear kept my grandmother and me awake. It was, or should have been, a combination of the two for me those summer nights. I was hard-pressed to comprehend the fear portion. If I had, I still wouldn't have slept, but I probably would have stayed in bed.

Aunt Winnie's stunning pronouncement, which had silenced everyone, would keep me awake for a long time. How were we to get in the Liquidation Store, and what would we find out? (I couldn't help but make it a "we" situation.) What would we do about it once we found out about whatever it was that was there?

"Winnie is right," Aunt Patti finally said after a long silence, all of us still at the dinner table. "We need to do something, for Chris' sake, even if we do little!" (Not that Chris, whoever that was, was actually mentioned.)

Anyway, it actually wasn't much of an idea by itself, even when Aunt Winnie had said it. The only idea it launched was Aunt

Ellen getting up and bringing out her homemade chocolate mousse, which spurred a lot of talk (no one could ever be silent over it; it was the dessert which had to be praised), but not about how to beat AH. It had lifted our moods immeasurably, even Aunt Winnie's, even my dad's. Maybe it wasn't something that could win the war for us, but it had a remarkable morale-boosting effect.

"Wherever did you get this recipe from, Ellen?" Aunt Winnie probed, but Aunt Ellen only smiled as she ushered Davey to the sink for another hand-washing.

"She won't even tell me," Uncle Frank said, licking his spoon. "She only says, 'From Shangri-La, from Shangri-La.'"

As the mousse vanished, a few desultory remarks came and went. The leaders all wondered whether or not they should just go visit the Liquidation Store; go there and talk to Hilde, appeal to her, appease her if necessary. The mere suggestion quickly died at the table, however. It was known that AH would be on her guard, would keep us at bay, would only accept abject surrender for terms, anyway. We could only go in forcefully, and for that we would have to be prepared.

So the day had ended. We walked home in silence, partway with Aunt Winnie. I had no chance to ask her what she had planned for AH. It would be nasty, I knew. It would have to be. I wanted it to be. I also didn't want to miss it. All I could do was wonder what it would be.

All day Tuesday I had to spend at home, though. It was my punishment for listening to the radio after Mom had said no. While I didn't disagree with the punishment—it was only more gardening, and my thumb could only become greener if it had lived on Mars—I objected to the timing. Why immediately the next day? Weren't most petty crimes paid for somewhat after they were discovered and the criminals apprehended? Wasn't there a trial, a court date, probation, a cooling-off period?

I desperately wanted to go over to my aunt's house. I tried every weaselly way I could think of, without resorting to tactics more worthy (or rather, less worthy) of a different aunt. Mom was determined, though. There was just something about her sister (Aunt Babs) that irked her.

Years later I found out that Mom had been close to Aunt Babs when young, much closer than to Aunt Hilde, both in years and in sentiments. Aunt Babs had left home early, though, before even graduating from high school. Mom had never understood why and I guess she never forgave her sister.

When my mom's family had lived in town, before my two grandfathers fought, I think only Aunt Hilde had been born. By the time they came back, in time (luckily for me) for my mother to meet my father in high school, Aunt Babs had already gone.

Once while snooping (I'm not proud of that trait, but I'm honest about it), I discovered a couple dozen postcards stuck in a shoebox in the back of my mom's closet. Aunt Babs had sent them from everywhere on the planet: Europe, South America, Africa, Asia, Australia. They didn't say much apart from things like the weather and an explanation of what famous building or scene was depicted on the front, but they obviously meant something to Mom. Perhaps she always hoped that Aunt Babs would return home and maybe settle down and they could be sisters again. Thinking back on the postcards, it was probably Aunt Babs' way of saying, "Please come join me. I'm sorry. I'm lonely."

There's something sad in all that.

But betrayal has long and bitter roots in the county. Feuds erupted all the time, and as the townsfolk all knew, they sure were great entertainment. They were usually small and of short duration, with little lasting memory. This one, ours, was already much larger in proportion than anyone had imagined it could be. No one had expected Hilde to buy the radio station and the bank—no one would have thought any one person could have afforded both—but otherwise, it had been delightful for those not involved (well, maybe not the marina blowing up). The appearance of Barbara Rose was a mania in town, outside the family, that is. Lawrence Welcome, who had had her twice in his taxi, seemed delirious with joy and was himself a minor celebrity because of it.

For my mother, this was not cause for celebration. Outside of telling me which patches I still needed to weed, she only told me one thing: "Barbara Rose only tells lies, Johnny, and she only breaks hearts."

Be that as it may, I was up to my ears in turnips at the time and I knew I was missing out on something exciting being planned by a different aunt. The day was spent by the time I was finished, and there was just no helping it. Wednesday too I was kept busy, mostly by Dad, down at the Five and Dime. I tried to sneak away, but they seemed to be keeping a close eye on me (which was unwarranted, really).

Thursday I was finally able to secure some freedom of movement. Dad left early for the Five and Dime, while Mom busied herself with the laundry. Temptation arose first from the dining room radio. I could tune in quickly, quietly, just to see if Aunt Hilde or Aunt Babs dropped any hints, but I demurred. What were the chances of that? Slim compared to the opportunity to get out on my own. The outside beckoned brightly.

I tiptoed across the house. I had the front screen door in view on a bright sunny day—I could even feel the mild breeze and hear the busy birds—when the practiced footfalls of my mother climbing the stairs from the basement reached my ears. For a split-second I froze, then bolted like the Road Runner outside, only I didn't leave a hole in my outline in the screen door, but rather just smacked it open. I was at the end of the drive before I heard it bang back into place. I kept running and got far enough away from the faint and growing fainter cries of, "Johnny?

Johnny!" that I would probably be believed when I said later that I hadn't heard my mother at all.

The town seemed a busy place that morning. There were always the "Regulars" roaming around, hunkered down in Roy's Barbershop, or strolling back and forth between Rudder's Goods and the Five and Dime. In addition to these few, one could always count on seeing a farmer or two in town for a variety of reasons. More than that and it would have to be a holiday or national emergency. In those cases, there would be a reason why so many folks congregated on the streets, and there surely were dozens!

Then I remembered about AH foreclosing on so many farms. That plus the marina fire was still the talk of the town; when I watched the people long enough, I could tell that they all kept meandering toward the river, toward the marina (well, the ex-marina) and back from it.

I stopped and took in as much as I could, sitting on the one open bench in Quincy Park (named for John Quincy Adams, of course). Another pattern of movement seemed to gel in my mind after a time. I blinked hard, jabbed my fists into my eyes and even pinched my forearm. Farmers (well, ex-farmers) were moving by ones and twos down Hancock Lane, at the end of which I well knew was the Liquidation Store. I didn't believe that, and further didn't believe that they weren't coming back! Then I thought I saw them all heading down Hancock from the direction of Madison and Washington, which was our main intersection (it had a stop sign).

My curiosity was piqued, and whenever that happened, I knew better than to try and head it off for it simply could not be helped. I've tried. Lord, how I've tried. Every time the Five and Dime got a new shipment of goods, I was there. I had to see if there was anything new, anything different. There never was, and Dad always got into such a snit every time I showed up, snooping around the crates and boxes. He'd ask every rhetorical question he could think of, from "Why are you down here again, as if I didn't know?" to "What are you expecting to find, since we never order anything different?" He didn't seem to understand that the suppliers could make mistakes, maybe sending us something exotic like tennis rackets, or maybe they'd miscount and send us extra packets of Juicy Fruit and Dad could give me those because otherwise his books wouldn't balance. Honestly, sometimes the guy just didn't have an imagination! Or hope.

I scanned the roads for what we kids always called "traffic". This wasn't cars, it was any adult related closely enough to us who was capable of handing out a chore. My dad's cousins were usually okay—two of them were "Regulars" downtown, so that was good—but Aunt Ellen's niece Joharriet on *her* side of the family (who was much older than me, so we never felt she was in *our* generation) was always looking for someone to help her can her tomatoes. Why she got to boss us around was a lifelong mystery, but each of us kids only ever disobeyed her once. After that, our parents made sure our bottoms were sore for days and our minds much clearer on the subject.

The streets were clear of said "traffic" so I ran to the other side, dodging a car and two more of those big trucks hauling stuff across the river. Every man, woman and child coming from around the corner had one fist around what looked to be an ice cream cone and their eyes glued to a flier. When I was close enough to them, the ice cream was confirmed, but I was unable to make out what was on the fliers that could possibly be so engrossing.

Around the corner appeared a vision in velvet (how in the world could he wear that in this heat?). I should have known. In our town, if it involved ice cream, Uncle Benny was sure to be around. He was not only around, he appeared to be behind it all.

I approached him and maybe I shouldn't have done so, but my need to know superseded all precautions. The crowd thinned. By coincidence, it seemed, all the strangers and stragglers in town had already been and left Benny's outpost.

He had a picnic table and umbrella set up on the sidewalk, and I could see an ice cream churner on the table—not his rain barrel one, though, but something new and store-bought—along with a small stack of the fliers, held down on the table by a small stone. As he bent down, packing something in a crate—possibly the fruit for the ice cream, or extra cones—I noticed a placard standing at his feet.

Free Homemade Ice Cream!
"Goose-steppin'-Berry"
Take a Flier!!!

While bent down, he grabbed the placard, folded it and placed it in a briefcase. He straightened and put the briefcase on the picnic table. I sensed a lost opportunity as he slid the rest of the fliers into the briefcase as well, then without looking whipped the stone behind him.

"Ow!"

I rubbed my forehead and remembered last summer when Uncle Benny had complained at one of our picnics: "There's so many nieces and nephews! Throw a rock and you're bound to hit one!" Who knew he'd be right?

He spun around when he heard me though, and watching him jump and scan the sidewalk (for Uncle Frank or Aunt Winnie, I knew) was something of a payback. Seeing I was alone seemed to restore him, and he flashed me a full smile, holding out one hand, empty, like a magician might, while feeling for the lid of the briefcase with the other.

"Oh, Gianni!" he said with mock delight.

Gianni? Where did that come from?

"Hey, I'd-a give-a you some more of my ice cream, but I-a am-a very late!"

Another uncle with a phony accent? Maybe it was another disturbed attempt at distancing himself from Uncle Joe.

"Hi Uncle Benny. What are you doing?"

"Oh, you kids, you-a are-a everywhere! Just throw a rock!"

I rubbed my forehead again. I decided to try a different tactic.

"What are you doing, handing out desserts?"

"Just desserts!" he said and gave a mangled laugh because he seemed to try and suppress it completely.

He turned then and slammed shut the briefcase and quickly fiddled with the churner before rounding on me again. His smile remained constant, but he took out a handkerchief and dabbed his forehead.

"You a good boy, Gianni. Why-a don't you-a go play now, eh? Ciao!"

Maybe he played dumb (I think he was playing), but he was also dumb like a fox, because he knew where my loyalties lay. In my code, he had just become the Dessert Fox.

I wasn't going to get any information out of him, I knew, but I stood my ground anyway, playing innocent like a little kid. It would make him the most nervous. I'd give him both barrels, then I'd run for Aunt Winnie's.

Three times he dropped the ice cream maker as he tried hoisting it with one arm in order to grab the briefcase with the other. He settled on throwing the briefcase on top of the churner and picking that up with both arms, toting it while he waddled away, precarious, anxious, but unwilling to talk to me anymore.

I did my best "harrumph" (which I had learned from Grandfather Treat when I was three; he always got a kick out of me imitating him) and took off in the opposite direction. The Dessert Fox headed for the other side of the river; I went toward the Liquidation Store. No, I wasn't planning on paying a visit to Aunt Hilde, but I ran as fast as I could toward the backs of the crowd still walking that way.

They ambled and I flew, so I caught up to them easily. Mostly, these were people Aunt Winnie had been sheltering. I knew them by face and somewhat by reputation (though I didn't really *know* any of them, even their kids, very well). They seemed like sensible people, but one can never tell what ugly ideas hide in people's brains. All these people were going straight to one of AH's strongholds. Didn't they know what fate surely awaited them?

Actually, I didn't know either, not really. I hadn't been in it for months, well before the feud started. Who knew how AH had changed it? It was just a store, though, so what could possibly happen?

As I thought of talking to them, reasoning with them, pleading with them, my mouth went dry, and I became mute. Then a little girl, her face smeared with melted ice cream and bits of gooseberries, dropped her flier as her arm was pulled by an impatient parent. The family continued on, the girl seemingly conscious only of her messy treat, so I quickly swooped in and snatched the fallen flier. It looked and felt somehow familiar, except it belted forth bizarre announcements:

Down and Out? Mortgage Foreclosed? Farm Bankrupt?
Don't despair! Jobs and shelter await you!
Join the Greater East Dodge Co-Prosperity Sphere!
Apply at the Liquidation Store!
Fabulous Prizes will be given at hourly drawings!
No purchase necessary!

It was unexpected, but it filled me with trepidation, and my knees wobbled tremulously. I'd bring it to Aunt Winnie or Uncle Frank. As it was almost lunchtime anyway, and as I was close to the Five and Dime (but some ways from Aunt Winnie's), I decided to find Uncle Frank first. When Uncle Frank worked days, he usually had a mound of sandwiches available for any family member who pitched in (or, if one were sneaky enough, just showed up). Aunt Ellen made them, of course, or nobody would have touched them. Uncle Frank was fine at lots of things, but not food that didn't involve the grill. Aunt Ellen was a culinary genius. I stuffed the flier in my back pocket and scampered toward the haven of the family store.

"It's a nightmare is what it is!"

I arrived as Uncle Frank pounded the front counter, scowling and pacing, slamming his cane on the tile with every other step. Aunt Patti and Dad sat on stools at the head of separate aisles, chomping on egg salad on rye. There was another farmer there, too, his back to me. He looked a little familiar, but all the farmers could end up looking the same after milking cows and spreading manure. All I could really tell about him was he was tall, lanky and bald, with standard denim overalls and, with the way his elbows bent at his sides, his thumbs were probably holding onto his suspenders. As it seemed I was unnoticed upon entering (the door had been propped open), I quickly skittered around the front counter, grabbed two halves of a sandwich and sat down on the floor at the entrance to the Back Room.

"It's not like you need it now," Dad said as he wiped his mouth on his sleeve. Mom would know what we had for lunch.

"I do need it now," my uncle snapped. "The election isn't that far off, you know!"

"Heck, you'll be swept in on a landslide vote, that's for gol darn sure," Aunt Patti said, though I'm not quoting her verbatim.

"A fat stinking lot you two would know about it," Uncle Frank said, continuing his pacing and stomping. "I've been so busy with this feud, I haven't even been able to put out feelers about who might run against me. The mayorship is important to me! It's important to the family! I need to see this town and this family through these difficult times."

"Well, then you can do it the old-fashioned way, door-to-door, never mind this printing press son-of-a-biscuit."

"Patti, it's strategically important. If I try knocking on every door, I'll wear out my soles. And my soul, I know it. With leaflets, then I can hop from one island of important mailboxes to the next, bypassing points of known resistance. Now, see, you really don't know anything about higher strategy like this, so that's why I've brought in Isaac to be my campaign manager."

I peeked over the counter and took another look. The man turned slightly and I got a good profile picture. Now I recognized my dad's cousin Isaac from the countryside. Everybody called him Ike. I had not known a lot about him before the feud, but I was to see him around plenty between then and the pivotal mayoral election. I wasn't positive what a campaign manager was, but it sounded serious; it wasn't anything Uncle Frank had ever needed before.

"I wondered why you were here, Ike," Dad said.

"Ike will plan the overall strategy and get everybody on board. I don't have time to take all these calls, but Ike can build the consensus I need."

I shuddered as I slunk down and went back to my egg salad. I got the sense that business had turned serious. Was Uncle Frank in danger of not winning the next election? Who wasn't going to vote for Uncle Frank? Many, it seemed like, based on the groans I heard from the other adults.

"I was pulling for our cousin Montpelier," Aunt Winnie said of Ike's appointment later on, "but Isaac's a good choice, too. We can all work with him."

Montpelier—or Monty, as we always referred to him—was another farmer from the outskirts of town (and not Isaac's brother, but from another sibling of Grandfather Treat's, though they were both rather thin on top). We visited Monty's farm exactly twice each year: Once in the spring, to see if he had survived the winter and was still alive, and once in the fall, to gladly take in some of the corn he had produced. As a bachelor farmer, he didn't need much and was always happy to supply the family. Slow and methodical in his farming ways—as he was in all things—he mostly got the job done right in the end. His steady, repetitive completion of his annual crop made him a hero in Aunt Winnie's house, at least, though my dad and at least one uncle had long nicknamed him "Plodder", though for years I thought that had to do with his very large, flat feet.

There was no way Plodder would've gotten the job over Ike, whom everybody liked. I kind of liked him, too, and I contemplated him as I found an angle where I could see things better while remaining hidden.

"The first thing we need to do," Ike said while Uncle Frank continued pacing around him, "is find the printing press. We need it and we need it bad."

"Plus," Uncle Frank added, "the press belongs to the town and it's missing from the Town Hall basement."

"Well, how about the gosh durned importance of my missing boyfriend!" Aunt Patti interjected, pushing her cousin Isaac aside, just as he donned an old cap. "He keeps going on these trips! He was due back from this last one Saturday night. Here it is Thursday and I've had neither sight nor sound of him!"

Finally, Uncle Frank stopped moving. Ike came back into view, but Uncle Frank maneuvered in front of him as my uncle rubbed his temples and waved one arm at Aunt Patti in a placating gesture.

"Norman is just fine," he said. "He agreed to go on a mission for us."

"Us? Who's 'us'?" Patti cried and Uncle Frank gesticulated wildly between himself and Cousin Isaac.

"Us!" he said emphatically. "Look, Norman will likely be back this weekend. He's traveling on my dime. What he's doing is important, Patti. I don't want to hear another word on the matter!"

The last bit he roared. It stunned me that it worked in silencing Aunt Patti. It seemed callous, but Uncle Frank had a lot on his mind. I had forgotten that the mayoral election was almost upon us. Uncle Frank always got in a bind over it. No one in town had ever been mayor longer, though, and we all expected him to continue in that capacity indefinitely. Who else would run against him now? Oh, some traditionalists in the town had made a fuss last time out, I recalled (though I was too young to take much notice of the elections prior to that), saying if Elizer MacSheedy our town founder hadn't been mayor more than twice, then no one should be, although Elizer had died in the middle of his second term. This time out, I think we all figured he would be unopposed. From my vantage point, though, I could see that his face was lined with stress, his brow wilted with worry. He seemed old, really old, for the first time to me.

It struck a chord in me to see and recognize my uncle as having frailties, as being human. He had always scoffed at help, but he needed some, even if he didn't exactly want any. I suddenly made a connection in my mind and realized I could help him.

Gulping down the last vestiges of my purloined lunch, I withdrew the crumpled flier from my back pocket, flattened it out as best I could on the floor and stood up. I must have appeared magically to Dad and Aunt Patti, for they both stared wide-eyed at me.

"I found this, Uncle Frank," I said as I walked it over to the counter where he had stopped, Cousin Ike gaping at me in awe.

He took it without looking at me or the paper and mopped his forehead with it. When it finally hit him that it didn't feel like his handkerchief, he stopped and smoothed out the crumpled sheet. He looked at it quizzically, then his eyes widened in realization and he dashed over to the telephone.

"Get me Dodge six, six. . . . Yes, all right, Cora, I know you know it's me, and yes, you're right, I do want Hilde's number." Uncle Frank rolled his eyes. I imagine Cora LaSee, our operator, had been waiting for this call. My uncle mumbled under his breath as he waited for the connection while Ike read the flyer, then, "Hello? Hilde! You listen to me! What? What? Now, listen!"

This was tense. I felt in awe over this battle where the combatants never set eyes on one another, groping about to deliver a blow. Uncle Frank yelled and yelled into the mouthpiece. He gave some pretty good shots. "Belly up to the bull!" was my favorite, even though I didn't understand it. He fumed whenever Aunt Hilde screamed back at him; we couldn't tell the exact words, but we could hear it was loud and screechy. It made us cringe.

After several minutes of the back and forth, Uncle Frank decided to disengage. He slammed down the receiver and yelled, "Scratch one Flat-top!" which is what he had taken to calling Aunt Hilde (I always focused on her little mustache, but Uncle Frank must've concentrated on her head). He seemed alternately pleased and shaken by this engagement. We wanted to speak, but kept a respectful silence as he seemed to lick his wounds, contemplating his next move.

"You stay here!" he shouted as he dashed off as fast as he could, and while I didn't interpret that to include me, Dad did and my attempts to follow Uncle Frank were foiled.

"Johnny," was all he said when I was halfway to the door. It stopped me cold, even though there was no anger or threat attached to it. It was simply an order, so I obeyed.

I knew I had seen little blue fliers somewhere before. The town press would churn those out every once in a while. The last time I recalled seeing them—after thinking about it—was the last election, with Uncle Frank's motto (he wanted it adopted as the town motto, but so far, the council had opposed him): *It's Great to Be Here!* It wasn't much, but most people admitted it was better than the established town motto: *It's a Good Place to Be.* Someone, years ago, had come across a cheap supply of 10,000 reams of 5" x 7" blue paper and given it to the city (nobody remembered who, which was a little odd for us). The town council had quickly enacted a law that allowed anyone in town to use the paper (the council members wanted their home attic space back). As far as I knew, there were 8,000 or more reams remaining. Aunt Hilde and Uncle Benny had used a few more, it seemed, and it also seemed like they had taken the town's press.

Uncle Frank was going to do open battle against AH and the Dessert Fox, I knew it. What a shame not to be there. It could all be over any minute. Pastor Evers had been right to look for good things in the midst of bad: Uncle Frank had reached his breaking point and would clean up my naughty relations for good!

After I finished my sandwich, Dad made me clean up some more Coke bottles while he minded the store (there weren't many as the store was almost out of Coca-Cola). Aunt Patti left, saying she was going to try and telephone Norman, though she didn't know where he was at; Ike busied himself with paperwork. When I finished with the chore, Dad grilled me on what the flier had said, then fished out two quarters from the till and told me I had done a good job on the bottles.

"Thanks. I usually only get one quarter." Me and my stupid big mouth.

Dad seemed ambivalent. I thought he would ask me for one back. Then he nodded and said, "Well, you get double for combat pay. You met up with Uncle Benny, didn't you? Now get along to Aunt Winnie's. She needs more help. She said you could have dinner there tonight, too. I have to try and find out what's happened to all our deliveries."

I turned and left, pocketing the fifty cents and wondering (not for the first time, not for the last) why I had so many cousins but did so many chores alone.

*　　*　　*

When I arrived, Aunt Winnie was steaming and fuming and in one of the foulest moods in which I had ever seen her. Her garden was fine in that there were no new weeds. However, most of the plants had been trampled. I hadn't been there since the night before the *Arizona Kid* blew up, but it looked like her place had been at the marina. Inside her house, things were even worse, if that were possible. Everything seemed in broken disarray, except her kitchen which seemed to have sustained only minimal damage.

"What happened here, Aunt Winnie?"

She (that gallant woman) did not lash out at me, but barely paused as she bustled about the place with more fervor than anything. She held up two fingers in a V shape and winked at me.

"Give me two hours of hard work, Johnny, and we'll have this place picked up and put back together again."

"I don't know, Aunt Winnie. They couldn't do it with Humpty Dumpty. . . ."

I trailed off and stopped shaking my head, instead bending and picking up shreds of towels and crumpled magazines and whatever else I found on the floor. Soon, I had great swaths cleared, but also big rubbish piles (which I knew Aunt Winnie wouldn't just throw out, but had to go through first), so I wasn't sure how much better off we were.

"When we get done, Johnny, we've got a good stew on the stove to get through. Then we'll turn on the radio and listen to the tramp and make fun of her!"

Aunt Winnie had shaken off her mood and her renewed high spirits carried me through the *four* hours of lifting, carrying, sorting, sweeping, *et al*. It was late already, my stomach groused incessantly and, when it seemed that I paid it no nevermind, enlisted the aid of my brain which soon clouded my vision until I nearly blacked out.

I found a chair, showed Aunt Winnie my most pathetic look that I saved for truly special occasions (of either hunger or greed), and thankfully it swayed her. The stew was hot but not scalding, it was available immediately and there was plenty of it. I overlooked the fact that in three bowls I had found only two small bits of meat. Times, I knew deep in my bones, were hard.

Aunt Winnie tuned in KOBG while we ate. For twenty minutes Aunt Babs babbled on and on, promising music and entertainment, but instead reciting some essay about the history of our county. It wasn't what I had learned, and it amazed me until Aunt Winnie started shrilly yelling at every other word of Aunt Babs'.

"The original land grant for the county was nearly four times the current size—"

"Balderdash!"

"—and it was from the site of our town that Lewis and Clark first encountered Sacagawea—"

"Unmitigated rubbish!"

"—and were told that the surrounding valley had been set aside by the gods for future prosperity."

"What in blazes does that mean, you lying mouthpiece on legs!"

And what did that slur mean, Aunt Winnie? I got a weird mental image.

After she shut off the radio with one final nasty word (technically not an expletive), and after allowing a minute or so of silence to wash it all away, I finally remembered to ask again about what exactly had happened to her place.

"It was those ungrateful wretches!" she cried. "I mean, they're poor souls and all, but it's not like I'm running the Ritz here. They had no place to go. We have to open our homes, Johnny. Well, but here's the danger: This isn't their land, their house, their things, so they treated it all like dirt. I didn't say anything against them because I knew they had been wronged by those thieves. I wasn't going to make a sacrifice that cost me nothing. Everything can be repaired or replaced, at least eventually. No, I only regret the loss the garden sustained."

I remembered the state of the garden I had seen. With a shudder, I asked if we had to pick up the outside yet that night.

"Good gracious, I should think not. It's almost dark already! No, there's no sense, anyway. Most of it is simply gone."

Wow. Gone? Picked by people other than Davey? But no, Aunt Winnie said some of it was picked and eaten, but most of it was not ready yet. It had been trampled by people not knowing where to go or how to live with other people.

"One would think they would know how to treat vegetables, though, most of them being farmers."

"One would think," I assented.

"One would be wrong."

So we sat for another minute, the stew gone but not fully digested, the sun firmly down in the horizon, streaking the sky with only a few fuzzy rays of light or hope. The day was done. There was something left to do, I felt, but my body was tired and sore.

"Hey, Aunt Winnie!" I said with a sudden jerk that nearly toppled me from my precariously leaning chair (she was so sleepy herself she had not noticed me engaged in the sitting *faux pas*).

"What? What's that? What's happening?"

"I just remembered!" I told her about the fliers Uncle Benny had been handing out, about getting people's attention with free ice cream, and also about Uncle Frank's reaction.

She nodded but didn't seem impressed. In fact, she stifled a yawn (she didn't stifle it very well, either). All in all, I was a little crushed. She threw me a bone by asking me what flavor ice cream Uncle Benny had been dishing out. I told her, but I still wasn't happy.

"It's a little late for gooseberries," Aunt Winnie pondered, rubbing her chin. "I'll lay wages they were sour. Anyway, Johnny, your uncle called me a few minutes before you got here from the Five and Dime."

"He called you then? That must have been right after I left there!"

"Yes. He wanted to know why I hadn't put in any hours there lately, er, but that's neither here nor there. He did tell me about the flier, however, as well as his visit to the Liquidation Store."

"What happened?"

"No one was there."

"What? That's impossible!"

"So he thought, too. He said he was so angry he tried to kick in the door!"

"Holy crap!" I shouted and I immediately wished I hadn't.

Aunt Winnie wasn't scandalized by my vulgar language, but terribly disappointed. Perhaps she didn't blame me as her best efforts at calming the wild tongues of my father and another one of my aunts had never worked, but she did not see the setbacks as a reason to refrain from putting forth renewed effort on the next generation. I felt with vigor on my backside her feelings on sensible speech and plainly wondered how old I would have to be before my punishments could simply be monetary instead of corporal (twenty-three, as it turned out).

Walking a little gingerly, I helped Aunt Winnie clean the table and begin the washing up. Generously, I only had to do the clearing and the drying.

"Yes, I was amazed at Frank's spirit, too," Aunt Winnie said, picking up her story thread. "I thought the old fool would have a heart attack. Plus the fact that he's mayor, attempting breaking and entering, even one's sister-in-law's establishment, is more than a bit unsavory. He said he thought he did a little bit of damage, too, even though he didn't get in."

"Are you going to spank him?"

She gave me her version of The Look, took my towel and handed me her brush. I was unregenerate, I was.

"In broad daylight! I ask you!"

But she didn't ask me. She dried her dishes slowly, wiping the towel around and around a plate so that I was nearly hypnotized. Even succumbing to the deadening effects, I soon found myself half a dozen dishes ahead of her, with only the flatware remaining (Aunt Winnie always used the maximum amount of dishes possible, much to my chagrin).

Finally, she nodded to herself, quickly finishing the task at hand and peering outside. She motioned me to follow her. With dried hands, we went to her front hall closet where she pulled out two dark-brown raincoats.

"Let's go, Johnny!" she said to me, handing me a raincoat and donning the other one. Her voice quivered with excitement and her knees were noticeable by their shaking.

"Go? Where are we going?" I asked, dumbly putting on the coat, though I knew it wasn't raining and it certainly wasn't cold.

She rummaged around the top shelf of the closet, mumbling to herself (which she normally never did). Finally, she gave a satisfied grunt, pulled something out and handed it to me.

It was a flashlight.

"Let's go to the Liquidation Store, Johnny!"

*   *   *

While still on the outskirts of town, she talked in her normal manner to me, passing the time by talking about George Bernard Shaw and something she had read by him or about him, I couldn't follow. It was something about America and England being two countries separated by the same language. It was a puzzler, but maybe only because I was sweating so profusely in my raincoat—the thing just didn't breathe—and so I had to ask why.

"Well, it's very simple. Take this flashlight, for instance. In England, they call it a 'torch'."

"No, I meant, why am I wearing this awful raincoat?"

"Oh. Yes. Well, it's camouflage, isn't it?"

It took a minute for me to understand. I thought: *Of course! We wear the dark raincoats at night to keep us from being seen.* Then I thought: *We're going to the Liquidation Store.* A further thought: *The Liquidation Store is closed at night.* Then I understood, and it all came together like a grand scientific theory: *We're going to bust up the Liquidation Store!*

Even in the dark, I think Aunt Winnie could see me struggle with these thoughts. Perhaps my eyes opened wide and the whites could be seen like oncoming headlights, giving away my position while she wanted blackout conditions. Whatever the reason, she averted my questions and protestations (especially the moral ones, regarding a certain spanking I had gotten over some lifted mail) by clapping her hand over my mouth (a move that surprised me to no end).

"Now, Johnny, I'm sorry to be dragging you into this. However, it is apparent that of all the next generation, you stand out as being the most mature."

The most mature? Would she swear an affidavit to that? At least to my mother?

"I mean you see what's right and what's wrong and you're not afraid to choose between them. That takes courage, boy. It's a testament to how well you've been raised by your folks and me."

At that last "and me," I thought I saw her look away in embarrassment, because she knew she didn't deserve very much of the credit, but if medals were being handed out, I don't think she'd be averse to getting in line. Still, she actually had taught me a lot about right and wrong; she had taught a lot of us kids. Not just by spanking, either. There had been lots of lectures, too.

"Ultimately Johnny, it's a choice, and it takes courage, like I said. One either wants to stand up to tyranny or succumb. This is not a child foolishly lashing out at a strict parent because chores and lessons are not fun! No, Hilde and Benny are up to no good, to dominate the family, and more than that, the town and the whole county, too.

"It also takes courage to act on those convictions, Johnny. Frank has assured me that we are doing all we can with legal means, but we're going to see if we can't add our own little shot to the feud."

"What are we going to do, Aunt Winnie?"

"It's just a little bombing run, Johnny. I wouldn't have brought you, but I need the cover."

We were in the town proper and her voice became a whisper. With no lights on this late and the sky dark and cloudy, we couldn't see anyone (and hopefully no one could see us). I barely saw Aunt Winnie's outline. I wouldn't have believed it had I not been there, but she walked lightly, as if on feathers. Hard-pressed to imitate her, I engaged in an exaggerated tiptoe, reminiscent of any myriad of cartoon characters trying to sneak up on Bugs Bunny; I felt I would be caught at any second with a blazing spotlight blinding me in my tracks.

"Me?" I whispered, chancing the noise. "Why me?"

She put a hand on me to stop my tiptoeing. She leaned in close so we could see each other's face. Then she gave me a penetrating glare. "Because your eyes are good. You don't," she said this quite slowly, enunciating, "miss much."

That may have been the biggest compliment Aunt Winnie ever intentionally gave me.

I forced my mouth shut (to keep from exposing white, shiny teeth; yes, I did brush twice daily, thank you very much) and we continued on. It seemed we walked (tiptoed) for hours. Every time a dog barked my heart made for the emergency escape route up the esophagus; each time I had to swallow hard and often before I could continue, convinced that AH lurked in the darkness or around the next corner.

Finally, Aunt Winnie stopped us and pointed a finger downward. I squatted and, with a break in the cloud cover exposing a half-moon, I saw her creep up to a building I recognized as the Liquidation Store.

She moved stealthily on cat-like feet. This too I would not have believed, an extension of her light footfalls when needed. As I watched her try the door and peer in through each window, something seemed odd about the front and portion of the side that I could see. I figured it out just as Aunt Winnie heaved a brick at one of the windows and it bounced back with a dull thud; the windows were boarded up. It appeared that Uncle Frank had had at least a modicum of success. As unbelievable as it was that Aunt Winnie would heave a brick at a window in the middle of the night, I was even more dumfounded when she tried it again, this time aiming at the boarded-up glass on the door barely visible down the steps to the cellar.

I remembered my job as lookout when Aunt Winnie apparently succeeded (for I didn't hear glass breaking), as she raised her fists in triumph and, turning on her flashlight, launched herself down the steps. Jerking my head from side to side, sweating bullets and feverishly dodging imaginary ones shot by AH's defenses, I thought I caught movement around the far side of the Liquidation Store, heading toward Aunt Winnie.

Another flashlight shone and I knew it wasn't a friend to either of us. What to do? My heart beat wildly and my hands sought frantically for hope or something more solid to grasp. Finding a small chunk of broken pavement, I whipped it as hard as I could, over the head of the enemy patrol (who it was I couldn't tell for sure). It landed with a hard smack against a garbage can, knocking off the lid which rang like a cymbal crash. The light turned away immediately and disappeared back from where it had come.

Then a ruckus of crashes and dog barking erupted from the cellar of the Liquidation Store. A hustling Aunt Winnie bounded up from the steps, practically defying gravity, time and various other laws of physics. She made it to me in seconds flat and the last thing I saw before she grabbed my arm and yanked me with her was the return of the other flashlight, but even if that person pursued us, Aunt Winnie outpaced him, forcing me along at speeds I had rarely seen outside of Aunt Patti's cars. We didn't slow until we were out of the town proper and closing on her house once more.

When she finally spoke (and let go of my arm—wow, did that woman have a grip!), I could tell she was as out of breath as was I. "She . . . had a big . . . German . . . Shepherd . . . in there!" she gasped.

Inside her house again I saw immediately that Aunt Winnie told the truth, for something big had taken a chunk out of her raincoat and part of her dress, too. This was a very embarrassing situation for a nephew, but Aunt Winnie seemed ruddy with enthusiasm.

"Hah!" she said, covering up the hole with her hand. "I'm bloodied, but still in one piece. Hmmph, I guess Frank was being literal when he said the 'dog' chased him away. I thought he was speaking metaphorically and meant Hilde."

We plopped down on good furniture—not caring about mussing the fabric up on this night—and neither of us said anything more until our breathing had finally normalized. With a few hand motions as encouragement from her, I went to the kitchen and found some lemonade in the ice-box. Aunt Winnie, I understood, enthusiasm or not, would not be leaving her armchair and risking a breeze for anything. I would sleep there tonight (I sometimes did after having dinner there; Mom and Dad knew this well) and I knew where everything for a guest nephew was, so I figured she would get up from the chair after I went to bed.

I brought Aunt Winnie a glass and sat and sipped mine glumly. The excitement of illegality was flimsy and ethereal. Right and wrong were drilled into me from an early age and, not having teenage rebellion to prod me (not yet being a teenager), I didn't find delight when it went unaccompanied with instant success.

Sure, I had stolen some U.S. Mail, but that had felt like detective stuff, Dick Tracy versus comic archenemies. Mostly, it had felt like a sudden and swift blow, landing victory like a surprise uppercut in a prize fight. Our night adventure felt like a quick retreat with our tails between our legs.

"It's not so bad, Johnny," Aunt Winnie said as she surveyed me, her voice again full of its normal resonance. "We've taken the fight to her. She knows we'll be watching her day and night, and that she can't hide behind her storefront like a good citizen of the world. We're onto her, and that she's got that blasted guard dog only goes to show she's frightened of us."

"But Aunt Winnie, we just wasted our time and nearly got caught, too!"

"Now, now, remember what Pastor Evers said. Or think of Shakespeare: 'If you can look into the seeds of time, And say which grain will grow, and which will not, Speak then to me, who neither beg nor fear Your favors nor your hate.'"

"Macbeth?"

Aunt Winnie raised her eyebrows. "Not bad! You're finally learning something. You could work on memorizing some of it now."

Maybe I could at least try and remember what Pastor Evers had said. It was about focusing on the good, I remembered that much. It was about hope.

"Besides," Aunt Winnie continued, "it wasn't for naught at all. I spotted the printing press in there, so we've confirmed she's got that. And we'll keep up the pressure, this time to her home base."

"What do you mean her 'home base'?"

"She had a scale model set up there. I got enough of a look before I got bit to recognize the layout. There's something big going on with Treat's land."

CHAPTER 6: NORMANDY

I't rained most of the next couple of weeks after Aunt Winnie's raid. Ten times or more I went outside to play after it had cleared, only to be sent scampering when it immediately started back up again. I'd wait through the opening drizzles easily enough, to see which way things were headed, but each time the clouds opened up with another full barrage and a seemingly endless supply of wet ammunition. It felt like the brief interludes between downfalls were merely the dark clouds' chance to reload and fire indiscriminately again.

The baseball season was in serious jeopardy.

We didn't have much in the way of organized baseball, but every year the kids around town managed to get two teams together (ages 10-14) that played against each other twenty or thirty times a summer. The best players merged to form one team whenever we were able to play a team from another community, and the mergers became permanent when the fourteen-year-olds moved into the high school league.

The family feud affected everything in town, and our baseball games were no exception. The foreclosure of all the farm properties had forced some kids to stop playing as they helped their families work and put food on the table, which to me seemed about even with baseball (maybe a little behind) on the priority scale. Others stayed away due to intense pressure, co-opted or drafted into positions they'd rather not have, like my cousins or dependents of Uncle Benny and Aunt Hilde, told to stay away for whatever reason. On the days we could play, we were left short-handed, flipping coins all the way up to 8 out of 15 in order not to have "Shorty" Fred Pedersen and "Three-Toed" Franky Gathway on our team (those two, along with Jack "Flip" Fulsome and Francis "The Wetter" Gordon were known to us collectively as the "4-Fs"; for good or ill, we pitied their inability to do anything but bunt and that not intentionally). Nine on a side being required, we eventually bowed to even this ignominy and everyone played or attempted it at least.

Some adults who walked by the ball field cheered us for our spirit and innocence and our overall lack of discrimination. Perhaps it was a bit egalitarian, but as it was forced upon us by circumstances rather than being chosen, it seemed hypocritical to accept any honor around it. We just wanted to play ball and get on with having fun before there was no more time for it; something even I could sense approaching ever more swiftly.

I still thought of the feud as something of an adventure, though. What a grand human drama unfolded before me, brought on by people's choices, right or wrong and for whatever intention. Each day brought new vacillations to this view, naturally, as I knew how evil AH had become (having long suspected it). Still, I had had several heart-pounding adventures since the opening salvo, as well as having been privy to major meetings amongst the heads of my family. Adventures of such magnitude were rare in our town, though I had always had my share of fun but benign times.

Remembering these things buoyed me somewhat during the rains. It didn't always last and I was left longing for normalcy. Sitting inside, looking out and watching the water stream out the end of the downspout—and patently NOT listening to the radio—it seemed as if life had changed for good (though whether for true good or bad I couldn't say for sure). Then the phone rang, breaking my reverie. It was Uncle Frank, inviting us all over for supper.

This meant a conference, I knew, as soon as Dad hung up the phone and told us to go get our coats and get in the car.

"Oh," he said, probably intending this for Mom who was busy fidgeting with her appearance in the mirror, "and Norman's back. He's at Frank's."

"Well, I just talked with Patti today and she didn't say anything about him being back!" Mom replied. And I thought she hadn't been listening. I'd need to file that tidbit away for future use: *Warning, she CAN hear you even when she looks distracted!*

"Don't make faces!" she suddenly snapped, and I quickly pulled in my tongue and unfurrowed my brow. Geez, she could see out the back of her head, too!

Oh wait, she was using the mirror.

"No," Dad said, apparently not party to our digression, "I don't think he went to Patti's. I think he went to Frank's first. He's probably calling her now."

"Why Frank's first?" I blurted out, which was a doubly-compounded error, since not only hadn't I called my dad's brother "Uncle", but it was likely a question Mom would have asked anyway, leaving me as an unnoticed (mostly) eavesdropper.

"Jonathan," Mom snapped. Then, "Yes, why Frank's first?"

"He found out something about Benny and Hilde. It's big. That's why we're going over there."

Fantastic! Finally, there would be movement. Then I wondered, *We're still going to eat, aren't we?*

When we got there after a short drive (we would have walked if it hadn't been raining), I could tell the atmosphere was charged. I could also tell that, yes, we were going to eat, but that this time would not be like after the marina explosion. The dining room table was not set up with all the extensions, while the card tables were up in the kitchen. The kids would be eating with a closed door separating us from the action; the adults looked like they would have their conference first, then eat.

My glum face probably stuck out to my cousins like the KOBG radio tower over town, and most likely they teased me over it, but I couldn't change it and didn't really notice them (well, I tried not to; they could be heartless). Would I have to sit idly by after having done so much for the family? I had earned the right to sit at the grown-up's table! Plus, I just didn't want to miss out.

I peeked into the living room and caught a glimpse of Aunt Winnie, Uncle Frank and even Uncle Joe (which was weird, because I hadn't seen his kids, my cousins). Then I saw Norman. Aunt Patti was with him and had her arms around his neck, holding him tightly. He seemed alternately pleased and embarrassed before finally separating himself from my aunt's embraces.

"Everything's going to be all right, Patti," he said, but he seemed to have a hard time making eye contact.

"I was just so worried about you! You didn't even call me, you lousy son-of-a-gun." Once again, my paraphrase.

"Patti!" Aunt Ellen cried in practiced shamefacedness.

"I just want to be where you are," Aunt Patti said, defiantly.

"That's just not always possible," Uncle Frank said. "Now come on."

"Yes," Cousin Ike said, "let's sit down and dissect what Norman's brought us."

The goodies already! If I could just slide my way along the wall, I could reach the couch, settle down and not even be noticed.

"Children, you'll have to leave the room."

I looked left and saw my second cousin Kirk standing there with a finger half-way up his . . . well, never mind. Suffice to say, Aunt Ellen grabbed him and me and force-marched us to the kitchen sink (she picked up Davey along the way, too), detaining us there until we had each washed hands four times thoroughly (even though I hadn't had my fingers up anywhere).

"Have a seat," Aunt Ellen said, pointing at the final spots at the card tables. "There's a platter there to start on and I'll get your food straight away."

"Oh boy, veggies!" Davey cried and sat down with relish.

I slithered into my seat, longing for redemption to a world I thought was better. My cousins didn't even want to talk about baseball (and to be fair, we hadn't had a good game in a long time due to the rain and the feud). To top it all off, Laura asked Aunt Ellen if we were having more of her marvelous mousse for dessert and the answer was a resounding "No."

Then, when the pit of my stomach felt rock-hard, came a distinct cry from the other room: Aunt Winnie calling my name. A summons! Maybe I was being singled out for my heroism, applauded for my bravery, asked humbly for my views on the next campaign!

"Johnny! Johnny!" She poked her head into the kitchen. "Bring me a glass of water."

Davey sniggered as I skulked out of my chair and over to the sink. I carried it with red-hot anger boiling behind my temples and expected to thrust the glass into Aunt Winnie's hands just beyond the door to the living room. When I looked, however, she had maneuvered herself to the sofa farthest away and I had to step delicately around and through the various adults and pieces of furniture to get to her.

"This keeps getting worse!" Uncle Frank said. He seemed to be in the middle of a litany. "That printing press was the town's. I need to use it for the campaign coming up. By this time I should have had two fliers printed up for my supporters already."

"Well, if she's stolen it, why not get the county sheriff over here?"

"She hasn't stolen it, that's why! I just found out the council voted in favor of turning over possession of the press temporarily in Hilde's favor. She has it legally!"

I wondered how that could possibly have transpired with Uncle Frank being mayor?

"Dog gone it! I told those people to wake me if anything interesting came up in that meeting!"

Oh. Anyway, I walked as slowly as I dared, painfully trying to be invisible or, barring that, appearing as if I were interested solely in keeping Aunt Ellen's knick-knacks and antiques from taking any clumsy childhood damage. I reached Aunt Winnie nonetheless and handed her the glass.

As I started to turn, to make my way back, she barked out softly, "Sit down."

Colonel Prescott at the Battle of Bunker Hill would have sent a steady volley my way with how wide my eyes got. I backed into a seat on the sofa next to my aunt and she whispered, half under her breath to me and half in explanation to the rest of the room (they weren't paying attention, however), "You can return the glass when I'm finished with it."

I settled in, nervously looking to where my parents sat, but as the conversation progressed, it appeared I was safe under Aunt Winnie's auspices. She took a great gulp of the water (I regretted not letting the tap run and get a little cooler) and casually slipped some papers into my lap.

I looked down at an official looking letter addressed to Norman with a Washington D.C. P.O. box number. It was from an attorney in Manhattan. Goose-pimples sprouted from everywhere on me and I realized that Aunt Winnie disagreed with Uncle Frank about there being no kids allowed, and was a faithful ally. What a great aunt!

I read the letter with zest, but surreptitiously:

Mr. Norman D. Beech
P.O. Box 6644
Washington, D.C. 20005

Dear Mr. Beech:

Enclosed are the pertinent pieces of data concerning Outwits Corporation, which actually started as a subsidiary company to a larger conglomeration set up with the same principal holders called the Greater East Dodge Co-Prosperity Sphere.

Both entities have caused something of a stir here on Wall Street, with two magnificent IPOs and the news of their successful product test. Their failure to follow up their early successes with the necessary filings regarding their land redevelopment, however, has left many investors skittish. That and the fact that most investors seem to have bought shares in each company, while they together produce only one product.

However, all recent news releases have promised formidable advances. Government and industrial magnates are all nervously awaiting these developments.

Thank you for your prompt attention to my enclosed invoice. Please remit to my New York office.

Sincerely,

Oscar S. Stimson

Bizarre. I turned it over, but there was nothing else there, so I quickly moved on to the other pieces of paper. One was a newspaper clipping, with the intriguing headline: "Corporation Product Test 'Successful'", but it didn't state any specifics and couldn't hold my attention. The other paper was a colorful brochure, obviously not done by our town's press.

Outwits Corporation
Makers of Military and Industrial Products

Before I could read further, Aunt Winnie ripped the brochure from my hands, stood up and addressed the loyal family.

"We have to act," she declared. "This isn't about the printing press anymore. It's bigger than that!"

"It's about our land," Dad said.

"It's bigger than that," Aunt Winnie said, and we all looked at her. Saving the land had been her crusade.

"What Norman brought us fits with everything we've gone through these past couple of months. He told us he met some investors who have actually spoken with Hilde and seen a sample of this . . . this . . . what are they calling it again?"

She flipped through the brochure and mumbled as she moved her finger along the lines. Then she stabbed it when she found what she was looking for.

"Here it is. Product 'V-1', whatever that stands for. Norman, tell us what they said."

Norman sat up from the other couch, slipping out from Aunt Patti's arm (though I saw him pat her knee affectionately; he was a nice guy). He cleared his throat and I bet he wondered what he was doing in the spotlight and whether he was part of the family or not. I knew we all looked on him as part already, especially as how he had uncovered information about AH.

"Well, they said they had seen before and after pictures of a pier, which supposedly demonstrated the effectiveness of the Outwits product."

"The marina!" we all breathed.

"The *Arizona*!" Uncle Frank wailed.

Norman nodded. "Yes, I'm afraid so. These people are all interested in explosives. Some for industrial use, mining, road construction and the like. Others for military use. Still others for somewhat obscure reasons, which I sensed may have been nefarious, since I received information that one of the main investors had once faced federal smuggling charges."

"But that still doesn't explain why there's such a keen interest in New York on what Hilde cooked up way out here."

"Well, from what I gathered, their product is cheap to manufacture, safe to transport, is easy to work with being . . . let's see, how did they describe it? Oh yes, 'not quite a liquid, not quite a solid, but like a gelatinous batter'. They promise even bigger things for their follow-up product 'V-2', which according to their literature is 'rocketing toward completion'."

"Anything else?"

"Not really. Oh wait. One fellow did mention that when he saw a sample of the V-1 he was almost tempted to eat it. Said it smelled like chocolate."

Chocolate? I thought. *Explosive?* That could mean only one thing.

"It's Aunt Hilde's fudge," I said. Oh, for crying out loud!

Not for the first time in my life, all the adults in the room turned their heads as one and stared at me as if I were the Lindbergh baby jumping out at the trial of Bruno Hauptmann yelling, "Surprise! I was hiding in the closet all along!"

That was that. I was a goner. The heat from the stares seared the bleeding that was my tongue. One day, I felt, I would learn to put a stopper between my brain and the outside world. What few successes I had had seemed pitifully insignificant compared to speaking out of turn at a place I was not supposed to be. I regretted this for breaking Aunt Winnie's trust in me, because not missing out on things truly meant a lot to me.

"Yes, that's what they said."

Who said that? My head had dropped to almost between my knees and rose like a submarine letting loose ballast. It was Norman saving me, great, grand, wonderful, hopefully future Uncle Norman. All the parental heads swished again, over to Norman. Their collective gasp was world-class.

"What?" Uncle Frank said in a slow, droning syllable.

Norman waved a finger at me (*a* finger, not *the* finger). He nodded his head emphatically as he explained.

"Fudge is what the investor said it reminded him of. It looked like fudge batter and smelled well, overpoweringly like chocolate. He said he thought it was a joke until the Outwits representative took a small amount and put it under a can of Sterno and it blew a hole in the conference table three feet wide."

I was stunned by the stunned silence in the room, the remarkable reaction to Norman's confirmation of my suspicion. The only thing that didn't ring true for me was that V-1 smelled "overpoweringly" like chocolate. Aunt Hilde's fudge only smelled mildly of chocolate. She must have hit upon a variation of her recipe, which we kids had always assumed to be somewhat deadly, and the new version just happened to smell right (for a treat). Maybe heating the ingredients initially, or reheating some frozen fudge over a flame for the first time, must have done some serious damage to her kitchen, and then I could only imagine the slow smile that must have crept up her twisted face as she tried to look pleased (which she couldn't accomplish, not ever having done so before), and how the idea burst in her mind on how she could exploit her creation and hit the big-time. Locked in the prison that was her kitchen (well, I had always thought of it that way), her struggle had produced a vision of a hellish future, in which she of course reveled.

The rest of the story fell into place as Norman, Aunt Winnie, Cousin Ike and Uncle Frank talked. AH and the Dessert Fox had formed a company called the Greater East Dodge Co-Prosperity Sphere, and a subsidiary, Outwits Corporation—because they had to rub our noses in it as they were doing it—and had launched it publicly, garnering six million dollars in capital, based only on the promise of their scheme. From that gain, AH had bought the radio station and the bank, and had foreclosed on all the surrounding farmland she could.

"This perplexed me to no end," Aunt Winnie said as she chomped on a cigar, first out one side of her mouth, then the other. "Why was she doing this? To what end? I could believe that it was just to make people suffer, but I sensed greater purpose to her aims. My suspicions were confirmed when I attacked the Liquidation Store.

"Before I was run off by that German Shepherd, I found a landscape model labeled 'Outwits: Final Solution', and on it, models of various buildings and roads.

"I knew she was up to something, and now we know what. She is building—or has built already—a factory to produce the V-1 for her investors, and maybe even a more deadly V-2. She needed laborers and quickly, so she rounded up as many as she could find, this year's crop be damned! And she bought the radio station to keep us all occupied and in the dark, to make plenty of trouble for us until she could finalize her scheme."

"And," Uncle Frank added, wiping a tear from his eye, "she blew up the marina as a test for her product."

I tugged on Aunt Winnie's dress and she sat down swiftly and leaned in for my comment (I had proved myself in combat to her). I said, "It wasn't just to show that the V-1 worked, but she had to get rid of our boats to keep us from going up to the land and checking it out for ourselves!" She nodded gravely and rubbed her chin with two stubby fingers.

The person most shocked by all that Aunt Winnie, Norman (and I) had said was Uncle Joe. He wept bitterly, and during the worst of his sobs even dropped his phony accent, though it came back anytime he spoke more than a fragment. He had joined the debacle having believed that Grandfather Treat's land would be converted to ice cream manufacture and chicken farming. Now he admitted to all of us how bad things were for him, giving us details and not just accusations and innuendo.

When he told us how he had sent his kids to North Dakota to visit their grandma, I understood why they weren't around, either at Uncle Frank and Aunt Ellen's or at the soggy baseball diamond. The why of it still escaped me until, through tears (could they actually be real ones, from Uncle Joe?) he said how he was living in a tent in the back Forty, on the outskirts of his land, and how AH had taken over much of his property, housing a horde of itinerant workers in his house, eating all his chickens and building a road from his place through a wood to their own place (Uncle Joe's driveway was a long, straight and narrow gravel strip, but it led directly to Hamilton Street—that's all on the other side of the Obeg, of course—which twelve miles down hit Route 55, from which one could get anywhere).

"Ah'm fightin', Ah say Ah'm fightin' back!" he bellowed. He regained his stoic façade with a good deal of effort then before continuing.

"Ah have hired me a fine, Ah say a fine set o' lawyers to repruh-sent mah interests. They've filed a brief to get mah deed back which that vam-press stole!"

That was Aunt Babs he was talking about, and the fact that she had made off with the deed to his property.

"But if y'all dohn' join the fray soon, Ah say soon, then Ah shall shorely perish! Them fine lawyers say Hilde's got lawyers and money o'plenty. They've falsified the deed to make it look, Ah say, to make it look like Ah've sold it to her! It could take me months just to get mah own home back, and Ah could be overrun in the meantime."

"Joseph is right."

Uncle Frank and Aunt Winnie both said this at the same time. I fought hard and successfully resisted the temptation to shout,

"Jinx!" as it would not have added anything meaningful to the conversation.

"We've hit the Liquidation Store time and again," Uncle Frank said, "but it's just not doing enough."

"Her operation is too big," Ike added.

"Agreed," chimed in Aunt Winnie. "Anyway, I believe her store has become nothing more to her than a recruitment station for the V-1 factory production. No, we'll have to bring the battle to her."

"Ah say, y'all can't get near her home, not with all them thar German Shepherds guardin' the place. They's mighty vicious!" Uncle Joe said and surreptitiously rubbed his rump.

"Indeed. No, we'll have to go see this factory that's built or being built on our own land."

"But how are we supposed to do that?" Dad said. "I'm not sure we can get there by land, not unless we cross Hilde's land, and as Joseph says, that won't be easy."

"We shall have to go by boat," Aunt Winnie said and the whole room (including me but excluding Uncle Frank) gasped and started exclaiming many things along the lines of, "That's impossible! All the boats have been destroyed!" until Uncle Frank raised a hand for silence, and the cries gradually died.

"I believe there is still one vessel down at the marina capable of carrying us across," he said and looked pointedly at Norman.

Aunt Patti sat up straight and slapped her boyfriend's arm. "You've got a boat! It's in Maurice's garage!"

"But it's not finished yet."

"But it floats," Uncle Frank said. "Ike and I went down and inspected it ourselves. It's big enough for six of us, although that may be a little bit of a squeeze, and plenty of oars survived the blast. It may not be a fancy trip, but we're going there to put a stop to this and take back our land!"

The room erupted in cheers, but it died quickly except for me—this was great stuff!—as I didn't realize until later that they all quickly understood what sort of an adventure had been proposed and agreed upon. It felt deadly and great all at once, a massive undertaking that could mean victory or defeat. Time was crucial. We had to get across before AH consolidated her gains and found the means to solidify them through legal machinations, bringing her weapons of vengeance into play to defeat us.

Quickly they picked six of themselves to man the oars: Aunt Patti, Dad, Uncle Frank, Aunt Ellen, Aunt Winnie and Norman (Uncle Joe said something about seasickness, then something about his arthritic hands being no good for rowing and finally something about rheumatism—that was the first I had heard that he suffered from those conditions, poor man—so he was left off the boat).

"Good, that's three oars to a side," Uncle Frank said. "That should be enough to get us there."

"Frank," Aunt Winnie said and cleared her throat.

"Yes? What is it?"

"We will still need someone to steer the boat."

"We'll just have to manage as best we can with the oars, Winnie. There's no room for a seventh."

"There is if he's small," Aunt Winnie said and she dropped her hand solidly on my shoulder.

*   *   *

My mother protested my inclusion vehemently, of course. I felt a strange ambivalence to that. On one hand, as a young boy, I felt ready for most challenges and resented my mother's thumb (and its concomitant long arm). On the other, in a rare glimpse of maturity that would plague me off and on over the years, I saw her protecting her own, arguing that it was still my time to be a child and not to be encumbered by all the worries and cares of adulthood. I liked that about her, but I still wanted to go.

In the end, Aunt Winnie won out with her persuasiveness. She actually touted me as a champion of the family, which made Dad's remaining hair stand up straight in surprise. By extracting a promise from me that I would stay in the boat when it reached Grandfather Treat's land (a lousy oath I didn't want to keep, but I had to swear on the Bible—my own family making me swear on the Bible!), I was reluctantly allowed to accompany the adventurers. Dad even caught my eye and gave me a wink and a nod, having gotten over his surprise. Even years after his death, each time I remembered his silent lauding, I felt a surge of pride and a gush of tears.

We planned to go early in the morning. The 5th was that next Tuesday, and Uncle Frank said he was ready to go, but the weather turned inclement (again), so we postponed until the 6th. I actually thought this was good, as it was AH's birthday. This would be a great present for her. To celebrate, she and the Dessert Fox usually hunted grouse on the far side of their property (even though that seemed like cannibalism to me, based on how much they liked to complain). If we were lucky, they would be well away from us when we "hit the beach"; that was the plan, anyway, as Cousin Isaac drew it up.

"Alright, listen up!" Ike shouted as he approached the table. A hole was made for him—even Uncle Frank gave way—and he threw down a large roll of paper that he spread out, two of my aunts grabbing hold of the sides to help it lay down flat. It was a map. Fleetingly, I had hoped it was something official from the county surveyor's office, like official blueprints with minute details and sterile descriptions about elevation and geology, but it was immediately evident that this was a hand-drawn affair. Was it in crayon?

"This is the objective. I want you to study it, commit it to memory; you'll need it to survive."

"Isaac," Aunt Winnie said, "we've all been there."

"In the heat of battle, it's only your training, your equipment and your fellow trooper you can count on!" Ike said, glowering in his cousin's direction. I could imagine a cousin of mine and me exchanging such a look. I smiled like an idiot through most of the rest of this intense meeting.

"Skip the pep talk, Ike," Uncle Frank interjected. "What's the plan?"

Ike leaned over the map and put a finger on the Obeg River. "You'll approach from the south by boat." The finger shook, belying the resoluteness of his voice. He had been practicing the talk, at least, but seeing that nervous finger made my smile droop for a bit, until more of Aunt Winnie's scathing commentary intruded.

"Of course we approach from the south, Isaac, the land is in the north of the county!"

"Winifred," Uncle Frank said under his breath.

"All right, all right. Just get on with it."

"Remember, you're going upstream, so you'll have to paddle in unison. Just make sure you save some energy for the real fight. When you round this bend in the river, the beach will be in view. If you're lucky, you'll arrive from a direction they're not expecting."

"But they could only be expecting us from the south!"

"Winifred," Uncle Frank said again, this time not quite so quietly, but a bit menacingly.

"Oh, all right!" she snapped at her brother before turning to their cousin. "It's a good plan, Ike, just skip to what we need to know."

Ike moved his hand along the purple stretch with the word "Beach" written across it. Remembering Treat's land, I knew it wasn't really a beach, *per se*, the kind with lots of sand, but I wasn't about to argue the point.

"When you approach the beach, you need to get the boat as close to the shore as possible. You're vulnerable out there in the water. Expect rocks and other obstacles, but don't jump out too soon. Wait until your boat scrapes the shore; that's a far different sound than hitting a rock too far out. You jump out when you hit one of those and you could be floating back to Dodge."

Ike moved his finger from "Beach" a couple of inches inland to "Wall". My smile drooped again at that word. What the heck had my double-aunt built there?

"Now, we don't know what this really looks like at this time, but we know they've been building a lot in this area. We expect they've constructed a defensive wall where the bushes start. Or it could still just be bushes. Regardless, it would be a good place for guards to spy you out . . . or even worse."

"Good Lord, Isaac, you don't think they'll be shooting at us, do you?"

Ike's grim visage wavered. "Oh, shooting? Oh, yeah, I guess that would be even worse."

"Even worse than what?"

"Well, we've had those reports of dogs, likely German Shepherds. Maybe Alsatians."

"I don't like Alsatians," Uncle Frank said coarsely, clearing his throat.

"Yes, but what if there's shooting?"

Ike ignored my aunt and kept going with renewed vigor. "So, hit the beach hard, get over this wall—or bush—and head inland. Don't group yourselves together, but stay with your assigned partner. Reconnoiter the area around each flank, then move in and destroy that factory. Destroy it, and they're finished. You'll be home by Christmas."

"It's still summer, Isaac."

"It's just a metaphor, Winifred," Uncle Frank said as he grabbed the map and rolled it up. He handed it to Ike. "Burn this later," he said seriously, and Ike nodded just as gravely as he took it. "Let's go," Uncle Frank said to the rest of us, and that short statement chilled my bones.

At least my mother hadn't been there for the briefing. We all looked a little green around the gills, but with a last hearty (and perhaps forced) nod of approval from Uncle Frank, we all silently pledged ourselves to the cause. Then, jittery but strangely silent, the six adults who would be in the boat marched two by two to Maurice Peters' garage, with me in tow behind. Ike tarried last.

Ahead of me, Uncle Frank used his cane, of course, and I doubted that the limp was affected this time. Still, with the sternness of his face and the squaring of his shoulders, the hard, protracted gait of his march only added to his apparent toughness. He could be a flibbertigibbet at times—and I never counted his blubbering over the loss of his boat against him—but he had led in business and politics and naturally took the lead in war, too. He carried a length of rope with him, looped and slung across his shoulders, and sported his wide-brimmed white Panama hat. He wore his usual white suit, too, though it was dingy and even I thought it smelled a bit (the result of a lack of detergent and soap deliveries to the Five and Dime), even though everyone else save Aunt Winnie wore overalls, nylon or denim.

Aunt Winnie, giving up nothing but a modicum of respect for Uncle Frank's preeminence as the acknowledged patriarch of the family, wore an unusual (for her, it just wasn't her color . . . not that I knew anything about people's colors) yellow dress, perhaps symbolic for her of the outcome we all longed for. As a bow to the inevitable workload ahead of us, she marched in a pair of combat boots (Lord knows how or where she obtained them). She carried no other visible accoutrements, but she chomped down on one of her cigars, and as we marched I could see its tip jutting out to her right, swaying up and down with every other step, keeping a bizarre time. Somewhere in the golden glow of her outfit (like the sun, too bright to be looked at directly), I knew had to be hidden a stash of more cigars and matches; she always came prepared.

Aunt Ellen and Dad followed, and Aunt Patti and Norman came last, save for me. Dad and Norman each toted two oars, while Aunt Patti and Aunt Ellen each held their own. Aunt Ellen had packed sandwiches, which she had deposited in her ornate wicker picnic basket that she used practically every Sunday; I think it had been a wedding gift from Grandmother Versey, but I wasn't sure.

I carried this, of course, and it was a beast. It didn't matter that the family had been rationing for weeks due to the delivery problems. Aunt Winnie's ruined garden had only despoiled her own crop, and we always had enough fruits and vegetables to spare for her. No matter what, we always found plenty to eat. No mousse, no desserts of any kind, and not even half the people of a normal picnic, but Aunt Ellen only knew one way to prepare a picnic basket: overloaded.

Lunging back and forth under the weight, as if on waves or in a turbulent wind, I struggled to keep my head up. I had been too excited to eat breakfast and, as I carried the great pack, my legs felt like jelly and my head a woozy mess. I pondered dropping out, if only to be sick. *Let me reach that beach,* I prayed silently to God and forced my feet to keep moving.

I don't know why I had to carry the basket, though, as the rest of the family gathered from their various residences and followed us a couple of steps behind, including all my cousins on this side of the river. They could have made Davey or Laura haul it between them, but I guess Mom, left in charge of them and maybe still stinging from her inability to keep me out of the fray, didn't think to make them work (that very concept staggered me, however).

As we marched through town, headed inexorably toward the remains of the marina, what few people were out and about at that early hour stood and stared silently, reverential and respectful as we passed. They too were caught up in the great excursion, if not about to join it, for they had been hurt by AH, too, their lives disrupted or worse, their homes taken and livelihood denied. Every one of them had the look of people who had had to do much soul searching: Live under tyranny or fight for freedom?

Against AH, my choice stayed clear and easy (the follow-through not quite so easy), and I hoped that my choices would always stay so focused.

When we were within sight of Maurice Peters' garage, just down from the charred ruins of the marina, he saw us from the window in his room above the garage and came rushing down to meet us. He was a sight in his Coke-bottle glasses, the ones the doctor said he didn't need. They must have been to help his farsightedness, for when he got close to us he halted abruptly, took them off and stuffed them in his pocket.

Uncle Frank stopped us suddenly, grabbing an oar from Dad and planting it like a flag as he held out his other arm dramatically. We piled up behind him like cars in a freeway collision, three separate cousins slamming into me with loud complaints. We all quieted quickly, though, and Uncle Frank didn't make us wait for it.

"People of Dodge, I have returned!" he announced to his hushed audience of one in front of him, and I knew this promise meant something to him, coming back to where he had ignominiously retreated from losing his precious pearl, the *Arizona*.

"Are you going to start rebuilding the pier?" Maurice asked.

"That's a stupid question," Aunt Winnie said pointedly, dispelling a myth as she shoved ahead of Uncle Frank.

"No, Maurice," Uncle Frank said, lowering his arm and oar. "We're here for the boat."

"Boat? What boat? What's left of the *Arizona Kid* is at the bottom of the Obeg."

"No, Maurice," Norman said, stepping out from the back of the line and heading for the garage. "We're here for mine."

As one, we pushed on past poor, befuddled Maurice, opened up his garage and hauled out the sleek, half-finished boat, hefted up between the six adults. I couldn't help with this, unfortunately, as my hands were already full.

It took about half an hour to get the boat in the water and all the oars and the rudder situated correctly. Norman tied it loosely to a lone post with Uncle Frank's rope. Looking down at it, the boat didn't appear the instrument of freedom that my uncle had said it would be. Seats where we would all sit were temporarily hammered in by Norman and Ike. Dad directed me to set the basket down on the walkway. "We'll put that aboard when we're about to go," he said.

"Gather round, everyone," Uncle Frank called, holding his arms open in a big C. He shooed away Maurice and a couple of other non-family members, then had us all fold our hands and bow our heads.

"This seems an appropriate time to pray," he said. "Dear Lord, we ask You to oversee our endeavor. Look with kindness and mercy upon we six—"

"Seven," Aunt Winnie mumbled.

"Ahem. We seven who set forth on this mission. Be in the proud of our boat—"

"Prow."

"Ahem. Be in the prow of our boat, gird up our loins and equip us for battle—"

"Where is—?" one of my cousins, I think Laura, started to say, but was instantly hushed up by Mom.

"Ahem. Equip us for battle and lead us safely back home again. We humbly beseech You—"

"Golly durn, Frank!" Aunt Patti cried (once again, she only said something like that). "The Lord knows whose apples we're going to go kick. Just get on with it!"

"Ahem! We humbly beseech. . . . Oh, very well. Guard all that You are over, Lord. Amen."

"Amen," we all said and we broke like football players leaving the huddle, heading directly for their places. Cousin Ike came up to each of us, teary-eyed, sniffling mightily. Handing each of us a typewritten and carbon-copied half-sheet of paper that we were to read in the boat, he said, "And now, after all this planning, you set off and I, I am suddenly powerless." All the adults stuffed their copies of his note quickly into a pocket, except Aunt Winnie who had none, so she stuck it in one boot as she scowled. The aunts started climbing aboard, then Dad hefted the picnic basket into the boat.

"Gracious, Ellen! What did you pack in here?" he cried, but Aunt Ellen apparently didn't feel that this deserved an answer. I thought Dad lucky to escape The Look from any of the women around. He then turned for a kiss from Mom, but she turned her back and found Cousin Ike two inches from her.

"Tell me again why you aren't going?" she asked him as she created some additional distance.

"Oh, my old war wound on my left arm is acting up. It doesn't allow me to hold a paddle," he answered, his face drooping to severe depths as he quickly put away a handkerchief and grabbed his right arm with his left hand.

"I didn't know you had fought. Which war was this?"

"Well, that big one everybody was in." He rubbed his right arm fiercely.

"I see. I thought you said it was your left arm that was hurting you?"

"Uh, grabbing my right arm and moving it about helps relieve the symptoms."

Mom scowled at him but said nothing more, fiery eyes under short brown curls. She gathered up all my cousins with the loving demeanor of a prison guard as I took my place in the back of the boat. I hefted the rudder and patted it gently, as if it were an old friend, as if I knew what the heck I was doing. This was, of course, to show confidence to my younger cousins so that they wouldn't be afraid at all.

"Aunt Bess, where is—?"

"Oh, let's just get on home!" Mom said, oozing exasperation. *En masse*, she and the kids turned from the remains of the pier as Norman and Patti pushed us off, then clambered aboard. As we floated out toward the middle of the river, I looked at the paper from Cousin Ike.

Soldiers and sailors! it declared, while an ethereal silence of some transcending kind gripped me.

You are about to embark on the Great Crusade. Your task will not be an easy one. I have full confidence in your courage and devotion to duty and skill in battle.

Good luck! And let us beseech the blessing of Almighty God upon this great and noble undertaking.

Shaken and awed, I mourned as the wind whipped the paper out of my hands. I think I was the only one who had read his. Six oars started dabbing the water, a tentative movement before full organization. Grabbing hold of the rudder, which felt heavy and unsettled, I looked back over my shoulder as our line was cast off. My mother and cousins were trailing away, while above them in the darkening skies I caught a glint from the cross of our church, still solidly above our town. Somberly, I turned back, concentrating.

The wind picked up considerably once we were out on the water. Even though the Obeg wasn't the Mississippi or the Missouri, it was still about the length of a football field wide, or maybe a little more, in places. During the spring melt, we of course stayed away from the river due to the temperature and also the extremely strong currents. Over the summer, however, as it warmed it also slowed. Most days, that is. As we wanted to get about five miles upstream without a motor, even a small current would be aggravating, and today it flowed darkly and dangerously.

"Keep rowing! All together! Keep rowing, I said!" Aunt Ellen shouted (I wouldn't have guessed her, either, except it turned out she had been captain of the first women's rowing team at State College). Immediately in peril once out in the center of the river, the six strove against the current while I floundered with my responsibility.

"Stop hitting me with your elbows, Norman!"

"I'm sorry, Patti, but I'm not that good from the left."

"Stroke! Stroke! Stroke!" Aunt Ellen boomed.

"I think I'm having one!" Aunt Winnie cried and looked about her. No one, not even me as I wrestled with the rudder, allowed her the slightest sympathy, so she pulled out another cigar from (I wish I hadn't seen it) under her bosom, chomped on it, unlit as the matches fell behind her, onto the picnic basket. Looking down, the matches had already disappeared, swept over the side, perhaps, and Aunt Winnie had returned to a furious paddling, keeping time with no one, especially not Aunt Ellen.

"Stroke! Stroke! Stroke!"

"Good night, woman!" Uncle Frank yelled out. "You're driving us too fast! We can't keep up."

"But we'll lose ground to the current if we don't!"

"But we can't work together at the pace you're setting."

That was truth, so Aunt Ellen, the dreams of her youthful college experiences fading quickly from her eyes, started over. The pace slowed, but she challenged everyone to row better than the freshman co-eds whom she had guided (but to last place at every tournament, I later found out, to Aunt Ellen's chagrin). All of them wanted to best Aunt Ellen's memories, so with renewed dedication, they worked as one. Thoughts of the impending battle dampened spirits as arms and backs strained with the task at hand.

Progress, I felt, was being achieved. It even seemed to make steering easier.

Being in the back held certain advantages, like the ability to see everyone and know instantly who wasn't keeping time. However, Aunt Patti and Norman, being next to last, were the most enthusiastic of paddlers. Though they kept time, they doused me considerably so that soon I was drenched. The wind picked up and cut into my skin. I wanted to cry and scream and most of all to let go of that rudder (I felt a splinter; it was right up under the middle of my palm, the soft spot that's always so sensitive). Just when it seemed the lowest point of our journey, I saw that familiar bend in the Obeg, a jut of land maybe fifty feet long, rocky and wooded. Beyond that was the beach (such as it was) where we could land. Norman once said about the place, "That's not a beach. A beach has sand! This is too rocky. If the bluffs were higher, it would remind me of Utah, maybe the river valley by Omaha." Norman had traveled a lot.

"There it is!" I cried out and immediately wished I hadn't. All six oars stopped and six heads looked up. The current caught our craft and instantly we started slipping away.

"Stroke! Stroke! Stroke!" yelled Aunt Ellen, so on the six rowed once more.

As we reached and then rounded the promontory, I expected the scene I had always seen, the unspoiled land of pines and red oaks and bush and wildflowers, with giant boulders among the fallen remains of formerly glorious trees, lending an ethereal beauty and delicacy to the place, a sacred plot of land, good for camping or communing. That's what had been there. The sight of it now shocked me. Beyond the bordering row of trees, where there should have been tall grasses and small copses great for playing all sorts of games (except baseball; too rocky), there was row upon row of one-story shacks and a larger building—the factory, back a ways, sporting a dozen small chimneys, all puffing small gray clouds into the steel sky. To the side and beyond were skeletons of more buildings and various construction vehicles and equipment. She had cleared a lot of land, all right, and constructed more in months than anyone had seen built in town in years. How much had been done! How much more was planned?

With a last, draining effort, we glided our craft within a few feet of shore. The boat scraped the bottom—a chilling sound—and Aunt Patti jumped out, splashing me one last time (though she was fine in her hip waders), and pulled the boat in enough so that everyone could get out. Dad and Norman got the boat more securely on the beach (there was too *some* sand, Norman!), and Uncle Frank used his rope to tie the boat to one of the larger rocks. It took a moment more for Aunt Ellen to help Aunt Winnie out; they seemed to share a quiet moment between them, Aunt Winnie likely revising her opinion upward of her eldest sister-in-law.

"Where do you think you're going?" Dad asked me.

"I'm just going to sit up front," I said. Just because I had stood up and had one foot over the side of the boat didn't mean I wasn't moving only to the prow.

"See that you stay there," Dad said as he turned to head inland. "And keep your head down!" he added, though I wasn't sure why. Would there really be shooting?

From my vantage point (a lousy one, of course, even with my head up), there didn't seem to be many people about. Apparently, we had caught AH off guard. The "wall" ahead that Ike had warned us about was planks with holes for lookouts (or maybe just rotted out spots in old wood), but if anyone had been behind them, they had fled. My six family members spread out in three groups of two and each headed directly for some of the closest buildings where I lost sight of them.

I caught fleeting glimpses of action from then on. There must have been some people in the shacks because somebody screamed, and there were figures running away, toward the main building, the V-1 factory. Calls and whistles echoed from various places; signals from my family to each other, I thought (or hoped). My heart beat thunderously, the pulse a crescendo in my ears. Above it, I heard more people yelling, then engines erupting and someone banging on metal quickly, like a drum, sounding like machine gun bursts.

All of a sudden, the boat swayed and a sharp bang behind me startled me. In an instant, before even whipping my head around, my mind had conjured a thousand horrible tortures for what had sneaked up behind me. Most of these were horned apparitions that looked remarkably like my double-aunt godmother. I was almost the youngest person in the county to ever suffer massive myocardial infarction. Climbing out from the picnic basket which had tipped over was my cousin Gracie.

"Are you going to help me up, or what?" she said as she struggled in the bottom of the boat, her legs still clearly pinned inside the wicker basket.

"What are you doing here!" I yelped, holding a hand to my heart. When she reached out one open hand to me, the other clenched in a tight fist, I nonetheless grabbed hold and yanked her out of the picnic basket. Her foot had kicked a hole in the side of it. Under a different set of circumstances, I would have mercilessly teased her about the trouble she would be in for ruining the basket, hoping to get some good tears out of her, but I couldn't think of anything mean to say.

"What are you doing here?" I asked again, still yelling, still unable to think clearly, but needing to fill the void.

Gracie climbed to the front of the boat then, pushing past me, her normally sedate pigtails frazzled, coming undone and blowing in the wind. She swung her legs over and hopped down, clambering quickly on all fours up the rocks.

"It's no fair you get to do everything! I wanted to see, too!" she called back and then disappeared.

One foot went up onto the rail, but it stuck there. I had promised. On the Bible. I wasn't to leave the boat. I couldn't. I'd be flayed alive if they found out.

But wouldn't they flay me alive if they found out I let my younger cousin go off alone into the fray? I mean, even if they had already gotten done spanking her into oblivion for stowing aboard Norman's boat?

I stood up and tried to catch sight of Gracie. In the distance, a large yellow truck—it must have been a bulldozer—went crashing into one part of the factory. Timber and dust flew everywhere in the tremendous crash. When the bulldozer backed out, I saw the driver stand and raise a fist, then let out a whoop of delight that carried all the way back to the riverbank. I knew it was Aunt Patti.

She sank back down and the treads of the beast kicked up dirt, sending everyone who approached her flying. I followed the glint of metal as she took it on a flanking maneuver around the far side of the factory. Every few moments I'd lose it as it went in a depression. Rising again, I'd see it knock down a wall or partially built structure, grinding furiously, belching smoke and coughing up destruction.

I felt a thrill at the sight. She was doing it! Aunt Patti was destroying AH's compound! Truly she was the greatest Woman of Action in the history of the whole county. Soon, however, more commotion arose. A new crowd appeared from the woods. From what I could tell, it looked like they had a chance at outflanking her and sweeping her off the whole beach. The ominous sound of trained dogs carried over the field and my heart sank. She would never be able to destroy the buildings, not all of them, not enough of them, before she would be stopped.

I stood stock still in the prow of the boat wondering what was to become of us. It was an eternal moment. Why did the mean people prosper as we suffered through tragedy after tragedy? How much could be endured? If we lost that day, would we ever have the courage to confront AH again? The town would be hers, the whole county. The destruction of the marina, the takeover of the radio station and the bank, the foreclosure of so many farms, all the dreadful lies she had spread, all of it would go unpunished. She would reap the rewards of industrial manufacture while we toiled away in the heat of her kitchens. Where was the good news in any of this?

My mind lingered and thought of my world going up in smoke. Blinking away my tears I realized that my world literally was going up in smoke. First one strand, then another, flew in dark flumes up to the heavens. The fire spread from the outer buildings to the factory. They were quickly all ablaze.

People screamed and I caught glimpses of figures heading into the woods, of dogs whimpering and scattering, their tails between their legs. Lost in all this was the sight of the bulldozer, my dad and the others. I felt frightened and hated being the only one in the boat. A lone figure crested the outcropping of rocks directly in front of me. She jumped down and ran to the boat.

Gracie looked white as a ghost. With wide, scared eyes she looked up at me and held my gaze, like a peaceful picture of a beautiful angel caught against a dark background, her tousled hair a modernist halo. Then she whipped Aunt Winnie's packet of matches as far as she could into the Obeg, pulled herself into the boat and dove as best she could back into the picnic basket.

"God bless you, Pyro," I breathed with awe.

CHAPTER 7: BATTLE OF THE BULGE

When my dad, Norman, one uncle and two of my three aunts reached the boat, I still stood in the prow. I held up my hands skyward, mimicking the plume of smoke from the buildings, and I guess also of surrender.

I said to them, "I did it! I set fire to the factory!"

They stood ringed around the front of the boat, silent and stupefied. They all breathed heavily and were covered with dirt and sweat. Dad and Norman each had holes in the knees of their overalls. Finally, Aunt Winnie threw up her hands and shook her head as she stepped toward the boat.

"Oh for crying out loud, Jonathan. We can all see Gracie's legs sticking out from the picnic basket."

It was true; there was no hope in hiding her. It had, I knew, been a desperate gambit to save my poor, young cousin. Being only six, I didn't think she merited the repercussions that were sure to follow for charring Grandfather Treat's land to a crisp. I felt no matter what Dad would do to me, Aunt Winnie and maybe even Uncle Frank would intervene on my behalf because of the feud, leaving me short of paying the ultimate penalty (which would include giving up my baseball mitt . . . oh, and likely some kind of paddling on my rear, too). My heart cringed in fear, imagining them all taking a turn beating poor Gracie. Tears welled up (though later I would claim it was just smoke in my eyes) and I grabbed Aunt Winnie as she tried to climb aboard and shook her.

"No! It really was me! Okay, I admit, Gracie got hold of the matches like she always does, but I'm the one who did it. I took them from her and made her stay here and I got out of the boat even though I swore not to! I did it!"

Aunt Winnie stopped trying to get into the boat. She grabbed my hand (what a grip on the old gal!) and forcibly removed it from her person. Grimacing, she motioned me to stand aside.

As she came on board she said, "You've done a good job for us, Johnny. There's no need for you to claim credit for what your young cousin has done. We don't think any less of you."

Credit? Less of me? What was this?

"And I kept a pretty good watch on you," Aunt Ellen noted as she too got on board. "I promised your mother I would, so I made sure to get a view of the boat every couple of minutes. Though I didn't see the little whippersnapper get loose. By the way, dear, what happened to all my sandwiches?"

"I put 'em in the river when you were praying so I could fit in here. Help me out?"

"That was naughty," Aunt Ellen said as she helped Gracie out of the basket.

That was naughty? What kind of lame punishment was that for starting an inferno? I thought I was about to take the beating of my life for that?

As the rest clambered aboard, I stumbled back to the rudder. When I sat down, mouth agape at what had transpired, I remembered that one of our number was missing. Then it hit me that the smoke seemed to be clearing and that the ring of trees surrounding the compound all still stood.

"What?" I started, but immediately decided to try a different tact. "Where?" which also seemed inappropriate, but I guess was understood.

"Your aunt Patti is all right," Norman answered me. "The fire got the factory and, unfortunately, most of the other buildings as well."

"Unfortunately?"

"Yes," Dad said, backing up Norman. "Apart from the factory, those were homes, more or less. Well, temporary shelters anyway. I think everyone got out in time. It's all new wood and didn't burn fast, but everything's pretty well destroyed. Most everyone was working down the road, clearing more land or something, and everybody in the factory got out as soon as Patti drove through it with the bulldozer. So, no loss of life, but what little these people had is gone."

"True," Aunt Winnie said with a hard expression, "but the main point is the factory is destroyed. Their production is set back months! That buys us time to press home our advantage, which I feel is time Hilde and Benny cannot afford at all. Patti put a hole in the wall, but their guards and dogs were coming and would have driven us away without doing lasting damage. Instead, Gracie's fire drove *them* away!"

"Yes, we stopped a couple of the fellows—not from around here, so they were cowardly," Uncle Frank said. "They just wanted to 'get out of Dodge', so to speak, so we let them go, but not before they told us that today was the first day the factory was operational."

"Good thing, too, or the fire would have ignited ready V-1 and blown us all to kingdom come!"

"So where is Aunt Patti?"

"I said she's coming," Aunt Winnie told me in that accusatory tone of hers that so wasn't one of her endearing qualities. And she hadn't told me that at all.

"She's putting out the fire," Norman said. He explained that they had built a road around the compound, and that had kept the fire isolated from the trees, since the wind had died almost as soon as we had landed the boat (another of life's ironies). Aunt Patti was finishing up plowing dirt over the remaining cinders.

The heavy smoke had cleared, but the wisps from each pile of ashes or remainder of a home or the parts of the factory skeleton would most likely smolder for days. They were right, though, that the fire hadn't spread to the wooded areas. My double-aunt godmother had quickly developed a lot of this land surreptitiously (what could she do with a free hand over time?), but there was still wilderness left. I felt a welt of sadness in my heart thinking of the difference in visions that Grandfather had versus what AH had put into practice. My cheeks were splattered with wetness and I thought I must have started crying, but then I saw Aunt Patti running toward the boat.

"The rain should take care of the rest of it," she said as she climbed aboard. Dad and Norman pushed us off with their oars. She was right; it started raining hard then. Soaking wet and with no sandwiches to eat, we made our way back to town. The adults talked animatedly about their exploits—none more so than Aunt Patti who was neither shy nor humble. They sheltered Gracie and promised her a piece of the rationed candy from the Five and Dime. I steered us home and blew rain off my face every few seconds.

*   *   *

My frustration lasted most of the next few weeks. Not only was Gracie the toast of the family (not to mention the shrubs, since she was setting small fires almost hourly), but my folks had drafted me to go out and work on their and others' gardens. That's right, they had sub-contracted me out for ten cents an hour (I got to keep half; not the best deal, but I've had worse). The days were filled with fighting the weeds, plodding through hedges to get to different fields of my relatives or neighbors, all to go through the exact same thing again. Johnny the slug, the grunt, the good foot soldier, marching off to battle, obeying orders that couldn't possibly make sense or align in any way, shape or form with my grandiose strategic thoughts. What did one stinking field have to do with crushing AH? How pointless could it be expending my life in the fields when I would much rather be at home?

At night, after long hours of marching and fighting and marching again, we listened to the radio both during and after dinner. It was nice to have it back, even though it was Aunt Babs and not Stewart Swisland. Mom still wasn't happy about it, but had agreed with Dad that they needed to keep tabs on what was going on, and the best way to do that was still the radio (even if it also contained a lot of lies). There was some talk between my folks that Aunt Hilde would have to sell the radio station, what with her V-1 plant destroyed and all, but if she were contemplating it, it didn't show up on the radio waves.

Aunt Babs played more music than she had the first few days of her tour of duty. Even though she interrupted the string of songs often enough to blare some truly nasty and dyspeptic rhetoric, about "certain villains" who had "taken away the economic advantages" our town could have had with the factory, and that the "Greater East Dodge Co-Prosperity Sphere" was still intact, I was still glad to have something to fill the air.

The feud had gone on longer than we could have ever imagined, and been much more costly to us than we could have known. If we had known, would we have made the same choices? I hoped we would have, though the temptation to stay out of a fray loomed large.

I wasn't the only one whose life had been interrupted, of course. Things were so bad and so busy that I caught my father often patting his oatmeal dishearteningly at the breakfast table.

He'd sigh and mumble something about most likely missing the turkeys this year. It was one of his true hobbies, and his passion for it neared mine for baseball.

One of his cousins, a widowed farmer named MaryAnn, raised turkeys to Uncle Joe's chickens. Her husband had owned the biggest tract of land in the county and had cultivated only a small portion of it, spending all his time and money on erecting a fence to surround his entire property. It took him nearly twenty years, but he did it, a feat to rival the Chinese emperors of old, most folks reckoned. We never found out why he did it, or what he planned to do after the fence was finished, for a week after he finished it he fell dead of a heart attack. My dad's poor cousin was left with land, land, more land, plus more fencing than one could fathom, and a debt that looked like it belonged on government books. So she decided to raise turkeys.

She didn't know much about it, so after she got a few pairs she just let them run all over the property, breeding free and easy. Maybe they could have flown over the fences, but they seemed to like it there. If any fled, no one could really tell because she soon had hundreds—probably thousands—of turkeys running around. At first, she tried herding them into trucks to sell to the butchers, but it proved too difficult and time-consuming for her ("It's like herding turkeys" became a popular simile in town). Instead, she struck upon the idea of selling tickets onto her property, and renting out firearms.

Every summer, people would come from all around to go out and hunt down her turkeys. It didn't attract the serious hunter, but everyone who wanted either fresh turkey or a chance to fire a rifle, or just to join in a good time, came in droves. She built a billboard on the approach to her house, advertising the campaign as "MaryAnn's Great Turkey Shoot". She made enough each year to keep the place going, mend the fences, plus put something away for her son. The tradition lasted until I was well into my twenties when an accident—that really, we all should have seen coming—took the lives of two novice hunters, who had both been aiming at the same turkey from opposite sides. Apparently, the turkey survived. The feud year would be the only year Dad missed until then.

As the summer wore on, my annoyance with my cousin Gracie and how the older generation had handled her actions dissipated. It dovetailed nicely with new shipments of sugar, candy, soap, fresh oranges and other items to the Five and Dime. Dad said he had sorted out the difficulties with the shipping companies a while back. "We met them midway, sank their hopes of overwhelming us and set ourselves on course for victory," which made no sense to me, but he seemed happy about it. Trucks started to get through regularly after that, and though sales still remained poor, Uncle Frank was generous to us. I loved the jaw breakers (boy, were they aptly named, much to my dentist's chagrin).

"I'm feeling good, Johnny!" he confided to me as he doled out the sweets. "Your double-aunt tried to hoodwink the town again, just like she did with the printing press, but I nipped it in the butt! Oh, pardon my language. Anyway, she submitted a written request to have the downtown area re-zoned for development to the council. I sent it on to the Downtown Land Redevelopment Sub-Committee!"

"Who's on dat, Unca Fwank?" I asked with a huge bulge in my cheek, slurping on goo.

"Just me!" he barked and guffawed. "Now run along, Johnny. I like you, but you're bad for business just now."

The sub-committee report was about all I heard on the feud during those weeks. Some nights we had Aunt Winnie over to eat. When it was just us, we would listen to the radio without much comment. Once in a while Dad would get annoyed and say something, but Mom took his comments about Aunt Babs too seriously, transferring the family's anger at Aunt Hilde and her cohorts onto herself, just because of her heritage. Aunt Patti had said no one in the family blamed her, or (by extension) me, but I began to see or at least imagine my cousins and others around town casting baleful looks at me, knowing I was the one doubly related to the prime troublemaker. I'd hear snippets of conversation about how my eyes were set too close together, so that it was obvious to all that I would be a troublemaker, too. I should be penned up, locked up, guarded night and day. Though I had proven myself loyal time and time again, it was not enough to shake the fear that "Willie's blood" (as I thought I heard it called by somebody as I worked in their garden under a hot sun) would always rise and rear its ugly head. Mom must have felt a lot of this, too. Maybe people just couldn't help themselves from being mean.

I understood my mother's agitation and quick temper in ways that Dad just couldn't (at least, not without trying a lot harder). I knew she felt the glares even more acutely. It made me angry, naturally, but also more resolute to stand firm against AH. It also allowed me to feel tenderly toward Mom in ways that growing boys sometimes forget about.

Anyway, Aunt Winnie never listened to the radio without having a conversation with it.

"Rest assured that our glorious station owner will never rest or tire of the fight. She will raise up new places of work, rest and play for the town and the surrounding countryside."

"Excrement!" Aunt Winnie thundered, slapping the table with one solid hand. The dishes rattled but we tried to get back to our meatloaf with little aplomb.

"Even though ignorant brutes try to derail your happiness, you can feel safe knowing that someone will fight for you."

"Balderdash! Come down here and say that!"

"The enemies of our fathers' land will never stand. They are ready to tumble. Valiant listeners, heed the advice of our great station owner: Boycott the Five and Dime Store and vow to stay away from Patti's Autos."

"Charlatan! Where do you come off saying these things?"

"And coming up, after our next selection of soothing music, an important announcement of historic significance. The announcement that will change your lives forever, and will forever rid our father's land—our fathers' land, that is—of the totalitarian refuse that has dominated innocent folk for too many years. And now, here's some Bing Crosby."

"Vile seductress!" Aunt Winnie screamed. "'Tis a tale told by an idiot, full of sound and fury; signifying nothing!'"

Mom sighed heavily as she stared at her plate and picked over her meatloaf. Dad felt shut out by Mom's sullenness, I knew this instinctively, and he too stared dejectedly at his plate. Aunt Winnie glowered over the whole scene as Bing crooned across the room. I sat with my hands in my lap, with a half-slab of meatloaf left on my plate, and my milk glass barely touched.

"It's okay, Aunt Winnie," I said. "No one believes Aunt Babs, anyway."

Aunt Winnie grimaced and went back to eating. "Your attempts at mollifying me are misguided, Johnny. I don't believe her; none of us here do. But the masses, Johnny, oh the masses. I fear for them, I do. Some of them do believe her, probably many.

"It is human nature to wallow in ignorance, to take the path of least resistance. Scripture indeed says wisely that broad is the path of sin, and many are on it, while narrow is the way of righteousness."

I scratched my head. "I don't think we've gotten to that one yet."

"What? Are you sure? Harry, you better have a word with that Sunday School teacher, Mrs. McCormick."

"Yes, all right."

"Listen here," Aunt Winnie continued. "I tell a dozen people most days that Hilde is a liar and a thief, but she—through her mouthpiece—tells *hundreds* of people *every* day the exact opposite. It's easy to turn on the radio and have fed to you what you should think and feel and believe. It takes energy and diligence to winnow the chaff from the wheat."

I frowned. Clearly, this conversation wasn't what I had intended in simply trying to say something nice to my aunt.

"So, radio is bad and we shouldn't ever listen to it, right?"

That sounded pretty good. The parents and aunts and uncles would rejoice at any child who displayed the least bit of desire to give up any radio time.

"What? That's not what I'm saying at all. Radio is a thing, an inanimate object. Remember your Scripture lessons, boy. The Bible does not say that money is the root of all evil—"

"Sure, we've done that one. Money *is* the root of all evil, right?"

"No! The *love* of money is the root of all evil. Money is good or bad based on how it is used. Radio will be the same thing. You might hear the truth from it, but how are you going to know, Johnny?"

"Um, I don't know," I said and, without thinking, shrugged my shoulders.

"Attention, good fair folk!" It was the first and only time I felt grateful toward Aunt Babs for not playing more music.

"Well, what is it going to be, you miscreant?" Aunt Winnie said, crouching low in her chair like a tiger about to pounce.

"This town is at a crossroads. We can look back to the past, or we can forge ahead into a beautiful future. This town is in your hands. It is time for you to stand up and be counted. For a very limited time, a special chair has been constructed and will be available—for a small fee—to all the townsfolk to climb into and be hoisted up in comfort and ease to nearly the top of the KOBG radio tower. There you can sit and survey the splendor of the world. When you come down, you can take a bow, for you will have seen our present, and also our future. The way will be clear and you will vote for Hilde . . . for mayor!"

"What?" we all shouted.

"That's right," Aunt Babs said. "Our glorious station owner is running for mayor. It is time to be rid of the stagnant, oppressed policies of the past! Move into the future! Come to the tower and survey the great world in which we live, then give the mayoral authority to the one who will run this town to greatness! Vote for Hilde!"

*　　*　　*

Uncle Frank's good mood of the past few weeks had vanished by the time the four of us had jumped up from the table and rushed over to his house. Obviously, he had heard the announcement himself.

Although he had fretted publicly about his inability (due to AH's machinations) to campaign the way he normally had (via a broad leaflet dispersal on the town), we could all tell that he felt relaxed about his chances in the upcoming election. Up until AH's announcement, he had been running unopposed. The town took him as an institution. It was a "business as usual, lazy-fare attitude" (as Dad put it once, strangely) by a town that rarely rocked the boat. Watching someone else rock the boat, however, delighted everyone in the county. Uncle Frank understood that implicitly, which was why he was now worried.

Within a few hours, the whole family on our side of the Obeg (this excluded Uncle Joe, of course) had gathered at the Five and Dime, always a headquarters of sorts for us. Everyone was confused by the sudden, vicious, scathing political attacks on the radio. We kids, and even quite a few of the adults, huddled in small groups, our heads downcast, our hearts routed and despairing.

Nothing ever woke Uncle Frank to such fury as when he was cornered politically, though. He didn't get that from his father, so it must have come from Grandmother Verity. Grandfather Treat's traits shone through when Uncle Frank ended up sleeping through council meetings, but the fire and savvy must have come from Versey. Striding through the Five and Dime, he upbraided us for our own slumped shoulders and praised us for our as yet unseen ability to grasp victory from the jaws of defeat. He appeared to us as a fierce screaming eagle, surrounded and harried, cut off from supplies with no foreseeable hope, yet refusing to give in.

"The gauntlet has been thrown down!" he cried, raising his cane in the air and shaking it. I don't think he noticed that he almost burst three light bulbs on the ceiling. "This is the last desperate gambit of a cornered and hungry dog! We have proven ourselves against this foe time and time again. Times have been darker than this, and yet we prevailed then! So don't hang your heads. Hold the line and they will never break us!"

I felt inspired. I also wondered if we were all to get deputy mayoral status out of things. I clamped my mouth shut on this question, though, since I knew it would take an act of God to get Uncle Frank to share his chair.

Cousin Davey ran in, breathing hard and quickly doubling over as soon as he stopped. He held up a flier (that same blue paper so we all immediately knew that Aunt Hilde had printed it up on "her" printing press) and shook it ferociously. Cousin Ike grabbed it and brought it over to Uncle Frank; Aunt Ellen handed Davey a carrot which he instantly started devouring.

"'Vote for Hilde!'" Uncle Frank read, sneering at the note as he took it from Ike's hands. "'A vote for Hilde is a vote for prosperity and peace. Show that you are against "King Frank" and his desire to hold the office of mayor for life. Demand that he surrenders his position immediately. By siding with Hilde, you will show "King Frank" that his position is hopeless. Hundreds have already signed the petition demanding his removal! Join them today. Remember, a vote for Hilde is a vote for development and jobs!'"

Uncle Frank steamed in anger. He crushed the paper magnificently and shouted defiantly: "Nuts!"

Davey looked up from polishing off his carrot. "Do we get nuts, too?"

*   *   *

It wasn't an easy assignment. We all had our basic outposts surrounding the Five and Dime. Some of them were for two of us, some for only one. The adults hadn't wanted the kids involved at all, but they all saw the workload and therefore the necessity. They told us to treat this like a game, somehow with that keeping the innocence and gaiety of childhood intact. I appreciated their sentiment, not that the idea worked. The idea *was* work, and there was no way around it.

However, it was the feud, and there were only a couple of days before the election. We had to help Uncle Frank. He had to win the election again. If we gained the upper hand against AH, we all felt that she should quit. Apparently that wasn't in her nature, so it wouldn't be in ours, either.

We held the line against AH's onslaught as best we could. Dad and Aunt Patti rummaged around the basement of the Five and Dime for any remainders of election material from previous years. Aunt Ellen did the same back at their place. The next day we were sent off in ones and twos with buttons, pamphlets and hats emblazoned with Uncle Frank's name for mayor. The years were wrong on every single item, but it was all we had.

Davey and I were given a cardboard box with straw hats with red and white stripes, like the kind a barbershop quartet wore, a bunch of buttons and two pens. We were told to go to Washington Avenue and hand out everything to anybody we saw. If possible, we were to scratch out the old years and write in the current year.

"This is really hard," I complained to Davey as I tried to write on a button. We had quickly decided that as I had better penmanship, I would correct the years, and as Davey had a bigger mouth, he would hawk our wares.

"You're a sissy," Davey said.

He took a hat and a button (I hadn't finished with either) and ran up behind a middle-aged man—it looked like Mr. Puferoy, the principal of our school. Davey jumped up and plopped the hat on the man and stuck the button in the back of his shirt.

"Hey! Ow!" the man yelled. It was indeed Mr. Puferoy. "What in blazes are you doing?"

"Vote for Frank Smith!" Davey shouted and ran back to our post to get more ammunition.

Mister Puferoy paused for a moment before calling out, "It doesn't look good for you!" Then he stomped off, throwing the hat into the gutter (but he forgot about the button).

Davey continued on with his sneak attack advertisement style, which I felt was ineffective and possibly illegal, but I didn't want his job so I stuck to mine. Davey had probably already received detention at the start of school from Mr. Puferoy, plus had been slapped by Mrs. McDonald (he had pinned the button somewhere inappropriate). It was dangerous work. When I suggested we go back to the Five and Dime, he shook his head and said as long as we had a single button to hand out, he wasn't leaving his post.

That shamed me, so I remained with him, scratching and writing on buttons and hats as best as I could. On other corners, my folks and cousins and aunts and uncles worked just as diligently. For all that had transpired, I was bound to help them. Just days earlier I had been feeling like we would all survive the feud, that it was close to collapsing. After all I had done, all we had all been through, I thought we had won. To find myself again on the front lines, fighting feverishly, writing, pushing hard with my pen until both hands and all fingers were numb, disheartened me. To see all the passersby either wearing AH's insignia—or at least discarding our hats and buttons as soon as Davey plunked them on them—discouraged me. For the first time in my life probably I relied on Davey. He was there with me, sharing this frustration and danger with his own thoughts swirling through his head. I had offered the opportunity to flee and he had rejected it out of hand. I forgave him his foibles and thanked God for his stout heart.

As I did so, we had our first triumph. Pastor Evers saw me first (and shuddered), but then Davey got to him. He said he welcomed the chance to wear Uncle Frank's hat (he wasn't quite as enthused about the button, though).

"Well, boys," he yelled through a grimace as he extracted the button's pin from fairly deep inside his arm, "I admire your spirit! The Good Book says 'The harvest is great, but the workers are small. The Lord loves a child who will go to them all!'"

We stood and stared at him. He carefully folded the button pin into its clasp and pocketed it.

"Yeah," I said. "Or something like that."

"Exactly! Something like that," Pastor Evers acknowledged, apparently wondering which book said what he had quoted. When he wondered, it was the only time his voice strayed from top volume.

"Hey, here's a new one, boys!" he said. He tucked his hands under his armpits, bent down ever so slightly and yelled magnificently, "Squawk!"

Davey and I looked sheepishly at each other.

"Parakeet?" I ventured.

"Nope! Good guess though, Johnny! No, that was our dear friend, the black-throated sparrow! Anyway, I don't believe those lies about Frank! You can tell him I'll be voting for him! Now, if you'll excuse me, I have to go see a man about a tetanus shot!"

After he left us, we heard a blaring noise at the end of the street. From the other side of the Obeg, thundering across the bridge, came Uncle Benny's car, replete with loudspeaker horns strapped to the top and decked out in red, white and lavender streamers (someone had been filching town supplies again!). The horn honked at passersby and, as it neared us, we could make out some of the words, almost hidden behind the loud march music.

"Vote for Hilde! Watch your town be transformed! Vote for Hilde! Everyone will work! Vote for Hilde! Free sausages and beer at the 'Hilde for Mayor Rally'!"

"Hmmph. Sausages," Davey sneered as the car rolled past us.

Davey wasn't impressed, but sausages and beer would go down well in our town, I knew. Aunt Hilde would have a huge turnout. If there was more time, and had I any energy, I was sure I could do something to stop the rally. As it was, I was out of ideas and dog-tired. We would have to wait until we had more and better campaign supplies before going on the offensive. If we could get those supplies in time, that is, which seemed doubtful.

The car passed us twice more before we ran out of our old hats and buttons. I couldn't tell who the driver was—I had expected Uncle Benny, but it was probably one of the displaced farmers from their side of the river, and I didn't know many of them by sight. We didn't speak about the car and we walked only slowly back to the Five and Dime (and I had to carry the empty, but unwieldy, box by myself the whole way). There was no need to run since we didn't have any news that the others didn't have; that car had made the rounds all right, and with its loudspeakers had gotten to everyone.

Back at base, we saw the wear and tear of small-town political battle. We were almost all there except for Uncle Frank and my mom and aunts. Dad said they were getting supper ready for us, and the mere mention of food sent my stomach into somersaults of hunger. We looked longingly into the candy aisles (save for Davey), but found very little to tempt us. Not that we could have had anything, but it wasn't worth the risk of begging from the adults if the possible reward was only some year-old Bit o' Honeys, and not any Hershey bars.

"We handed them all out," Dad said quietly behind me, sensing my thoughts. "What few we had, anyway. They were needed for the effort."

I thought of the mindless masses munching on our Hershey bars as they loped along to the free sausages and beer at AH's after seeing the county from the top of the KOBG tower. That wasn't fair, though. They didn't know the trap that awaited them. We could only tell them so often and in so many ways. It would have to be one more way, too, to keep the tide from turning.

"Why don't you children wait outside," Aunt Winnie said. As it wasn't up for debate, we complied.

The clouds hung heavy over the center of town, darkening our mood. I thought about rounding up some kids and trying to get a ball game together, but it felt a little useless. Either it would rain or we'd be called in to eat or we wouldn't even get enough together for a game, even if we used ghost runners and girls in left field.

Two couples passed us wearing Hilde garb—red armbands or hats with intermingled Hs—and talking animatedly. They seemed not to notice us, and their talk confused us.

"She'll win that challenge for sure!"

"I can't wait for those sausages and beer!"

"Neither can she!"

"I bet he'll wish he never heard of sausages!"

"I'm voting for her in a cinch!"

"Too bad that chair-lift didn't work."

The only thing we understood was the comment about the vote, and that depressed us. Otherwise, the gaggle was so loud and annoying we couldn't even think straight to try and trip them as they passed. We watched them go and silently shared a common sneer. As we milled around, kicking at pebbles, we heard a new commotion. Rounding the corner and heading quickly for the Five and Dime came Uncle Frank and, lo and behold, Uncle Joe! They shouted at each other simultaneously so that we couldn't comprehend them. Uncle Joe raised his fists and thumped his chest, while Uncle Frank brandished his cane.

"This conniving will never stand—"

"Without me y'all'd be nowhere—"

"I'm the candidate here—"

"Ah'm the one making progress—"

It was a jumbled mess of threats and evocations, worse than the Hilde supporters. We kids parted like the Red Sea in front of Moses as my uncles bore down on us. Still arguing, they launched themselves at the entrance to the store and got stuck together in the doorway. It was the only thing that stopped their shouting. They both struggled like fish out of water, their cheeks puffed and red as sweat poured down their brows. Seizing on the idea of sucking in their guts at the same time, as we watched, they both inhaled and with a mighty pop burst through to the inside of the store.

My cousins and I wasted no time flying inside ourselves, Aunt Winnie edict or no, and just barely managed escaping the same imbroglio of the uncles because of the relative lack of girth in our guts (but that many of us at once was a tight squeeze). We watched open-mouthed as the two faced each other and continued their shouting match.

"No one would ever vote for you—"

"They ahr all tired of you—"

"You are not well received on this side of town—"

"Y'all would benefit from mah lead—"

Aunt Winnie approached them with complete temerity. She reached out and grabbed hold of an ear of each of them and yanked hard without letting go.

"Ow! Winifred!"

"Oh! Sis-tah!"

With these pleas, they quieted, except for their labored breathing, and Aunt Winnie finally let go. When they both gathered in air for another attack, Aunt Winnie beat them to it by slapping the backs of their heads. I knew Aunt Winnie must have sneaked off to the movies now and again to see the Three Stooges, as her routine was both smooth and classic, but I'd bet she'd deny it.

"Be quiet, both of you!" she snapped. "It's been nearly thirty years since I've spanked either one of you, but I'm not afraid to start up again! Now what is all this nonsense about?"

"I told him—"

"Ah know that—"

She slapped the backs of their heads again.

"Joseph!" she shouted, choosing, and Uncle Frank looked deeply dismayed as he rubbed the back of his own head.

Uncle Joe took one step back and gave her a stiff nod of his head. He hiked up his pants, stuck out his chin and proudly declared, "Ah shall be the candidate!"

In the distance somewhere, a lonely cricket chirped.

At least, it seemed that way, based on our reaction.

"What?" everyone except Uncle Frank replied after a few seconds.

"See what I mean?" Uncle Frank said, but we didn't.

"Frank!" Aunt Winnie barked.

Instead of speaking again immediately, Uncle Frank surveyed us with a seasoned eye. He must have understood our lack of comprehension (I helped him out by giving him my most stupefied gaze, the one I usually reserved for when I really wanted to annoy my parents) as he pointed at Uncle Joe (who still looked smug) and started explaining.

"He wants to run for mayor!"

We looked at each other. Dad ventured a guess: "Against you?"

"No! In place of me!"

"What?!?" we all cried. This shocked us and smacked of the same initial treachery we had felt when the feud started and Uncle Joe had sided with Aunt Hilde and Uncle Benny.

"You must stand down, Brother!" Uncle Joe cried, pointing one finger in the air in a mock posture of the polished politician.

"Joseph, you can't be serious?" Aunt Winnie said.

"Ah am a hunnert percent serious, Sis-tah. Ah have retaken my home and property—with no thanks to y'all—"

"What!?!" we all cried again, outraged, but Uncle Joe noticed it not.

"Ah have that ghastly woman on the run, I say, the run. Besides which, if Frank drops out o' the race, why then she'll have campaigned, I say, campaigned in vain!"

"Have you been eating chicken feed again, Joseph?"

It was Uncle Joe's turn to look deeply offended at Aunt Winnie. We all knew she had caught him eating the pellets once, many years ago when he first started chicken farming. He claimed that he had been testing it to make sure it was safe for his birds, but he knew no one bought that. Aunt Winnie enjoyed telling that story often, but usually when he wasn't around.

Uncle Joe stared us down one by one. "Leadership of the family," he said softly and malevolently, "should pass to me."

My two uncles started yelling again, facing each other, nose touching nose. I didn't have a brother, but I wouldn't want to yell at a cousin like that. At least, not that closely. I mean, not with that much spit flying.

The shouting raged for what seemed like hours, though it couldn't have been nearly that long. Aunt Winnie intervened when she could, but they got so heated that every time she grabbed their ears, they simply slapped her hand away and kept on yelling.

We tried to follow along, but it was tougher than in a heated tennis volley. The shots fired from Uncle Joe roared like a host of rockets. What we could understand showed that he aimed most of them at Aunt Hilde (but indirectly attacked Uncle Frank, too, about what he felt was our lack of support), how he had taken over his land again (he mentioned that one a lot) and how his lawyers had filed several suits against AH personally. He was doing the most and winning the feud; therefore, he should be the next mayor. Uncle Frank exploded with rage at the insinuation that our actions in taking out the V-1 factory had nothing to do with AH pulling out of Uncle Joe's property. He felt most betrayed by the fact that he had sent large amounts of money and supplies over the river to Uncle Joe, and that that was what had kept Uncle Joe from being driven completely away and had funded his counter-suits.

Aunt Winnie circled the two like a boxing referee. After what felt like twelve rounds, she had had enough, and she cried the secret word of our family that sent shivers down our spines.

"Pies!"

Uncle Frank and Uncle Joe stopped in mid-scream. Their mouths clamped shut and they slowly turned their eyes as one to their sister.

"What did you say?" Uncle Frank breathed.

"You heard me," Aunt Winnie said slowly, her brow deeply furrowed and her fists clenched. "I said: 'Pies!'"

*   *   *

The pronouncement shocked us kids, traumatized us even. It was the first occasion in our lifetimes that the word "pies" had been uttered. Well, not just as a word, but as a challenge.

Whenever brothers fought in our family, if it couldn't be resolved, they had to eat it out. I knew on the playground boys were sometimes prodded to "duke it out" (usually by older boys, taunting the younger ones about their masculinity, but one time by this teacher who was later arrested), but Great-great-grandma Frieda Schnachtenvolkerfurstung (nee Oberhurstgemuellen- burger), back in Germany, had seven sons who couldn't stand each other (we were from the second son, and proud of it, or at least Aunt Winnie was). She couldn't stand the fighting, so she instituted a pie eating contest. Except once, it was always *mano a mano*. One couldn't leave the table without conceding. What seemed a ludicrous idea to the neighbors (and the boys themselves), quickly turned deadly serious. One could get into an argument with one's brother out of season, and in a flash, be sitting in front of a plate of under- or over-ripe lingonberry pie.

The bouts back in the old country came across the water as legends, the battles epic in length, the pies gargantuan in circumference. Coming out of a pie battle (it was related to us), one could not move for months. One truly longed to regurgitate.

Growing up with these tales, we were sternly forbidden to use the phrase "pie in the sky".

Grandfather Treat's father—who had endured many forkfuls of strawberry-rhubarb, pumpkin, apple, blueberry and other assorted baked tortures, all in order to be the one brother who got to ride up front in the carriage—had brought the tradition over to America. The scandal in the family goes that double-Great Grandma Frieda couldn't afford to feed all seven boys any longer (she had spent a fortune on baking supplies); someone (the next pie-eating loser) would have to emigrate. So they had one last *tete-a*-eat . . . and Great-grandfather Wolfgang pushed himself away from the table first. He climbed aboard a steamer the next day and spent four weeks with his head over the rail.

Grandfather Treat and my Great-uncle George had several pie fights, but Wolfgang didn't make them eat for every little disagreement. Instead, he reserved it for the most virulent quarrels. The aunts and uncles talked in hushed tones about the time Uncle Joe and Uncle Benny almost squared off, but it seems Grandmother Verity burned the first pie; when smoke filled the kitchen, everybody fled and by the time they could come back, the brothers said they weren't fighting any longer.

Dad always said that Uncle Joe was scared of the pie fight, had distracted Grandma Versey so that the pie got ruined, and quickly made a cheap peace with Uncle Benny. As we sat around our dining room table (it was deemed the most neutral place we could use) waiting for the first pies, we wondered if Uncle Joe would cave again.

"Two minutes!" Aunt Winnie hollered from the kitchen. She supervised while Mom and Aunt Ellen slaved away.

It hadn't been easy finding enough flour and sugar for a real contest. Deliveries to the Five and Dime had increased, but not enough. All of our homes had been scoured, and more than a dozen neighbors had been visited, one cousin or another holding out an empty coffee cup and asking if we could borrow something. As the showdown was set for my house, I had tasks to do inside, which included a lot more lifting than a coffee cup. I didn't mind (much), since I felt it would be a prime opportunity to eavesdrop and pick up some juicy tidbits. However, everyone hushed as they gathered round the table, eyes filled with secrecy and paranoia.

The first pie was cherry (a gift from heaven, I thought, which was from the very last of the previous year's canned selection, which Mom had hidden in our basement). Aunt Winnie chopped it apart with ferocity and served it up to them with a great slamming of plates and utensils. Uncle Joe had made it that far; he couldn't back out. Leadership meant too much to him.

"Ow!" he cried after one bite. "This sho' is hot!"

"Of course it is," Uncle Frank said. "It came straight from the oven! As will they all, if it takes more than one to down you!"

Uncle Frank took his own bite and furiously blinked back tears.

"Oh," Aunt Winnie said, clapping her hands mockingly, "we're a little low on sugar, so we had to stretch things a bit. And dear me, I've forgotten to pour you boys some water. How rude."

She didn't make a move to get the water. My uncles took the hint and kept on eating the spartanly sweetened pie.

Forcing back more cries and swallowing violently, they downed the cherry. They mashed their way through a strawberry-rhubarb. Two blueberries went by without so much as a belated belch. An apple and then a mixed-fruit pie were set before the titans. The apple vanished, but a little more slowly. They were on their second slice each of the mixed-fruit when I realized it was Mom cutting the pie. Where had Aunt Winnie gone?

"Drop this insane demand, Joseph," Uncle Frank mumbled as he huffed and puffed.

"Never!" Uncle Joe cried, though he looked paler than Uncle Frank to me.

Slowly and methodically, they munched their way through the last of the mixed-fruit offering. Their eyes moved from one empty pie dish to another, as if astounded at the damage they could do when provoked. Casting about for another pie, each one seemingly sure that it would do in the other, they started to get furious.

"Is that all?"

"Send in another one! Ah say, send it in!"

"I should eat your helpings with mine! I'm just getting started!"

"Ah shall have you and the pie for luncheon!"

Back and forth they went, talking about pies and putting each other in the trash bin. The kitchen door flew open and banged against the wall, stopping the threats. In strode Aunt Winnie. In one outstretched hand, she carried a pie. Vapors from it overcame the lingering scent of all the fruit flavors that had recently filled the house. We all blanched and took a step away, except for the two seated at the table.

"What . . . what is it?" Uncle Frank managed to gasp. Uncle Joe nodded assiduously.

Aunt Winnie set the pie down in the middle of the table, moving aside two empty dishes. She picked up a knife, held it in mid-air, poised above the pie, and looked them in the eyes, one, then the other.

"Water Chestnut Surprise."

Oh dear God! It couldn't be! She had transferred that recipe from cookie to pie, sending it to my uncles in a fate I'm not sure they deserved. Who was the enemy anymore? Shouldn't something so awful be reserved solely for AH?

My uncles sat speechless, turning heavier shades of green, one upon the other. Uncle Frank started shaking his head as he gripped the table, his knuckles shining white. Uncle Joe's eyes rolled into the back of his head and he simply whimpered.

"No, no," Uncle Frank muttered, and now his whole body shook. "It's not natural. Bring out something else."

"There is nothing else," Aunt Winnie said and defiantly started cutting. "We're completely out of baking supplies. This is the only filling we had left. This pie will decide it."

My uncles both groaned. They surveyed the wretched thing with revulsion and eyed the other. Slowly, with desperate resolve, they each picked up their forks as Aunt Winnie served them. They grimaced at each other, each defying his brother to take a single bite of the horrible concoction. Their heavy, labored breathing belied their bravado, but I felt a wave of family pride wash over me (followed several times over by nausea) as I realized the depths of their courage: They were going to eat it.

Looking back, it may have been foolishness and not courage that propelled them to bite into the Water Chestnut Surprise. Should one have yielded to the other? Of course, I knew Uncle Frank was a better leader for our family than Uncle Joe, but how far should Uncle Frank go to maintain that dominance? Could he go so far that I would feel differently, that I would think he gripped the reins of the family too tightly?

Uncle Joe's fork wavered as he ripped a piece off his slice and lifted it toward his nose. His whole mustache quivered as he sniffed mightily—a tactical error. Immediately he had to kick into suppression mode. So great was his desire that nothing came up, nothing was allowed to get to the surface. The grimace on his face turned to a snarl. He bared his teeth and foamed like a mad dog, finally slamming the fork into his teeth, forcing an entrance and clamping down again.

He shook and sweated with the sensation, worse than any flu. Dropping the fork and gripping the table, he stared past Uncle Frank into some cold, lonely, desolate place of his own imagining and whimpered.

Uncle Frank tested his own fortitude. We could all tell that he was trying to clamp his nostrils shut, without actually putting a hand to his nose (a sure sign of weakness). He took a piece of the pie and flung it into his mouth, quickly and completely, swallowing it without chewing. Slamming down the fork he cried, "Hah!" which probably was intended to come out differently than the high-pitched squeak that it was.

Uncle Joe fell to the floor, stiff as a statue. He rolled into the fetal position and didn't move. If he hadn't continued to whimper, we would've checked for a pulse.

After a moment, realizing that Uncle Frank still sat upright in his chair, the room erupted with cheers. We patted Uncle Frank heartily on the back (he didn't seem to enjoy the jostling, however). Someone turned on the radio for music to help us celebrate. Mostly, we were relieved that it was over. We had to finish one feud before we could start another; it was too much to think of to have Uncle Joe not be on our side anymore. So we bent down and patted him on the back, too, hoping he'd join in the celebration, but he didn't move an inch.

We danced around our dining room and spilled into the living room as a lively tune played. With the election dawning the next day, victory seemed surely in our grasp. All we had to do was weather the storm. I didn't know how we would finally end the feud, but I knew we would.

Suddenly, the music stopped. Aunt Babs came on again and I heard Aunt Winnie call her a name under her breath. Everyone in the room heard her first few words, and our joy vanished immediately. We hushed, even all of us kids, and the room seemed to close upon us, shrinking with the quietude of desolation and destruction.

"We are broadcasting live!" Aunt Babs wailed. "We are at the Town Hall, where a tremendous crowd has gathered! Everyone is enjoying the multitude of sausages and beer as we eagerly await our Leader! Listen to them toast success to our great owner, Hilde!"

In the background, we heard beer tankards clink and chants of: "For her! For her!"

"Yes, we all love her! And now, for the final time, we send out our challenge to the cowardly mayor, to meet Hilde in battle. Come down to the Town Hall, if you dare, and—"

We waited with clenched teeth and sucked-in breath.

"—accept the sausage eating and beer drinking challenge!"

The crowd erupted again. We didn't stay to find out how else they cheered but, as one, we lifted Uncle Frank and carried him out of the house, to a car, to be driven down to the Town Hall. It was a challenge that had to be met, we knew. The town was fickle, and its tastes were immediate. Before the crucial election, they fancied a sausage eating and beer drinking contest between the two candidates. Deep inside, I sensed a great distress over the pandering that the voters got, but in the desperate hour it was not something to be touched. We all piled into three cars, I in my parents' Packard with Dad, Cousin Ike and a very quiet and green Uncle Frank, and headed off to the center of town. Uncle Joe was left in our living room.

Poor Uncle Frank. He protested weakly that he was about to burst, that he couldn't possibly go through with things. Aunt Hilde had to be turned back, though. We would not let her snatch victory away from us, not when we were so close to defeating her utterly. Uncle Frank clutched his belly and moaned as he leaned out the window on the passenger side of Dad's car.

"Let's go!" Ike shouted, pointing an arm out the backseat window toward the looming threat. "We have to meet this challenge with whatever we've got left!"

Dad floored it. Nearing the Town Hall, we saw the assembled crowd surrounding a stage with massive banners proclaiming AH great. Dad beeped the car horn wildly, and we all waved our arms out the windows, saying "Hi" and also pleading with people to make room (our car's brakes were bad).

"Get out of the way!"

"Frank is here!"

"We'll meet any challenge!"

"For Pete's sake just get out of the way!"

For the first time in a long time, I saw my double-aunt godmother. Up on stage, strutting with the radio microphone half-shielding her face, her eyes wide with fear that her opponent had arrived and would actually challenge her for dominance and not cower in fear, she looked tremendously changed, like a house dilapidated from years of the elements and no upkeep. Her gaunt cheeks twitched as she spoke, and I noticed that she kept one hand behind her back at all times. (This worried me until I caught sight of her elbow wobbling continuously—she was sick; yes, twisted and mean, but also very ill. Should I feel any compassion or not?)

She recovered quickly. "Look! The prodigal returns to the campaign trail! Have any more buttons from yesteryear to give us?" Aunt Hilde bellowed from the stage. The crowd laughed appreciatively.

This riled Uncle Frank and no doubt about it. He brushed off our hands as they attempted to help him stand. Though he used his cane, and at times leaned heavily upon it, he stepped down from the running board and made a beeline for the stage, the crowd parting in front of him, the new Moses.

He reached the steps quickly and ascended while AH and her cronies on stage stepped back, giving way. One stooge quickly set up a card table and ran around like one of Uncle Joe's dangerous chickens as he looked for some chairs. A new keg was tapped at the far end—to the gasping delight of the crowd; an early Oktoberfest. The smell of cooking sausages filled the air, an overpowering sensation.

"Well, well," AH said. "It looks like we will do battle after all."

"Stop this nonsense, Flat-top! You'd make a lousy mayor, and we all know it!"

It was impossible to tell how the crowd felt about this (but Uncle Frank was right, she did have a rather flat head). The multitude murmured, but seemed anxious for a final, stinging comment from someone, anyone. I had a terrible image of sheep being led to slaughter.

"Let the sausages decide!" my double-aunt screamed, and the crowd erupted in joy.

What the heck did that mean, anyway?

I knew. It brought new meaning to the derogatory phrase "get stuffed". It was an eating battle, the second in as many hours for poor Uncle Frank. I just thought AH's crowd-pleasing was annoying, that's all.

Chairs were found and placed at opposite ends of the card table. A red and white checkered tablecloth draped the table for some reason. Eyes locked, my uncle and my double-aunt sat and stared, their eyes full of pure hatred. They each strapped a bib onto themselves and grabbed hold of a knife and a fork, holding them ready for battle.

What I witnessed that day may I never see again. Plates of steaming sausages and quart-sized mugs of beer appeared on the table. They bit and chewed, fighting with tooth and . . . well, other teeth. Boiling juice sprayed from every link, sending the bystanders reeling to the back, begging for mercy and hoping for morphine.

For an hour the combatants struggled for dominance. Their stomachs bulged under the strain, but neither gave way. The first to break completely would lose, had to lose. Plate after plate and mug after mug disappeared through the most disgusting belches and lip-smacking known to man.

Like a fly drawn to the light that will spell its doom, I found myself next to the stage, staring at the proceedings. Pellets of hot juice sprayed the ground all around me—how I escaped undamaged I cannot tell.

Unbelievably, my aunt spoke to my uncle, which, being near them I heard, but which was not broadcast as the microphone was nowhere close. It was a slurred, drunken sentence, but it was clear enough to pick out.

"Let's settle this amicably, Frank," she said, I swear it. "The whole east side of the river is under Joe's control. Our only chance is to link forces and march against him! Join me!"

Uncle Frank struggled to retain his composure, and the contents of his belly. He swallowed hard and belched three times before finally finding the air to speak.

"You'll never stop, will you, Hilde? I've told Ike, and I've already agreed with Joe. You've got to go. I will not rest until you're through!"

A wild, desperate fear permeated AH's normally maniacal glare. I knew why; she was used to having her way, used to people obeying. Something else there was, I thought, though. It wasn't just the incredulity of defiance, but she seemed truly astounded that Uncle Frank—against whom she had been fighting so hard—would not simply put the past aside in order to help her against Uncle Joe. What did she mean that Uncle Joe controlled the whole east side of the river?

She dropped her utensil. Her palsied hand that shook knocked over her beer mug. The crowd gasped and their eyes locked on Uncle Frank. Slowly raising his fork, he stabbed

215

another sausage, brought it to his mouth and bit off as much as he could chew (possibly more than he could chew).

The crowd cheered and everyone started hugging. Verna Lewitt, the young, pretty high school English teacher who lived about a block from us, grabbed hold of me and we embraced for maybe a minute. She kissed my cheek and turned to do the same to somebody else. I could only stare at her derriere as she swooped away, lost in adolescent, transcendent fervor.

When that passed (though I would dream about it many times in the coming months), I looked back on stage. Aunt Hilde had fled. Uncle Frank looked ill; I don't think he ever finished that last link. Dad jumped up on stage and I followed after him. We each took one of Uncle Frank's arms and helped steady him.

The microphone was brought forward and thrust into his face.

"I can't eat another bite," he mumbled, pushing it away.

I grabbed it quickly and yelled into it, "Vote for Uncle Frank!"

The crowd cheered this and I stood there bracing my uncle and his dangerously dangling, bulging belly, with a dopey grin on my face. I looked around for Miss Lewitt, but Dad started dragging Uncle Frank away, which pulled me along, too.

*   *   *

We got home late, so late that it was past midnight and technically voting day. Uncle Joe had crawled away from out of our dining room sometime during the sausage and beer battle. Mom sent me right to bed, and she followed suit, too. Dad had plopped in his favorite chair in the living room, however, and seemed lost in thought and perturbed as well, though I couldn't fathom why since we had obviously won a great victory.

In the morning, he was gone, at the Five and Dime Mom said, but I knew he would be at the Town Hall to vote, too. Mom said she would go after she had fed me breakfast, though it was only oatmeal as everything else in the kitchen had been used in the pies the day before. The air was still loaded with the heavy and somewhat noxious combination of odors, especially the last dastardly one from Aunt Winnie.

"After you eat, you just stay out of sight," Mom said as she stacked clean dishes. Normally, that type of threat was interpreted in my mind as something more akin to an invitation, but I think she meant it.

"I mean it," she growled and she snapped her drying towel. "Politics is nasty business. I don't know what else your aunt Hilde might try, but I don't want you nearby."

I patted my heavy oatmeal with my spoon, deeply regretting the paucity of brown sugar, and wondered why she was *my* aunt and not *her* sister?

The morning passed—though I wasn't sure the oatmeal ever would—and Mom dutifully went to the Town Hall (though I knew she wouldn't stay). By long local custom, our polls were only open until noon. No one really knew why; possibly because we had always been such a small town, probably because no one ever had much patience. Anyway, I had leave from working the gardens of the neighbors, so I made my way to the baseball fields. No one was there, so I started meandering. Only rarely did I encounter anyone, and then only briefly. Out of their own volition—I swear it—my feet directed me in a leisurely way into town. Resolution was in the air, and after all I had seen, it would be a shame to fall away at the very end, warnings to be careful and stay away notwithstanding.

I was glad my feet took over, for the commotion at the Town Hall and half a block away at the Liquidation Store was a first, even for the whole uproar that our town had seen. A huge crowd had gathered, and a string of eight black cars lined the side of Washington Avenue. The shouting increased as I gathered speed. A scuffle erupted as I reached the outer fringes of the crowd. Being smaller, I pushed my way inside until I kneeled one row behind the inner ring.

Lying on the ground, face-down—with another man's foot on his back—with his nose bleeding and one eye black and puffy, was Uncle Benny, the Dessert Fox no more. The hard boot that kept my uncle on the pavement was attached to a very official looking man in a dark suit with sunglasses. All around, the townsfolk shouted and shook their fists, while a few others, milling around the inner circle, tried to calm the crowd.

Uncle Benny caught my eye. Though I had thought many nasty things about him late at night before sleep (in lieu of counting sheep), seeing him in that stricken condition shocked me. Mom had been right—politics was rough. I didn't know how deeply though.

I saw Uncle Benny mouth, "You a good boy, Gianni," to me, but he also seemed delirious and spent. Who had done this, and why? It definitely seemed like the crowd had, though they had all been cheering Aunt Hilde the night before. And where was she, in some secret bunker somewhere?

Suddenly, into the circle walked Dad, Cousin Ike, Norman Beech, another man in a suit (sans sunglasses), and Mr. Miller, the chairman of the town council. The crowd quieted immediately; I tried to make myself as small as possible, hoping to God that He would strike me dead before Dad saw me there, because God would do that, wouldn't He, to protect a small boy?

Mr. Miller held up his hands for silence, though it had already been given. He held the pose too long, though, and a wag called out, "What?" which was what I had been thinking. Then I realized that it was me who had said it. I shrank down even lower.

"As some of you discovered with me, Benjamin Smith here was caught stuffing the ballot box."

A gasp came from those that hadn't known; curses flew down from those that had. A man near me said to the fellow next to him, "Any normal election cheat would have put in only so many false ballots. That fool stuffed the box with thousands of fake votes, all on five-by-seven blue sheets of paper. That box bulged with fake votes!"

"These other gentlemen here," Mr. Miller indicated the suits, "have arrived in Dodge investigating fraud by the Outwits Corporation, which according to Norman here has bilked investors out of over six millions of dollars."

A huge gasp from the crowd. "I don't believe it!" more than one whispered around me, but I knew it to be true.

"Hilde Smith, the president and CEO of Outwits, is nowhere to be found. These government boys have seized all of her and Benny's assets. Their resistance to the investigation has completely collapsed."

The crowd cheered this. Even those I recognized as having been supporters or workers for Aunt Hilde seemed heartened, as if a great dousing of cold water had slackened an eternal thirst, and they sighed in heady relief.

"They will also be investigating the fraud here and across the river."

Here *and* across the river? We weren't a big town and had only the two ballot boxes, one on each side of the river. Had Uncle Benny messed with both of them?

"How many times do I have to tell you?" the man next to Mr. Miller said. "We're from the Securities and Exchange Commission. We can't investigate voter fraud. That's for your state attorney general."

"Oh phooey!" a man in the crowd near me yelled out. "We've got feds here, we got all this local government, you mean we also gots to have the state involved, too?"

"I heard the county sheriff's on his way," piped in another unhelpful wag.

Mr. Miller held up his hands for silence again. He got it, but only after another smattering of murmurs.

"I'm sure these boys can handle it all," he said.

The suit next to him slapped his own thigh and looked about in disgust, but the crowd approved of Mr. Miller.

"I told you— " was as far as he got.

"Please!" we all cried.

"I simply cannot arrest—"

"PLEASE?"

"I don't have the authority—"

"PRETTY PLEASE?"

We waited breathlessly as the man scratched his head. He bobbed his head back and forth, a dizzying disarray combining a "yes" motion with a "no" motion.

"Well, I suppose we could take him into custody . . . just this once," the SEC man said.

"Hurray!" we all cheered, and they led Uncle Benny to one of the black sedans.

"Ciao, Gianni," he mouthed to me, and I wished he hadn't. I couldn't dwell on it as Mr. Miller started speaking again.

"Now, with the real polls closed, and the fake ballots discounted, I can announce the results. From the West Dodge polling station: Frank Smith 403, Hilde Smith 1, write-ins none."

Sustained cheering.

"From the East Dodge polling station: Frank Smith none, Hilde Smith 1, write-ins for Joseph Smith 402."

Huge gasp. A flurry of thoughts careened through our collective brains: How did Joe get all those write-ins? Were there really almost as many votes on the East bank of the Obeg as the West? How could Uncle Frank not get a single vote on the East side?

"As chairman of the Dodge Town Council, I declare that Frank Smith is the winner, 403 to 402 to 2."

The discombobulated thinking allowed us only to clap politely, the paucity of huzzahs an eerie premonition to what happened next. A shout of "Make way! Make way!" came from outside the circle. Breathless, my cousin Davey appeared. He stopped and doubled over momentarily. We in the circle around him waited anxiously while he gathered himself.

"I've just come from the Five and Dime!" he announced. As that was Uncle Frank's campaign headquarters, it was most likely where Uncle Frank had holed up, sipping some warm, spring water to steady his nerves. Of course, it was only two blocks away, and Davey was winded?

"Uncle Frank . . . is dead!" Davey shouted.

The gasp following this surpassed all the other amazing gasps our town had undertaken in its long history. Far surpassing the ensuing gasp of the vote results, the gasp around the revelations surrounding the destruction of the marina, even the Great Gasp of '08, when the first automobile had made its way into the village, a poor lost soul searching for a gas station, and the townsfolk thought he had bewitched a horse-driven carriage so they tarred and feathered him, tied him to a real horse and slapped it on the behind.

"What?" we finally all shouted together.

"Yeah," Davey said, still panting. "He's dead tired, he said. And awful sick, too, from those pies and the sausages and beer. He said as soon as he's elected, he's going to stand down."

CHAPTER 8: THE BOMB

I t was a beautiful, sunny day, unseasonably warm but with low humidity and a nice breeze, when my father dropped his bomb. No one saw it coming; it ushered us into a new age from which we could never return. Of course, the mop up of Hilde and Benny's mess took a while before Dad did his damage, duty-bound as he felt he was.

Cousin Davey had nearly been lynched by the crowd after his misstatement. He didn't understand why either, and I had to explain it to him about a dozen times.

"I was only saying what he told me to say," he kept saying in defense of his actions. "All I said was that he was stepping down, that he was tired."

"No, you didn't, Davey. You said he was dead!"

"I never said that."

"Yes, you did!"

"Well," he eventually conceded, shaken by my forceful admonishment, "maybe I did . . . once."

It was then that we heard a tremendous explosion. A gigantic bomb went off somewhere to the north of us, probably on the East bank of the Obeg, too. The ground shook and we all cast about in fear for something solid to hold, many of us praying fervently. As the tremors subsided, we looked to the northeast and saw a huge, brown plume rising in a mushroom-like formation. A scorching wind slammed into us, pelting us with dust and small bits of debris, carrying with it the unmistakable smell of fudge.

I knew in my heart what had become of Aunt Hilde, knew for certain that she had gone up with the last of her vengeful concoction. (Though we would never have proof of her demise, reports circulated throughout town that the charred remains of a small, squarish mustache were found near the crater where the explosion took place, not on Treat's land as we first thought, but just outside AH's farmhouse.)

When the dust cleared, we turned back to Mr. Miller. The confused townsfolk and displaced farmers harassed him from all sides, so he called an immediate session of the Dodge Town Council. The five pillars of our community huddled for the rest of the day, famously sending for Mrs. Willoby, the town librarian, to pull all city records and newspaper accounts of similar government crises since the town's founding. Shocked, she solemnly searched her meager archives, but was forced to respond that there were no roadmaps for such a conundrum.

By a 3-2 vote, the council approved a by-law that allowed them to name a successor to mayor when one was needed between election and swearing-in. The two members who opposed were both from East Dodge and they stormed off through the crowd, over the bridge and were not seen by us again. Then Mr. Miller and the remaining West Dodge members emerged from their conference and announced their decision.

They chose Dad as the new mayor.

Things had lightened up enough during the long council session that I had stopped hiding between peoples' legs (I was tired of getting stepped on was what really prompted me), and I had taken a place next to Dad. When he was told, his face went ashen.

He looked down at me and said softly, "A hard load has landed on me, John. Pray for me."

Which I did.

But not before—feeling an unstoppable welling of pride and joy, relief at the final ouster of my double-aunt godmother, the release of all my pent-up prepubescent angst—I shouted out for the whole assembly to hear:

"It's 'Victory in Dodge Day'! It's 'V-D Day'!"

And my father's hand shot from the sky and landed on my face, smothering my next words. A few minutes later, after Dad dragged me away from the laughing crowd, I was sent home, sore bottom and all.

Mrs. Willoby, still reeling from embarrassment at having unearthed nothing helpful during the crisis, had, in her mourning, received an epiphany. Her life's new mission would be to chronicle the town's legal proceedings. All of them. She had already gotten the council's meeting minutes notebook out. As soon as Dad had been declared mayor, she started following him around. The official records for Dodge that day still show the following entries:

5:05 p.m.	*Council Chair Miller announces appt. of Harry Smith as Mayor*
5:07 p.m.	*Mayor H. Smith spanks son*
5:11 p.m.	*Mayor H. Smith sends son home*
5:16 p.m.	*Mayor H. Smith showered with flowers and kisses from women (many young)*

I can't believe I missed that last one. I rued it for many years, sure that I would have gotten some of the kisses (but in reality I suppose only a few of the fallen petals).

At any rate, the town was hectic and pell-mell with outsiders for a fortnight. Government men swooped into every nook and cranny of Aunt Hilde's business ventures. The Liquidation Store, of course, was a biggie. Everyone in town was interviewed about it and everyone denied knowing anything about it or ever having been there; that incensed us, no one more so than Cousin Ike. The U.S. Marshal who had come in eventually got so sick and tired of that response from the townsfolk that he took Ike's suggestion and lined everyone up and took them on a tour of the musty building, into the dank basement and all. Seeing the models laid bare for all to see, of AH's evil plans, caused almost all the townsfolk to blanch.

The marshal also had to survey Grandfather Treat's land and the remaining structures there. I didn't know what would happen to the land, though, or when I would get to see it again. Dad made some comments—when he thought I wasn't around—that a new plan for "splitting it up for good" would probably happen. In fact, he thought it already had, "*de facto,*" but I couldn't tell what he meant and didn't want to ask outright.

The worst hit, for most folks, was that KOBG closed down. I wasn't sorry to have Aunt Babs' blasphemy finally ended, but it was our only radio station. Most everyone felt that they could live with some lies and hypocrisy, as long as it was still mostly songs and entertainment (I thought this rather prescient years later when I recalled this while watching television).

Then one day, a Wednesday, Aunt Winnie knocked on the door. Dad was already out, tending to a very busy Five and Dime, as well as his new mayoral duties. She told Mom and me that the whole family, what remained of it, would picnic that evening (we'd stay on the West side, however).

We had never had a picnic on a Wednesday night before, but we accepted what she said, and Mom went to go pack her basket. My aunt looked grayer and more tired than I had ever seen her before. She came inside and sat down heavily on the living room sofa.

"What's wrong, Aunt Winnie?" The feud had taken something from her, I knew, but wasn't sure what. She no longer had the fire in her belly or twinkle in her eye that had always defined her in my youth. I would always admire her, but I knew looking at her that the days of leaning on her were over. It wouldn't be Uncle Frank, either. Everything was squarely on Dad's shoulders.

"'Now is the winter of our discontent,'" she said thickly.

"Um, but summer just ended." As soon as I said it, I knew how stupid it sounded. I would be nearly twenty-five before I understood speaking metaphorically well enough to recognize it from twenty paces.

"I know, my boy, I know."

"Aren't you happy? We won, you know."

"Of course I know we won! I'm old, but I'm not blind like your great aunt Agnes!" She sighed and sank deeper into the cushions. "I only hope, for your sake Johnny, that it was not a pyrrhic victory."

I decided not to ask, but to make use of the dictionary later, in a quiet moment.

Aunt Winnie seemed disinclined to talk any longer, so I let her be. Eventually the three of us went to the West-side picnic grounds together, picking Dad up on the way. For the first time in a long time, the whole family gathered together peacefully. Except for Aunt Hilde. And Uncle Benny. Everyone else was there though, even Uncle Joe and his kids.

Uncle Frank was there, too, but he was in a wheelchair with a shawl wrapped around him and sunglasses on. Aunt Ellen sternly forbade all of us kids from talking to him, which was kind of creepy to an almost twelve-year-old.

We ate mostly in silence, macaroni salad, watermelon and fried chicken (cold, but not ones of Uncle Joe's). The youngest kids played, but mostly we all just sat there, the mania of the fall of AH having already receded while the pain of the scars remained.

After the meal, Dad and Uncle Joe, with a little input from Aunt Winnie, talked about family matters. They would each care for my cousins—Uncle Benny's kids, that is—and they would each "administer" part of Grandfather Treat's land.

It came out in subtle and not so subtle ways that Uncle Joe had already taken possession of Uncle Benny's farm and most of Treat's land, since it was on his side of the river. It would be hard for us to manage the land from where we lived, but Dad told Uncle Joe that we had paid a heavy price for it, so we should certainly take care of our own portion.

"Why don't Ah save y'all the trouble and admin-uh-stuh it fo' you?"

"Stop eating chicken-feed!" Aunt Winnie snapped, her last good put-down of Uncle Joe I ever heard.

"We'll manage it just fine," Dad said. "Even if we have to make a separate trip there every day."

Uncle Joe retreated coolly, but still smirked, so I wondered how many other plans he had. Dad didn't seem to mind, or at least notice, for he stood, walked over to where Mom was sitting, gnawing on a chicken leg and addressed the family.

Right as he started, I remembered that two weeks earlier, when he was appointed mayor, he had asked me to pray for him. I had forgotten until that moment, so I did it then, with a rock in my stomach, fearing I was too late. I looked up and all around, my mind awhirl, until my eyes rested on the familiar and comforting steeple of our church, so clearly in view at this picnic.

"We have been through a tremendous amount," Dad said between coughs to clear his throat. "We have worked and fought long and hard, standing up for what we felt was right. Unfortunately, it has cost us greatly."

He then listed the tally: Uncle Benny was in prison, with no hope of getting out anytime soon; Aunt Hilde's whereabouts were technically unknown; their kids would now grow up in different homes, divided; Uncle Frank was a shell of himself and most likely would never recuperate fully; the Five and Dime was nearly bankrupt (but would make a nice recovery); Aunt Winnie's home and land holdings were mortgaged five times over and she doubted she could keep it all—had, in fact, sold a couple of small parcels around town she had always owned, or owned for a very long time; Treat's land was devastated. Squabbles still remained, strongly evidenced by the fact that he and Uncle Joe couldn't seem to agree on anything. Treat and Versey's will, so much at the heart of matters before, had been swept aside, obsolete, imperfect, impractical.

Beyond that, however, challenges had been met. At every turn, victory was even more securely ours.

"However," Dad continued and his voice shook. I thought I saw him sweat, which was reasonable as he stood in the brilliant sunlight, but something I never saw him do before, at least when speaking. "However, this is now the second time that our family has been embroiled in a difficult feud. Both times they were caused, primarily, by one family.

"Now, we don't know where Hilde is today. I wouldn't think we'd ever see her again. To be sure, I have convinced Benny to file for a divorce, if he isn't granted a death certificate for her. Our brother will still be imprisoned, as he should be, but whatever Hilde's outcome was, we will not be tied to her anymore."

Dad then started shaking almost uncontrollably before he willed himself still. That was odd to me because, no matter what, we would be rid of Aunt Hilde for good. She was my assumed deceased ex-double-aunt still single-aunt godmother (could I get a bishop somewhere to annul the godmother bit?). It wasn't distressing at all. Still, he shook and stuttered for a full minute before steeling himself.

That's when he dropped his bomb. As it came down, I could see it, like a knife chopping carrots that slices one's finger instead, in slow motion, knowing it will happen, seeing it all unfold, unable to stop it at all.

"Even so, we're still married into that family," he said.

Please God, no. Please God, no!

He reached into his jacket pocket as Mom looked up and dropped her chicken leg. He took out some papers and handed them down to Mom.

"Bess," he said, "I want a divorce."

BOOM.

Maybe it was only my heartbeat, but there had been an explosion, somewhere. In the aftermath, Dad said something about, "For the good of the family," but I'm not sure if he said anything beyond that.

Please God, no. Please God, no!

My parents were getting divorced? How could this be? We had survived! We had triumphed! This couldn't be the only way.

And yet, I knew why he did it. Aunt Hilde had come into our family and nearly destroyed it. Just as her father had nearly destroyed Dad's father. The war had to stop. By any means; unconditionally! These families just didn't mix. Except in me.

We hadn't noticed in the interminably long time that it took for the debris to clear, while Mom shot continuous double *Looks* at Dad but couldn't find the words to speak, that Uncle Joe had left. I noticed out of the corner of my eye his kids, his picnic stuff, his empty blanket, but didn't connect it to him being gone until I saw him coming back.

He wasn't alone.

Strutting into our camp came Uncle Joe, arm in arm with a beautiful woman. Her jet-black hair simply cascaded down her shoulders, her tight blouse and skirt easily outlined her feminine body (the next day was my twelfth birthday, so I was starting to get filled with raging hormones that compulsively noticed things like that). Her face was painted to perfection, with dark, ruby lipstick and eyelashes that matched her hair. Her wide-brimmed hat shaded her face a bit, but she seemed content walking with Uncle Joe, if not happy. She looked a little familiar, but I knew I hadn't ever seen her before.

"Ah suppose now would be a good time to tell y'all," Uncle Joe said. "Barbara Rose and me is gettin' married."

"What?" we all gasped.

I gave that gasp a 9.5 out of 10 score as the rest of my mind reeled from the announcement of my mom's other sister, Aunt Babs, becoming my new double-aunt. She sat demurely on a blanket with us, her legs curled beneath her, and told us she just wanted to settle down.

We wouldn't be separated from Mom's family after all. Dad took back the divorce papers, but the damage had been done. Mom went home by herself, crying, completely shaken.

Eventually—I knew it even then—they would reconcile. Things would never be the same, though. How could they be? Dad's "Potluck Declaration" (as we came to call it later, though we never spoke of it when my mother was near) was an ultimatum Mom didn't deserve. It was a testament of her strong love that helped us through those closing days of conflict.

We parted from the rest of the family, packed up our belongings, walked Aunt Winnie home and made for our own shores. It was uncomfortable walking silently beside Dad, so I kept my eyes on the cross at the top of our church until it was behind me (but omnipresent still), and kept thinking.

Uncle Joe's announcements (not just the one about Aunt Babs) had sliced a cool, steely curtain between the families, neatly divided now by the Obeg River (apart from our small plot of Treat's land). I wondered in my lifetime if I would ever see it lifted. I thought of my cousins, how we would grow up apart, tainted by our experiences and burdened with our inheritances.

Mine would be heavy, I knew, knew it even then though not the shape of it. How would I respond? I didn't second-guess Dad, not even for what he said to Mom—though I hated it had happened—or question all that had been done by Uncle Frank and Aunt Winnie. They had done their duty; they had not let us be yoked into serving that which we couldn't support, betraying the faith of our fathers and the freedom which we had always enjoyed. Yet I wondered.

They were a great generation. Before my very eyes, they were passing. The feud had been settled, but how would we survive the new struggles? Would I grow up and have to battle Uncle Joe or his kids? Would other terrors and evils take AH's place? And the worst question: If they did, would I be able to stand? The fears remained, but as I thought about my folks and certain of my aunts and uncles, I felt hot tears on my cheeks and a fierce pounding in my chest. I knew that hope remained, too. It was strong.

"I wonder," I said to myself as I lay in bed that night, an hour or so after my bedtime, only a couple of hours away from my birthday. "I wonder . . . all the world wonders . . . will the hope we hold be enough in the days to come? Will the pain we endured buy us enough freedom that we find the sacrifice worthwhile?"

Heady thoughts for a near twelve-year-old. Admittedly, I also wondered if, in all the hoopla, my folks would remember my natal day? (Or, more accurately, would they remember a suitable gift? I wanted cleats and a new mitt.)

"I wonder," I said for a final time, shaking off the minor bout of selfishness as I shook off the sheets. On tiptoes, I snuck out to the hallway and crept downstairs. Silhouetted in the window of the living room, I saw Mom and Dad embracing. The past was over, but its effects would dog us for the rest of our days.

APPENDIX: EXPLANATIONS AND APOLOGIES

The Second World War has always fascinated me. It was also, always, in the distant past, for I was born long after the guns fell silent (but certainly not after its ramifications—not even my children have been born after those). The black and white photos I saw as a child never conveyed much that was real or anything very personal to me. Modern films like *Saving Private Ryan* and *Band of Brothers* do much more in that. Veterans have been honored for their sacrifice, and memorials have been built (all of I which I join in and applaud).

Still, I remain fascinated. What grew in me initially, as a boy, was the thrill of the machines, the bravery of the men and the whole sweeping power struggle. As I've grown older, I see the incredible human drama and magnitude of it all.

Another thing that has always fascinated me is family. Blood ties are strong in families that have bonded or have at least expended a lot of energy trying to bond. Families have their own unique histories that help explain some of our foibles, though they continually defy logic. Where have I come from? What triumphs and tragedies occurred—had to occur—simply so that I could be here?

It seemed appropriate then to end up writing about both topics at once. It encompassed two big subjects for me, and was in a vein that made the pain of the individuals who fought the war a little more palatable. It is a story of a family, one with both eyes of the narrator open, though the tongue is in place in the cheek more often than not.

That it tells the story of the Second World War—and that obviously very poorly and incompletely—is of course not meant to deprecate any veteran or any of the suffering. In fact, in many ways, I believe it highlights these things and shines a spotlight on them specifically because some humor and parody surround them. If it's a poor attempt at honoring and remembering those who lived through that war and those times, then I apologize. Family is important, history is important. Humor too is valuable in the human condition. It is something we use every day, a necessity, a coping mechanism, as well as a tool for learning valuable life lessons. This is how it's been for me, and so I wrote it that way for young Johnny Smith, somewhere in America, sometime during the 1940s, during an overly long summer.

One certainly does not need to be a student of history to read *War and Peace in Dodge* (it might, in fact, be a hindrance to enjoying it, if not least for a few of the anachronisms). I hope it can simply be read as an entertaining story of a family feud. Even knowing little of the Second World War, some of the representations are of the "bash you over the head" variety (sorry about that). Others are so subtle, my explanations here may provoke only groans (again, sorry about that). What with the Second World War being so vast, with so many historical personages and events, as well as uncounted millions of bit players, not everything is represented in this novel. Indeed, some things are blatantly missing and others are jumbled together in ways that you, the reader, may find annoying, or worse (once again, sorry about that). Finally, I will add that the story grew in the telling, and that in places I had to "draw outside the lines" of the established plot of the war in order to encompass what I felt should be told in this story.

Anyway, for those interested in the symbols, representations, hints and other assorted parallels, the following list is provided. It is not definitive, as that would not be much fun for you.

Aunt Hilde	Most of the aunts and uncles as characters are all pretty obvious, aren't they? Aunt Hilde, or "AH", is the ever-popular arch-nemesis Adolf Hitler. If you didn't get this one, you might need to read through things again.
Uncle Benny	He's Benito Mussolini, the weaker fascist married by treaty to Hitler. By code to Johnny, Uncle Benny becomes the "Dessert Fox," which calls to mind the "Desert Fox", who was Erwin Rommel really, but I couldn't afford to add another character to the book. That he makes "Goose-steppin'-Berry" ice cream is just another cheap fascist joke.
Uncle Joe	Stalin. He was from Georgia (the country, a Russian province at the time of Stalin's birth) so that's why I gave him a *faux* Southern accent. Honestly, envisioning Stalin talking like Foghorn Leghorn makes me laugh. Think about it, with that toilet-brush mustache wiggling up and down as he struts

through a speech. We always think of how evil Hitler was—and he certainly was—but we know less of this bastard who most likely killed a lot more people than Hitler did. One of my favorite vignettes from this book is Johnny thinking about how spending more time with Uncle Joe would have caused him to view Joe as worse than Hilde.

Aunt Winnie   Churchill. There was nothing intentional about representing this great man as an old woman. It just seemed like it would work better for the story, that's all. Now, making Hitler an ugly woman with a mustache, THAT was intentional. I highly recommend Churchill's *The Second World War* history for an in-depth view of the war from the vantage point of someone in a leadership position, showing the decisions he made at the time and how he arrived at them, though it's certainly not for everybody. As a whole, it ends up being more than a bit self-serving, with many holes. He was the only major political leader to write about the war (one of the few to survive it, even).

Uncle Frank   FDR, of course. Most likely you noted his "fireside chats" which FDR gave over the radio, one in which he famously illustrated giving aid to Great Britain by saying if we had a neighbor whose house was on fire, we would lend him our hose and not worry about whether or not the neighbor could pay for the hose until later. Obviously, toward the end of the war, FDR passed away. I only incapac-itated him as a character. His politics can be debated—most likely they will be for generations—but his leadership of the U.S. was as great as Churchill's of the U.K. That as his strength failed he kept Truman in the dark on everything (most notably the Manhattan Project) was a bit paranoid, and could have held disastrous consequences for America. This is hinted at in Uncle Frank's views of his brother Harry.

Harry   He represents Truman. Based on time involved, Truman was actually just a bit player, but the decisions he had to make placed him on a much bigger stage than maybe he otherwise deserved. As Johnny's dad, the boy gives him some sympathy he may or may not warrant, as well as some antagonism.

Aunt Patti   Vaguely represents generals Patton and Bradley; probably more Patton, though. Look, I know Patton wasn't involved in the Normandy invasion (except as a decoy), but I felt I needed a character like her, and she needed to cross the Obeg River. Her bulldozer driving hints strongly at Patton's tank corps.

Uncle Stan   Well, he's just a guy who doesn't appear much in the book; he just gives Aunt Patti the last name of "Bradley." So I guess Patti is

General Bradley when crossing the Obeg, and then General Patton when driving the bulldozer.

Norman D. Beech   Aunt Patti's new boyfriend is conveniently named and conveniently well-connected.

Johnny   Our narrator and hero. During "The Battle of Britain" chapter, he is representative of the RAF (also during Aunt Winnie's raid on the Liquidation Store). He plays many other important roles.

Aunt Babs   Her full name evokes Operation Barbarossa, which was the code name for Hitler's invasion of the Soviet Union. Prior to that time, Hitler and Stalin had been working together, or at least had signed a non-aggression pact. Philosophically, they had their differences. However, it's hard to see how fascism and communism are really different (the government controls everything and people who disagree are executed). They claim to be at opposite ends of the spectrum, but I think maybe the spectrum curves at each end and they meet behind our backs. It's hinted strongly that Uncle Joe and Uncle Benny are really identical twins, not fraternal. Barbara Rose, as a radio personality, also recalls "Tokyo Rose", the name G.I.s gave to female Japanese radio broadcasters who spun ridiculous propaganda.

Kirk   After the opening salvos fired by Hilde, Benny and Joe, Johnny is evacuated onto Uncle Frank's boat, along with his second cousin Kirk. In the story, I write: *"Done," Kirk said.* Get it? Dunkirk? Hello?

Liquidation Store In order to prepare for the invasion of Europe, and to debilitate Hitler's war machine, the U.S. started a bombing campaign that consisted almost solely of day-time raids. The British bombed exclusively at night. Uncle Frank "attacks" the Liquidation Store of Hilde's during the day, while Johnny sees Aunt Winnie do so at night. Obviously, as well as representing the German war machine, the Liquidation Store hints specifically of the concentration camps (as, of course, Joe's chicken coops are Stalin's gulags), as well as the Nazi party in general.

Chocolate Mousse Shortly after the withering Japanese attacks against Pearl Harbor, the Philippines, *et al*, America needed a victory, even a small one. Army bombers led by Col. Jimmy Doolittle were equipped to take off from aircraft carriers and they struck Japan, though with minimal materiel effect. The morale boost was terrific, though. When reporters asked FDR from where did the bombers take off, he replied, "From Shangri-La," a legendary Himalayan monastery from James Hilton's novel *Lost Horizon*.

Lebensraum

Hitler called the land east of Germany "lebensraum" or "living space", meaning for Germans, not for whoever was already living there. Treat's land suggests this, as the land is the obvious target of Hilde. The dividing of the land among the children of Treat and Versey is an obvious reference to the work of the framers of the Treaty of Versailles at the end of the First World War, a bitter contest whose effects are also still felt. The treaty makers tried. It's easy for us to say from where we sit that they messed up horribly, but it's not like the Dayton Accords did much better, and that only dealt with the Balkans, not the whole world. Those who do not learn from the mistakes of history are doomed to repeat them, they say, but they are only half-right. When much-maligned Neville Chamberlain adopted the tactic of appeasement to Hitler, on his mind was probably the fact that, had the nations appeased Austria-Hungary over Serbia, the Serbians would have suffered, but the First World War may have been averted. So, bad for the Czechs (thought Neville), but good for the rest of the world. The nations tried to hold firm against Austria-Hungary in 1914 (ironic that it may have worked on Hitler in the early 1930s, for a time, perhaps) but appeasement only convinced Hitler that he was strong and France and England were weak (morally as well as militarily). So perhaps Neville was applying the lessons of history (good), but avoiding the changing facts of his day (not so good). I do not live in Eastern Europe or the Balkans and so do not know if everything is hunky-dory or not there now. I suspect some people still have issues with how the land is divided.

Cousin Isaac | In a large family there are many cousins. Good thing, too, for there's always another character needed in a story like this. Isaac, Harry's cousin in the story, is known as "Ike", as was Eisenhower, the Supreme Allied Commander in the West. There were other cousins of Harry's and Frank's and Winnie's who played smaller roles that I regret could not be further expanded.

Operation Torch | This was the code-name for the Allied invasion of North Africa. There's not much of a parallel in my story, other than broadly as a continuation of the overall battle between the two sides and, as already mentioned, a touching on Rommel as the "Desert Fox". Also, this was perhaps my only chance to make a cheap joke about flashlights. When would that ever come again?

The Bomb | This was the hardest to parody, especially given the fact that I had condensed my feud basically to a one-front affair (with a number of large and small allusions to the Pacific Theater), so when Johnny's side had bested Hilde's, there was little of the feud left. In this case, the need for the bomb dropped by Harry is far less important than what the real

Truman faced (imperatively). But in this story, Harry was truly trying to stop the feud from ever flaring up again. He felt it had to be done, and Johnny knew it. It was intended to save greater pain. Was this so for Hiroshima and Nagasaki? There were and still are differences in opinion; probably always will be. I don't think the bombs on Hiroshima and Nagasaki were racist, as some may think (the bombs had been initially intended for Germany, after all). Obviously, Truman just wanted to end the war and save greater casualties with an invasion of Japan, and the American public wanted the war to be over. More than ending the feud, though, Harry's bomb in the story propels the family into a new age, as surely as the atom bomb did for us. Nothing would ever be the same again. There is forgiveness in love, but the sting from the bomb would still last. Truman ended the war, shockingly; he propelled us into a new age and possibly scared us from ever using the weapons in a war with the Soviet Union (especially once they had gotten the bomb, which they did quite quickly . . . but that's another story).

There are other parallels throughout, of course. They may or may not be important to you. If I have not made a specific reference to a favorite battle, weapon or personage of yours from the Second World War, I apologize.

For more explanations (and possibly more apologies), please visit the New Brevet Publications Facebook site or www.newbrevet.com

New Brevet books are published on Amazon.com KDP. Go there to find books by David Kurtz, or contact him at newbrevet@gmail.com

Thank you, gentle reader.

ABOUT THE AUTHOR

David Kurtz is a life-long history buff. By day he works as a sales analyst for Datasite Global Corporation in Minneapolis, MN, the numbers satisfying his analytical side. By night he is a sometimes writer and editor, fulfilling his creative side. He is the author of *Memoirs of Jesus as told to David Kurtz*, and the editor of *Dear Phil: A Collection of Letters to a Brother, 2013-2017*. *War and Peace in Dodge* is his first published novel. David lives in Coon Rapids, MN, with his wife and two children, attends church, pays his bills, complains on and off, but is generally happy. He is, however, painfully aware of another book with a similar title to this one written by a guy named Leo.